MISTER BILLIONS

A SMALL TOWN ENEMIES-TO-LOVERS FAKE MARRIAGE BILLIONAIRE ROMANTIC COMEDY

CASSIE-ANN L. MILLER

Enjoy Sommer and fall !

Christopher Walken

April 2021

PROLOGUE
CANNON

It's the plot twist of every cliched telenovela to ever get cancelled in its first season.

My best friend bolting up from under my Italian brocade silk comforter and flinging my live-in girlfriend's naked body clear across the king-sized bed.

Said girlfriend toppling over the side of the mattress and landing on the marble floor with the poise of a disgraced spider monkey.

Each of them spewing an array of nonsensical pleas and excuses my way.

"Cannon! You're home early!"

"D-don't do anything crazy, bro! I can explain."

"Baby, it's not what it looks like! You weren't supposed to find out like this!"

"I tried to say no but she threw herself at me!"

"I couldn't help it, Cannon. You work all the time. And it's been taking you *forever* to propose. Plus, my life coach said this sexual exploration thing is a healthy part of my natural evolution toward becoming the most authentic version of myself..."

I stand in the doorway stunned, frozen, as Margot scrambles around to unclip the gold-plated nipple clamps hanging from her tits like mini-chandeliers. Meanwhile, Carl kneels on the bed, hurrying to stuff his flaccid penis into his shit-stained white briefs.

I'm one momentary lapse in judgment away from torching the mattress with him in it.

Because there's no way in hell I will *ever* be able to lie on that bed with that woman in my arms again. Or sit on the couch in the living room and enjoy a Monday night football game with the hairy-assed asshole I built a billion-dollar software company with out of our college dorm room. Or take a deep breath of the hot, dense Manhattan summer air without choking on the putrid stench of this betrayal.

This is some fucked up shit.

I hear a faint whisper at the back of my mind. It sounds strangely like my grandfather's voice. *Why are you even surprised?*

To know who will betray you most devastatingly, look to the one you trust most ardently.

That phrase was underlined in red ink in a dog-eared book the grumpy, old man used to read over and over again when I was a child. I never fully understood it until right now.

Barely able to see through the red haze blurring my vision, my claws clamp down on the sheets and yank them from the bed. My roar rips a new hole through the ozone layer. "You motherfuckers!" I charge across the room and tear the bedside lamp out of the wall with blinding fury. Carl squeals like a terrified piglet when I raise it above my head.

But right as I'm about to do something dramatic—and

very, very stupid—I'm struck by a dizzying flash of clarity. A premonition, really.

I get a glimpse of myself, despondent and disheveled, being handcuffed and hauled into a cop car.

Then, I'm posing for an impromptu photo shoot courtesy of the fine officers of the NYPD.

And then I'm sharing a concrete holding cell with a chatty-drunk trucker named Jim for a state-imposed time-out.

Not worth it, man.

My mother already has one hot-tempered idiot spawn behind bars. She wouldn't be able to handle another.

Nah. Not worth it.

Thirty minutes later, I'm sauntering past the doorman—key fob spinning around my pointer finger, duffel bag hitched on my shoulder. I catch sight of Margot in my periphery, flailing and yelling hysterically as my building security drops her in a heap on the bustling sidewalk outside of my Upper East Side apartment.

Pushing her bleach-blonde hair from her eyes, she hollers after me. "Cannon, baby! You can't let them do this to me! You can't just leave me on the street! We love each other! Where are you going, baby?"

I sink behind the wheel of my sportscar and screech away from the curb without sparing a look back. *I'm going home, bitch...*

I always knew Margot was an opportunist. She first sank her fangs into me with a formidable blowjob at the house party where we met back at NYU. The minute my start-up got funded, she dropped her liberal arts classes like a knock-off handbag covered in questionable bodily fluids and made a name for herself around campus as my 'supportive girlfriend'. In other words, the whiny chick who spent her days online shopping with my credit card and then doing elaborate Facebook un-boxings to complain that the merchandise never quite lives up to the website product pictures.

But I was a horny college sophomore. And she was always down for morning sex.

By the time I was swiping my Black Card for her second rhinoplasty, she was sort of entrenched in my life. I was an idiot, so distracted by my success that I didn't realize how little she was actually contributing to our relationship.

As for Carl, he's dumb, lazy and as useful as the 'p' in pneumonia. But I put up with his inadequacies because he was with me in the trenches from the beginning, when we were getting doors shut in our faces by investors left and right. So despite his shortcomings, I didn't toss him to the curb like a dirty mattress the second our company made it big.

Because I believe in fucking loyalty.

Well, apparently, he doesn't feel the same. And I don't play that backstabbing shit, as he's about to find out.

I drive through the night, my tires eating up the dark lanes of the I-90 north. I don't stop once. Not to grab a hamburger. Not to take a piss. My only companion is the red hot pissed-off-ness that suffocates every other emotion that even dares to rear its stupid head.

Twelve hours later, the first flicker of daylight is breaking on the horizon. I slide on my aviators against the early morning sun. The meandering hatchback clogging the off-ramp up ahead is the only thing between me and the triple shot espresso I'll need to nail down the specifics of the comeuppance Margot and Carl have heading their way.

I crank the steering wheel sharply to the left and stomp down on the accelerator. My Tesla clips around the zigzagging Volkswagen Quantum barely holding its shit together under layers of duct tape.

When the startled teen driver looks up from the cellphone in his hand, our eyes meet. I shout in the direction of my closed window. "No texting and driving, Fuckface!"

I leave his ass in the dust.

Beneath my aviators, my gaze flicks up to the huge green highway sign looming above the roadway.

Welcome to Crescent Harbor.

I coast past the sign with the calm assurance of a man about to ruin some fucking lives.

But first...coffee.

1

LEXI

Some girls think that friendship is all about glamorous spa days, getting matching mani-pedis and gossiping about boys while sipping on mimosas. Or nights on the town, wearing sparkly dresses and taking Instagram-worthy duck-face group selfies in the washrooms of glitzy, pretentious nightclubs.

I know better.

I know that friendships are defined in the dark moments. The moments that come with snotty Kleenex and empty wine bottles on the floor.

The moments when your heartbroken bestie needs help moving the bodies.

Or the body parts.

The ten-inch, three-speed, silicone body parts.

Penny hoists the strap of her sweaty tank top up her shoulder and throws a horrified glance at the contents of the crumbling box we're hauling through the dark alley toward the backdoor of my bridal shop. "What are we gonna do with all these dildos?"

My stomach gurgles with anxiety. I'm the furthest thing

from a prude but this is not how I typically start my Monday mornings.

"Don't get your nipples all in a bunch, Penny." I scold her in my I've-got-this-under-control voice. "I'm gonna tape up the box, drag it over to the post office on my lunch break and ship it back to the seller for a refund. Simple as that."

...And right on cue, the bottom of the box gives out. Sex toys pour down onto the rain-drenched asphalt.

Ladies and gentlemen, I do not, in fact, have this under control.

Penny scoops a severed butt-plug out of the muddy puddle at her feet. She groans. "Remind me again how I got dragged into this mess."

My thoughts travel back to the weekend. I witnessed Iris on the verge of a complete emotional breakdown after her douchey (soon-to-be ex) husband came home with hickies on his neck, lipstick on his collar and a used condom clinging to the sole of his shiny leather shoe. He abruptly served her with divorce papers and hustled out the door, brimming suitcase in hand.

She showed up at my house in tears. And I'm never one to turn away a friend in need so I set aside my Friday night plans and took her in. Just like she took me in two years ago when I came to Crescent Harbor, not knowing a soul. A quick text message to Penny and she cut short her shift at the Frosty Pitcher to be there for her cousin in her time of need.

And yes, there were Lizzo songs involved. And wine. Copious amounts of wine.

My bestie got sloppy-drunk and stood atop my wobbly coffee table where she swore off men for all of eternity then committed herself to a lifetime of silicone peen. Penny and I sprawled inebriated on the carpet, showering Iris with compliments and words of encouragement and profound one-liners from Deepak Chopra books. 'Cause we're supportive like that.

At some point, Penny whipped out her wallet and produced a coupon to some random online sex store.

Penny always has the best coupons.

Next thing you know, there was a virtual shopping cart full of sex toys on my computer screen. Iris's drunken finger must have somehow hit the 'buy now' button. Because the UPS guy showed up at an ungodly hour last night, delivering a shit ton of x-rated merchandise to my door.

Now, Penny and I are in an alley. With a box of sex toys. At the crack of dawn.

We're trying to clean up this disaster since Iris is still too much of a hot mess to deal with life.

A classic case of Friday's-fun-ends-with-Monday's-consequences. Oops!

Anyway, I'm just glad Penny volunteered to help me walk the box over from my house five blocks away. I'm saving up for a car and there's no way I'd be able to handle this by myself.

Penny crouches down, piling muddy packages into her arms. She gives me a doubtful look. "Lexi, these are *sex toys*. Not T-shirts off the rack from Old Navy. I'm not sure the seller's gonna just hand over a refund. Plus, that website looked pretty sketchy, if you ask me."

Not getting the money back is not an option. Iris is in dire need of cash, especially with her impending divorce. We *have* to get the money back. I don't plan to leave my friend hanging.

"Well, we'll try to return them. And if that doesn't work, we'll think of something else, okay?" I twist the key in the lock and elbow the backdoor open.

"Something like what?" Penny shuffles past me as I scoop up the rest of the vibrators.

"I don't know. " I shrug, flustered. "Something..." I mumble under my breath. "I just hope I don't end up having to install a sex toy vending machine in the middle of my bridal boutique. If I have to, I will. But I hope it doesn't come to that."

I may have a reputation around town for being a notorious party girl but there are two things in life I take seriously; my friendships and my business.

Because my friendships and my business are the two constants that kept me going in my lowest moments, especially after my parents proved I couldn't rely on them for anything.

My friend snorts laughter through her nose and I silently wonder how she somehow manages to look like a pinup model even with sweat on her forehead and bags under her eyes.

Penny is an effortless bombshell. Every group of friends has one. Red hair, green eyes, a runway-worthy strut. Everywhere she goes, she unwittingly leaves a pile of slack-jawed, blue-balls'd men in her wake. Being hot comes naturally to her and it kills me that she doesn't even realize it.

Me? I always manage to come off a bit disheveled, no matter how hard I try.

I used to give myself a hard time for being a mess. Now, I've made peace with it for the most part. Every fun girl knows that sometimes you've got to sacrifice looking 'put-together' for the greater good.

We stumble through the fields and fields of satin and lace gowns cluttering the back room of Renewed Gowns, Crescent Harbor's only pre-owned bridal gown shop.

Penny and I dump the toys on the large table next to my

sewing machine in the stock room. A pin cushion, a pair of scissors and several old invoices flutter to the floor. I'd be embarrassed about the chaotic state of the place, but my girls have long come to terms with the fact that my organizational skills need some work.

Because high heels have never been my friends, I eagerly kick off those suckers under the table. They're already scuffed to hell from our little early-morning trek across the parking lot. I dramatically collapse into an exhausted heap on the pile of thick bridal magazines and dog-eared personal development books in my overstuffed armchair.

Meanwhile Penny drops onto a cushioned bench against the wall and curls up, fetal style. Her eyes flutter shut. "Promise me we're never letting Iris drink again. I love my cousin and everything but the girl can*not* handle her liquor."

"Iris's gonna need all the emotional support she can get right now." I throw Penny a solemn look. "And where I come from, 'emotional support' means tequila."

She tsks. "Whaaat?! I am all about emotional support. In fact, I firmly backed my cousin's no-men-for-life plan...Right up until she drunk-purchased Sixty. Seven. Dildos!"

I chuckle at the reminder. "You're *very* skeptimistic this morning. It's unbecoming."

Penny has already snatched a pile of silky fabric and balled it up beneath her head. "Sorry." She yawns. "Honestly, I think I just need coffee."

Energized by the mere idea of caffeine, I bounce to my feet. "Ooh! Coffee is the best idea I've heard all day." I glance at the wall clock. I've got half an hour before my first bridal appointment of the day. "Lattes from Jittery Joes? Walk with me!"

Penny cracks one eye open from her spot on the bench and turns her neck to look at me. "I'm just gonna take a little cat nap. Can't you go on without me?"

"Oh, come on!"

"I need to save my energy. Today is deep clean day at the bar. Hard manual labor," she whines. "Plus, I probably won't get any sleep before my shift. I promised Walker I'd go over to his house to help him with some online shopping because those lumberjack shirts of his need a break every now and then."

I grin like the Cheshire cat at the mention of Penny's big, surly, reclusive friend. "Walker, huh? I *bet* you won't be getting any sleep if you go to his house." I wink as I position myself in front of the mirror covering the wall.

I wiggled into my cute gray pencil skirt and the white camisole under my turquoise cardigan an hour ago, but I already look like I just got violently shoved over the side of a trampoline.

Despite my party girl tendencies, I try to look presentable for work. I am the face of my business after all. So I make the effort to keep it professional during business hours and limit my shenanigans to the weekends. Yet somehow it seems like the Universe is conspiring against my best intentions.

Penny slaps a hand over her mouth. "That came out wrong! It's not like that. Walker and I are just—"

"Friends?"

I've heard the Walker-and-I-are-just-friends routine one time too many. I'm over it. Those two need to bone. *Pronto*!

"Okay, back to the coffee..." Penny says, changing the conversation through a raging blush. "Vanilla oat milk latte. Pretty please? With two cane sugars and a dash of nutmeg." She wiggles a wad of dollar bills at me.

That bougie bitch.

I cut my eyes at my friend, trying to be annoyed with her but who am I kidding? I don't know how to hold a grudge.

I yawn and a tuft of messy brown hair falls over my eye as I snatch her money. "Only because I love you." I grab my purse and head for the door.

Still I find myself grinning when she calls out after me. "Love you, too, Lex!"

As I hustle down Promenade Street, I straighten my skirt that somehow is nearly backward and I re-tuck my shirt. There's mud on my knee and the back of my camisole is damp.

Well, shit.

Let's just hope I can make it to the coffee shop without running into anyone I need to impress this morning. But with the way this day has been unfolding, I'm not holding my breath.

2

CANNON

My lawyer's sleep-laden voice dribbles sluggishly across the phone line. "You want me to do *what*?"

I lift the bagel from the plate on the low coffee table in front of me and take a bite. Poppy seeds and oatmeal flakes and bacon bits—and whatever the hell else is going on with this bagel—rain down on the newspaper sitting on my lap. "Order the bank to freeze DataCo's accounts. Tell them you suspect fraudulent activities. That will temporarily prevent Carl from accessing the company's money while I figure out how to permanently screw that jackass over."

Across the phone line, Frank's chair squeaks under his shifting weight. "A-are you sure that's what you want to do?"

My temples throb with annoyance. "Did I fucking stutter, Frank?"

My lawyer chooses his words carefully. "Now, Cannon. I know that you suffered the ultimate shock last night. Two people you trusted betrayed you. I empathize. But let's not be reckless. Let's not be hasty. Let's think this through before we make any decisions we can't undo in the long run."

"This isn't a debate, Frank. There's nothing to think through. I've made my decision."

I leaf distractedly through the local newspaper. It's filled with ridiculous, inane headlines.

Sheep wander off Baylac Farm. Cause traffic pile-up on Park Road Bridge.

Hush money scandal threatens annual Onion Ring Festival

Local manure thief finally faces his day in court

Not exactly Pulitzer Prize material.

My eyes move across the empty dining room to where the shop's clueless counter staff crowd around the espresso machine, arguing and nudging each other back and forth.

A tall, clumsy hipster bro fumbles about with the screwdriver in hand. A young, jittery brunette holds up a phone in his face. Her ponytail sways around her as she bounces on her toes.

I kid you not—a YouTube video on coffee machine repair is playing.

I pull my broken wristwatch from my pocket and check the time. This nonsense has been going on for the past fifteen minutes. Meanwhile, I'm sitting here, getting more and more annoyed by the second.

Where the hell is my coffee?

When the barista's eyes meet mine, a fierce blush colors her cheeks. "Your coffee will be ready in a minute, sir," she promises. Again.

The only reason I haven't left is because this coffee shop is the only place in town that's open at this hour. And Heaven knows I need caffeine before I face my parents.

Once my mother gets wind of what's going on, there won't be enough Kleenex in the state of Illinois to control the waterworks. I may be an asshole but one thing I can't stand is seeing my Mom upset.

I bite into my bagel—quite possibly the driest hunk of carbs I've ever consumed—and trail mix falls into the neck of my shirt. Really fucking itchy.

I zone in and out of my lawyer's monologue. To Frank, I'm just being my usual reckless self. But DataCo is far from being the only asset in my sizeable financial portfolio, and we both know it.

I've diversified into real estate, pharmaceuticals, and even pet clothing and accessories. I make very handsome returns on my investments, and I'm not going to go broke over this.

Carl, on the other hand, is shit out of luck. With his shaky poker face, his fondness for escorts and his inability to count the loose change in his pocket without using a freaking calculator, I predict he'll be playing Mariah Carey's greatest hits on a bagpipe outside of Union Square for pocket change before the board of directors issues the next quarterly dividend.

Besides the truth is, this goes beyond money.

Yes, I lead a privileged life with expensive toys, homes in multiple cities, and more money than I know what to do with. But if I can't trust the people around me, what's the point of it all?

If the past twenty-four hours have taught me anything, it's that the two people closest to my life are some skanky hoes. And I need to teach them both a lesson before moving on.

Carl has called a few dozen times since I left New York. Margot has already filled up my voicemail with her whiny, pleading messages. Eventually, they'll both accept that I'm not going to call back. Ever.

In the meantime, I've granted my housekeeper free rein to go on a personal shopping spree in Margot's walk-in closet. In fact, I told the old woman she might as well move in to the vacant condo. Because I have no immediate plans to return to Manhattan and my disloyal ex has no reason to ever set foot in my apartment again.

I know Margot. The best way to stick it to her would be to leave her high-maintenance ass to fend for herself on the 'cruel streets' of the Upper East Side all while knowing that my housekeeper—who Margot always treated like a second-class citizen—is living her best life in my high-rise condo.

Now, it's time to deal with my slimy business partner.

"I need you to conduct a thorough search for any concealed assets Carl might have."

"Concealed assets?"

"Yes, any property you won't find declared on his tax returns or financial statements." I press the heel of my hand into my burning eye socket. I'm tired. I'm starving for food I can actually swallow. And I'm really starting to wonder how much longer I can wait on this coffee before I go apeshit in this place.

When I stare over at the counter, my gaze bumps into the barista's again. "Just one more minute," she promises, pressing her palms together in prayer.

I hear a tinkling chime and the grating hinges of the opening front door. I glance up...

And I instantly resent the rush of heat that dives straight into my cock.

Dark hair. Thick and wild as a forest. That's the first thing that catches my eye.

I can't see her face but I *definitely* see that hair and the ripe curve of her high, round, peach-shaped ass. Her turquoise cardigan cuts off an inch above her tight waist and her tiny gray skirt broadcasts an endless ream of long, long legs.

My cock throbs, eager and peppy, trying to convince me that, after the way the past sixteen hours have unravelled, I *deserve* to get my rocks off. With a hot piece of ass like the one currently leaned over the counter, moaning at the pastries sitting in the glass display case.

But there's 'something' about her. Besides her physical appeal. The way she lifts her chin and arches her spine, the way her kittenish laughter rises all the way to the rafters, filling the room with twinkling sparks of mischief.

This girl is a hurricane. I just know it. A storm of fierceness and energy and sass.

As she spins around to scan the dining area of the coffee shop, I catch a glimpse of her wide, baby doll eyes and her heart-shaped cherry-ripe lips. I drop my gaze back to my newspaper, narrowly avoiding eye contact.

Never mind, I tell my cock. I can already tell she'd be more trouble than I'm willing to put up with for a casual fuck. I have more important things to do. Specifically, making Carl's life a living hell.

I bring my attention back to Frank. "Find every last possession he owns and steal it or repossess it or burn it to the ground. Understood?"

The lawyer clears his throat uncomfortably. "Cannon..." The old man goes on another one of his rants, wasting precious time, trying to reason with me. I zone out.

My eyes go back to the girl at the counter. The urge to tangle my fingers in that long, messy hair surges something fierce. When my dick twitches, I glare down at him. *Not today, asshole.* I'm on a mission and I won't let my cock guide me off course.

Carl, I'm coming for you. Better warm up that bagpipe, motherfucker.

3

LEXI

When I step into the coffeeshop, my younger sister, Jessa, and her manager, Todd, are huddled around the fancy coffee machine with matching troubled expressions. Todd barely looks up at the sound of the door chime. But my sister glances up and her insta-grin goes as wide as the glass display case spread out beneath the cash register. "Happy Monday, Lexi!" Her sparkling energy fills the empty room.

Our friends like to joke that Jessa is an over-caffeinated Disney-Princess. The doe-eyed, brown-haired beauty is bright, sunny, optimistic. Obnoxiously enthusiastic about life. She's looking for work as a kindergarten teacher but she works this barista job to fill in the gaps between her current substitute teaching stints.

Jessa bounces toward me like she just finished drinking all the coffee in the tri-state area. I need some of that energy. Stat.

I collapse theatrically against the display case, spreading my arms to span the width of the glass. I groan loudly. "Oh my gosh, Jessa! I won't be held accountable for my actions if

I don't have an I.V. dumping coffee into my veins in the next sixty seconds. Caffeinate me!" I burst into a high-pitched giggle.

Her smile freezes on her face and her eyes widen just a touch. She leans across the counter and speaks in a quiet voice. "We've got company this morning, Lex." She lifts a brow and tilts her chin in the direction of the line of low tables and chairs positioned in the coffee shop's far corner.

That's when I see him.

The man sitting in the beat-up leather armchair has wide shoulders and huge paws for hands. His messy hair is in a man-bun, dark blond flyaways fanning out around his chiselled face. He's wearing suspenders and three days of stubble and the hottest, meanest frown I've ever seen.

No tie with his wrinkled button-down shirt. No socks with his scuffed leather shoes.

He exudes an easy, laidback kind of power. A zero-fucks-to-give vibe that makes me pulse between the legs. He leafs absently through a newspaper as he barks into his phone, frown lines digging angry trenches between his eyebrows.

Jessa's bright eyes blink amorously at the surly man. Her whisper floats across the counter. "He's gorgeous, isn't he? Too bad he's a bit of a jerk…"

I snort bitterly. "The gorgeous ones usually are." My cheeks prickle. I try to backpedal. "Not that *he's* particularly gorgeous."

She looks at me like I'm crazy. "Did you put your contact lenses on upside down this morning? That man is effing hot."

He must feel the weight of us staring because his head snaps up suddenly.

My eyes meet his and—*boom*!—it's like running head-on

into a brick wall. A hooded, deep-set, almond-shaped brick wall. Backlit by the fucking sun.

He scowls. Like my very existence is somehow offensive to him. But this is Crescent Harbor. Polite is the name of the game. So, against my better judgment, I give the man a polite chin tip and a good mannered "'Morning."

In one frigid, disinterested sweep, his eyes cover me from top to bottom, moving from my sweaty face and traveling over my tiny breasts and my disheveled cardigan before slicking down my wrinkled skirt to my bruised pumps.

Ouch!

His growly attention abruptly clips over to Jessa. He pulls the phone away from his face and pins my sister with an unnerving frown. "Am I gonna get that coffee any time soon?" He drums his fingers on the table next to his sunglasses.

Jessa's cheeks turn splotchy and red. "Of course. Y-yes. It'll only take a few more minutes, s-sir. I'm sorry for the wait." Her hands brace the counter like she's scared she might lose her balance.

The customer gives one more ugly sneer before going back to his phone call.

Jessa whispers apologetically. "Gimme a sec, Lexi." She spins back toward her anxiety-riddled manager who is now crouched down in front of the machine.

That's when I notice the angry red light hopping around on the front panel of the espresso maker. "What's wrong?" I ask, inching behind the counter to inspect the machine.

Todd flashes me a helpless look, on the verge of a very obvious panic attack. "I don't know what the deal is," he wheezes. "It's never given this warning message before, and it was fine ten minutes ago. It just randomly stopped working."

I check the clock on the wall. I'm officially running late. My first customer appointment is at 8:00 and I was hoping I'd have a few minutes to change my outfit and do something with my crazy hair before she shows up.

Also, poor Penny may be in a catatonic state on the floor from caffeine deficiency by now. But I feel a tug of compassion at the flustered expression on Todd's face.

Mind your business, Lexi, the little voice in my head says. *Don't get involved. You have places to be, shit to do.* Shit that does not involve continuing to play Captain-Save-a-Sister first thing on a Monday morning.

There's a gas station just off the highway. The brew in their self-serve coffee dispenser usually sits out overnight and tastes like lukewarm diesel exhaust. I should point the jerkface in that direction and be on my way. Because jerk-faces don't deserve good coffee.

But my eyes bounce from Jessa's nervous body language to the menacing expression of the man in the armchair and I know what I have to do.

On a sigh, I shrug out of my cardigan and hang it on the back of a counter stool. "Let me take a look. I might be able to fix it," I volunteer.

I elbow Todd out of the way and he glances at me with wide eyes. "What are you doing, Lexi?"

This wouldn't be the first time someone has doubted my skills. I don't exactly look like a handy kind of gal. But I don't mind proving people wrong.

Just last Thursday, I fixed Mr. Patel's copy machine at the office supply store. And when the microphones fritzed out at the Frosty Pitcher two weeks ago, I'm the one who rewired the entire system in the middle of karaoke night.

Despite my best efforts to do the whole posh, sophisticated boutique owner thing, I always find myself rolling up my sleeves and getting dirty, especially when it serves someone I care about.

I give Todd a smile. "My father could fix this kind of machine with his eyes closed and one hand tied behind his back." *Even while wading through one of his alcohol-induced fogs.* "Turns out I learned a few valuable lessons from Daddy Dearest." *Despite his earnest efforts to be a useless troll every day of the week.* I stretch a hand out to the manager. "Give me the screwdriver and step away from the machine."

Todd looks to my sister who nods in confirmation. He reluctantly settles the screwdriver in my palm.

"Thank you, Lexi," he whispers, beads of nervous sweat glistening on his forehead. "You're saving my ass."

My heart tightens with sympathy. "Hey..." I say in a soft voice, lowering my face to catch his eyes. "I can fix the machine. It's gonna be okay."

He nods slightly, inhaling so hard it makes his paprika-red mustache flutter with relief.

"Now, go find me a toolbox in case I need some pliers." I hip-check him out of the way.

"Yes, ma'am." He does a mock-salute.

"I'm taking my coffee free, by the way," I call out. "Those frothy fuckers are expensive."

Grinning, he gives me a thumbs up of approval right before he and my sister disappear into the back room.

As I'm carefully unscrewing the backplate of the coffee machine, the intriguing stranger's conversation takes over the empty room.

"The stock price will plummet," the person on the other end of the call announces at an ear-splitting volume.

The sexy devil bites into his bagel, totally undisturbed. "I'll eat the loss."

"The shareholders will be up in arms! The company will be in bankruptcy protection before the end of the fiscal year!"

"Not my problem."

"Spite is not a responsible investment strategy."

"Since when is revenge based on logic? I'm a self-made man, Frank. I'm not beholden to the board of directors or anybody else for that matter. I won't live my life in a snake den. Period."

Day-um. Mr. Jerkface is *pissed*. I feel profound sympathy for the soul who wronged this man.

Straining to listen in on the conversation, I'm not exactly paying attention to what I'm doing. The person on the other line continues trying to reason with him but the poor man's arguments are futile. Jerkface isn't having it.

I throw a look at the scoundrel sprawled in the armchair like a throne, legs spread wide, one elbow propped on the arm. Attention skimming the newspaper as he barks commands into the phone.

I glare openly. Who the hell does he think he is, ordering people around like that?

The machine wheezes, snapping me back to the moment. Brown liquid splatters the front of my white camisole. Surprised, I yip. I stare down at myself not sure how much more abuse my outfit can take.

So much for today's business world domination plans.

The man glances my way and gives me another irritated look before averting his attention back to the phone call. "Just get it done." He barks. He ends the call, slamming the device down hard. His jaw twitches and he pinches the bridge of his nose.

I power up the coffee machine. When I hear the steamy drips of liquid splash into my mug, I smile and screw the backplate back on. To celebrate my success, I brew myself a big-ass cappuccino. I finish it off with a dash of cinnamon. *Oh yes!*

When I take a long sip, I don't fight the moan that leaves my lips. I'm shameless, not even quiet about it. I glance at the impatient customer and I'm positive he's shaking with annoyance.

He glares in my direction. His eyes then flit around the counter, and I imagine he's looking for Jessa to serve him some of this caffeine goodness. If he weren't such a pompous jerkface, I'd happily help him out. But, again, assholes don't deserve the good coffee.

After a momentary standoff, he drops his eyes back to his paper.

"Waiting a few minutes for a cup of coffee must be a real hardship, huh?"

It's provocation to poke the bear but Jessa is my frigging sister. I do *not* just stand by and watch the people I love get verbally manhandled. That's not my style.

The patron doesn't even bother to look up from his newspaper. "Is it unreasonable for a customer to expect efficient service from a business where they're expending funds?" The growly tones of his voice rumble down my spine and resonate inside my panties.

I shake off the unwelcome visceral reaction and clear my throat. "It's *unreasonable* for a customer to be a jerk just because a struggling small business is having a machine malfunction."

"If a coffee shop can't manage to sell me a cup of coffee without having to declare a national state of emergency, then that pretty much sums up why it's a struggling business."

"I don't know how to tell you this, but..." I take a step closer and lower my voice like I'm trying to clue him in on a conspiracy theory, "No amount of money entitles you to boss people around like that."

"You sure about that?"

"True fact," I deadpan, my tone as dry as a cheddar cracker. And just as salty.

A scowl pinches the corners of his mouth as he casually flips a page on his stupid newspaper. He slowly scans the page and then flips again, on to the next one.

The asshole deliberately makes me wait.

My blood is simmering. Come on—I read that paper daily, and even I can admit it's not exactly hard hitting.

After a decade-long pause, he speaks again.

"And what do you suggest I do about the subpar customer service in this establishment?"

I twit back a sharp response. "How about exercising some patience? Some understanding? Some friggin' *compassion*? Just because you've probably got a million dollars in the bank doesn't mean you get to boss everyone around."

Finally, the arrogant jerk glances up. Those scalding caramel irises threaten to melt my kneecaps from right under me. "I've got a *billion* dollars, sweetheart...In fact, more than just one."

My chest twinges. My lips move wordlessly as shock dings through my system. I have exactly zero words to follow up that billion-dollar comment. *Good lord. Billions...? Of dollars...?* The guy can't be much older than thirty. Aren't billionaires old and bald and crusty?

But then again, billionaires probably have access to

the *good* Botox and all those unicorn milk beauty masks the rest of us never hear about.

He rolls back the sleeves of his shirt to reveal dark ink covering his strong forearms. "Tell me, Stormy. Are you the official crusader for justice around here, or can I expect to hear from the higher-ups at some point over the next few days?"

I try to stop myself from moving closer but I just can't. "Just a concerned citizen issuing a friendly warning...Here in Crescent Harbor, the locals don't take kindly to pompous assholes who stroll into town and act like they own the place."

"Is that so?" With a subtle twitch of his eyebrow, the man leans back in the beaten-up leather armchair. He crosses his arms over that broad chest. His palpable beast-energy is honed solely on me.

Mimicking his body language, I fold my arms, too. "Just last week a group of seniors at the farmer's market chased off a big city douchebag with their walking sticks."

His laugh comes from all the way down in the cobwebby basement of his dark, dark soul. But the way it lights up his face is almost mystical. It puts a row of perfect enamel on display. His eyes narrow to crinkly, dazzling slits and his thick Adam's apple bobs. "I'm terribly broken to have missed that."

I find myself smiling, too.

I have to deliberately remind myself that I'm trying to be mad at this guy.

It should be easy.

I should find him ridiculous. I mean, what's more pretentious than suspenders? Oh, that's right—a man bun.

Plus, he's got sesame seeds on his mouth. *Come on!*

But there's something about the way the whole package

comes together. Sesame seeds and all. It's masculine and rugged and impossible to ignore.

Our gazes merge for another long, twinkling silence. He's got me pinned in place by those powerful caramel eyes. Sticky and melting me from the inside.

On the outside, I don't flinch. I hold steady eye contact like a champ. Like a woman who can take on a king and bring him to his knees.

His phone bleats on the table beside him. From where I stand, I can see the gorgeous face and a head of bleach-blonde hair that lights up his screen.

His expression shifts. A tidal wave of hurt crashes across his handsome features.

The man drops his head and pinches the bridge of his nose. My curiosity spikes and I assess him, more closely this time. That's when I notice it—beneath the layer of brash confidence and self-importance—I see the fatigue. The weariness in his rounded shoulders, a tiny chink of weakness in his powerful façade.

Suddenly, I find myself wondering if there's more to this asshole. There *has* to be more to this asshole.

But when he lifts his face to mine, all traces of vulnerability are gone. His voice goes flat. "Well, thanks for the civics lesson, Stormy." He glides a hand into his pocket and glances quickly at a ratty, old wristwatch with a broken strap. "I'll keep all that in mind."

He rises abruptly from his seat just as Jessa emerges from the back room. Relief washes my sister's features when she sees that the espresso machine is in working order. She hurries to fill an extra-small to-go cup for the petulant customer.

Mr. Billions snaps his fingers at the barista like she's nothing more than a poorly-trained dog. I bite back the insult at the tip of my tongue as Jessa rushes across the room, looking equal parts terrified and hypnotized.

"Sir, I am so, so sorry about the wait," she says as she places the paper cup in his hand. "M-my manager says it's on the house. We couldn't *possibly* expect you to pay after all that inconvenience."

His towering height amplifies his intimidating aura a thousand times over. He levels my poor sister with a chilly glare that could give a penguin frostbite. A growly noise escapes his throat. "Damn right, I'm not paying for the coffee."

My forehead tightens painfully on a sharp frown. The nerve of that man. He brags about being a gazillionaire, and then he jumps at the first opportunity to worm his way out of paying for his coffee? That's why the rich get richer and all that shit.

He digs into his back pocket again. And this time, he produces a fat wad of cash pinched together by a solid gold money clip. Broke as I am, my throat goes dry watching him yank out a hundred dollar bill and fling it onto the table like it's nothing more than a used paper napkin.

He addresses Jessa. "For the bagel." Then, he throws me a challenging look. "And for the... *attitude*? My apologies." One corner of his mouth curls up into a barely-there smirk, silently daring me to say something.

For once, I keep my mouth zipped. My throat is too parched for words anyway.

Must be nice, being able to fling hundred dollar bills at lowly peasants to buy your way off the shit list.

Jessa stutters, obviously stunned to have earned such a hefty tip. "Th-thank you, s-sir."

Her face is an unflattering shade of red, but the gorgeous rascal probably doesn't notice because his defiant stare is still on me. His caramel eyes glint victoriously at my speechlessness. He leans close to my ear and his gravel-velour voice teases the hollow of my belly. "Don't let that smart mouth get you in trouble today, Stormy."

He steps back, slowly swiping his tongue across his lips, sweeping those sesame seeds away.

I can't help but imagine him using that tongue somewhere...*else.* "Will you quit calling me 'Stormy'? My name is—"

"Didn't ask," he cuts me off mercilessly.

My jaw drops loose like a trapdoor. This man's curtness stuns me silent. His severe stare pauses on my mouth for a half-second. Heat whips through me, head to toe, as he coolly turns and saunters out the exit. All the air gets sucked out with him.

Jessa slaps a hand over her chest and sighs audibly. "You two are gonna have the hottest, sweatiest animal sex. Mark my words."

I can barely hear my breathless whisper above the roaring of my heart. "Shut up, Jessa."

4

CANNON

The headquarters of Kingston Realty Holdings is a half-block down from that sad excuse for a coffee shop. I push through the finger-smudged glass door.

The messy, little creature with the big, sassy attitude is still on my mind.

She's loud, opinionated, annoying as hell. Sauntering around town at eight in the morning looking like she just got flung off a mechanical bull. And she expects people to take her seriously?

But why the hell am I still thinking about her? And more importantly, what's with this stupid grin on my face?

It's been a while since anyone's stood up to me. When I get into asshole mode—like I admittedly was at the coffee shop—people usually cower away. But she refused to back down. She challenged me. She called me on my foul-ass attitude. That takes fallopian fortitude.

And tits on a teddy bear—I think I like it.

A part of me is impressed. And fascinated. And curious to know more about her.

Another part of me says don't even think about it.

Taming that wild woman would be a project and quite frankly, I have enough shit on my plate. She's nothing but a distraction, which is exactly what I *don't* need.

I move across the lobby of Kingston Realty Holdings and something feels...*off*.

Although my family's business has evolved into a veritable empire over the nearly five decades that it's been in operation, this building itself has always been modest. My grandfather has always been a simple man. Low-key. Committed to his small town roots. But currently, the building is more than just 'understated'. It's rundown.

There's a thick layer of dust covering the abandoned security desk and the shrivelling potted plants are begging for hydration. I nearly face-plant when I trip on a mop-bucket forgotten in the middle of the elevator.

I shake off any lingering thoughts of my confrontation with that saucy woman from the coffee shop and I let myself into the office suite on the top floor. I flip on light switches as I travel down the hallway. The place smells musty. And sad. Thank god Gramps stopped coming into the office years ago. He'd be appalled.

I fall into a chair at the conference table and the sound of my ass hitting the cracked leather seat practically echos throughout the entire suite. That's how quiet the place is.

I pull out my beat up watch with the broken leather strap and double-check the time. The gears of the business world begin grinding at eight. Hell, that's when the grunt work starts. But if you're the boss, your ass better be in your swiveling chair before seven. Yet, my father is nowhere in sight.

By the time eight-thirty rolls around, I've only encountered three other humans here at Kingston Realty Holdings.

My father's grouchy secretary, Sally, an ancient realtor who's just killing time until he qualifies to collect his retirement package and some guy who is taking a nap next to an empty box of Cheez-Its at the staff room table.

My family owns the largest real estate company in the tri-county area, having snatched up almost ninety percent of the commercial realty in town. I spent most of my childhood here, watching Gramps teach my father the ropes so that he could one day carry on the Kingston family legacy. The place was always bustling with activity. Lease renewals. Tenant applications. New property acquisitions. Dull moments were few and far between.

But today? Today, I haven't heard a single phone ring. Through the conference room glass, I've got a clear view of the entire floor, and the whole mood is just fucking depressing.

I tap at a few buttons on my phone and swivel my chair back and forth as it rings. My youngest brother, Jude, answers with a grunt and I hear the clinks and clanks of exercise equipment in the background.

"Is there a holiday I don't know about?" I ask as I slide on my reading glasses.

Jude chuckles into the receiver. "I'm a professional athlete. What do I care what day it is? It's all the same to me."

My brother has a way of turning everything into a joke. He plays football for the Iowa Paragons and he thinks that gives him license to joke around all the time. And maybe it does. But after the type of morning I've had, I'm really not in the mood for Jude's flippant attitude right now.

At the grumble that pours from my chest, He goes half-serious for long enough to ask. "What is it, Cannon? What do you want? I'm with my trainer right now and—"

"Do you know what's going on with Dad? And Kingston Realties? I'm at the office today, and things just feel...off." I'm sifting through the legal documents Frank emailed to me a few minutes ago. Efficient as always, my lawyer has already started compiling a detailed dossier on Carl's assets. Mostly a list of rapidly depreciating consumer items. No real valuables. Nothing that will last in the long run. I plan to ruin it all anyway.

I hear the confusion in my brother's voice when he asks, "You're in *Crescent Harbor*? What are you doing back? Is everything all right with you?"

"Story for a different day," I mutter impatiently.

"Wait, this isn't about Margot, is it?" He sounds suspicious. "The girl's been blowing up Twitter all morning with cryptic tweets about heartbreak and true love and billionaires with small dicks." His chortle rips across the staticky phone connection. "Smells like a breakup to me. Please, make me the happiest man alive and tell me that you finally dumped that lunatic."

"Yes. Margot and I are done," I say plainly. I give my brother a quick run-down of last night's events.

Jude blows out a sigh of relief. "Well, all I can say is you're lucky you made it out of that relationship with your balls intact because that woman is nuttier than a barrel of pistachios."

Dropping my head, I massage the bridge of my nose. "Jude, I didn't call you to get into petty gossip." My temper snaps. "Tell me what's up with Dad. It's eight-thirty and he's not even at work yet."

A subtle note of worry creeps into my brother's voice. "How am I supposed to know, bro? I don't live in Crescent Harbor, either. Did you call Walker?"

"No, I didn't call Walker. You know how he is."

Our oldest brother *should* have been my first call but I didn't even bother trying. The guy is a damn recluse. I swear —he does more socializing with the sweet pepper seedlings on his farm than he does with actual, y'know, humans. Aside from his best friend, Penny, hardly anyone else can get a word out of him.

"I'm sure it's nothing to worry your pretty little head about," Jude says on a nervous chuckle. "Dad's been running things since Eli got locked up, and he ran things for a shit ton of years before that. I'm sure he's got it under control." I hear my brother's trainer yelling at him in the background to get off the phone. "Look—I'm with my team right now. Can I hit you back in—I don't know—an hour?"

"Yeah, sure. Call me back." My eyes surf over the empty cubicles again as we disconnect.

I take a deep breath, blowing it out slowly and forcing myself to relax. Jude may not know a lick about the family business, but he's probably right. Kingston Realties has been in the family for over four decades. I should have a little faith and trust that my dad has got things covered.

Besides, I didn't pull an all-nighter, crossing state lines, to meddle in small town real estate. I came to Crescent Harbor to plot sweet revenge against my treacherous business partner. So I shuffle the stack of documents in front of me and dive in.

After an eternity and a half, the loud elevator ding pulls me out of my work. I look up just in time to catch my father step into the suite. For a second, I have to stop and backtrack. Just how long has it been since I last saw him? Because he looks like he's aged a decade. His hair is entirely gray, as is the stubble covering his jawline. I can't remember the last time I saw a version of Dad who wasn't clean-shaven.

His secretary greets him lethargically. I check the time on my watch. It's almost ten.

I pull off my glasses and rise to intercept him before he disappears into his corner office. Dad's footsteps falter and his tired eyes widen in surprise. "Cannon...?"

"Hey, Dad," I greet him, patting his back in a manly hug.

My father pulls back and eyes me. "Your mother didn't tell me you'd be in town."

I flinch at the mention of my overprotective mother. I have enough on my plate without having to consider how stressed she'd be if she found out about Carl and Margot. "She doesn't know I'm here yet. I was overdue for a surprise visit."

Dad expels an unamused puff of air. "You were overdue for any kind of visit, son. When was the last time you came home?"

I laugh tightly. "I'm here now, Dad. Why does the last time matter?"

My father shakes his head and turns toward his office. Dad is a family man through and through and by his body language, it's clear that I've disappointed him with my long absences.

I follow him into his office and drop into a chair opposite his desk. "I have some *business* to take care of while I'm in town, so I made myself comfortable in the conference room. I hope you don't mind."

Dad's arm sweeps through the air. "Of course. Help yourself to whatever you need. The internet connection is shit and the printer is a prehistoric piece of junk, but all of our resources are at your disposal, Cannon."

There's an invisible weight in the air, making the entire room tense and heavy. I let it consume the office while I observe my father's slack face and sluggish demeanor. I know I'm not making this shit up. Something is wrong.

I glance out at the empty cubicles again. "Well, business definitely doesn't seem to be booming around here," I comment, keeping my tone as light as possible. "Where is everybody?"

Dad sighs heavily. He looks exhausted, plain and simple. "Well, when the CEO of a company gets hauled off to jail, employees tend to jump ship to save their reputations. I can't say I blame them."

Fucking Eli.

My brother went to jail a year ago for doing some shady-ass shit. White collar shit. It's been a real fucking nightmare.

My father worked hard his whole life. Now, he's in his golden years. He should be sitting on a yacht somewhere with Mom in the middle of the Mediterranean. Not being forced out of partial retirement to take control of the sinking ship that Kingston Realties has apparently become.

After my father took the company over from my maternal grandfather, he successfully ran the business for years while grooming Eli to one day take over the reins. That way, Dad could eventually slow down. Step back.

It never occurred to me to step in after Eli went to jail. I assumed that Dad could handle regaining control of the office now that Eli is out of the picture. This *was* his career for three decades after all. But as I sit here now, looking around the ghost town of an office, It's clear that shit is definitely not under control.

Maybe I *should* step in. Maybe I should find a way to help more. I start developing a plan in my mind. I could hire an outside firm to audit the books—to take inventory of the company's assets and liabilities. I'd probably need more admin staff and a team of realtors to rebuild our acquisitions department. Then, I'd focus on—

My cell phone rings, pulling me out of my head. It's Frank again.

Reality check.

I don't have the time to get involved in the family business. Not when I have ninety-nine problems of my own.

I'm rising to my feet before I've even accepted the call. "I've got to take this, Dad." I motion to my phone.

He nods unconvincingly. When I look into his eyes, I see the face of a drowning man. A man who needs help.

I turn and walk away.

I will not get involved I will not get involved I will not get involved.

The sole reason I'm in town right now is tearing down Carl and Margot. That's what I need to focus on until the mission is complete. Kingston Realties is none of my business. That was Eli and Dad's deal.

I answer the phone as I stroll down the carpeted hallway. "Frank, you'd better have good news for me."

Without skipping a beat, the lawyer picks up his usual speed-rambling, but my footsteps falter outside my brother's old office.

Everything in the room is just as it was before my brother went to jail. Smiling photos of Eli, his wife, and their daughter, Callie, cover every flat surface. Crayon drawings of stick figures are framed on the walls. There's even a child's stuffed animal on the narrow couch across from his desk. Eli truly was obsessed with his little family before epically screwing up his life.

Maybe for the first time, the loss of my brother hits me like a sucker punch. I pause and brace the doorframe. *You really fucked up, Eli.*

But screw these emotions trying to rear their head. I pull the handle and slam the door closed. Out of sight and out of mind is better.

"Repeat that, Frank. Bad connection," I lie as I turn my back on my family's drama and head back to my homebase in the conference room.

5
LEXI

The young bride-to-be stands on the platform in the middle of my boutique and eyes her reflection with a skeptical expression. "Do you *really* think I can get away with a mermaid-style?" She cradles her tiny baby bump as she twirls from side to side in front of the mirror. She lifts her gaze to mine.

"You look gorgeous, Kayla. Absolutely stunning," I tell the bride. And it's the truth. My voice goes softer as I speak to her. "But the number one most important thing on your wedding day is that you feel amazing. So, if you don't feel totally confident in that dress, I have a bunch of others I can show you." I roll over a rack of selections I set aside especially for Kayla when she called yesterday to set up her consultation.

I sweep a flowy hippie-style gown from the rack and hold it in front of me. This dress is cheaper than the mermaid-style and the sale would net me less profit but ultimately, I just want to see my customer happy, in a dress that will make her feel like a bazillion dollars as she walks down the aisle toward the man she loves.

I still remember the heartbroken woman who traded in this particular dress in exchange for a few twenty dollar bills. I remember handing her tissues across the counter as she explained that her fiancé called off the wedding at the last minute. She was trying to unload the dress quickly in hopes of lessening the pain. She said she hoped her misfortune would transmute into some lucky woman's happily ever after. I truly think Kayla might be that lucky woman.

A fresh set of tears spring up on the rims of her eyes. "Being pregnant on my wedding day was never part of the plan. It just...happened. And my mom and dad aren't being all that supportive. So, it means the world to me that you're being so nice, Lexi."

I feel my own tears tickling my eyes. I know what it's like to be disappointed by your parents. "Oh hun, I'm just so honored to be helping you make this decision." I give her a tight hug.

Kayla waddles into the changing room and eventually, she emerges looking like a bohemian dream. She couldn't be more gorgeous and she knows it, too. "How do you feel, hun?" I ask, peering at her over her shoulder in the mirror.

My customer nods happily, tears in her eyes. She hiccups a response. "Perfect. I-I...I feel absolutely perfect."

This is my favorite part of being in the bridal gown business. I love to get involved and make personal recommendations. To play such a big part in such a crucial decision for a future bride makes me feel purposeful.

I don't fit the profile. I know that. I don't look like those glossy, sophisticated boutique attendants on *Say Yes to the Dress*. My clients aren't typical, either. They aren't wealthy socialites with unlimited budgets. They're just regular women, trying to stretch every dollar to make sure their wedding day is special. Being a vital part of this process fills me with joy.

After a few twirls in front of the mirror, Kayla glides out of the dress. I carefully slip it into a garment bag as she counts out her money and hands me a fistful of cash. The dresses in here are second-hand. Most are seriously marked down. It isn't all that much money. But putting a smile on a bride-to-be's face, taking that worry off of her shoulders before her big day? That's priceless.

Peering down at the pittance in my cash register makes my stomach curl up with anxiety. I force myself to take a step back and look at the bigger picture. Business may be slow now but spring is right around the corner. The bridal season is about to pick up. Things will get better.

Finally, I'm walking Kayla to the door with her garment bag draped delicately over her arm. She thanks me with another quick hug. When she leaves, I kick off my shoes in the middle of the boutique. I stroll through the showroom, imagining the place through a stranger's eyes.

I won't lie—there's a lot on my to-do list. I want to replace the peeling pale blue floral wallpaper and the hardwood floors need to be buffed and varnished. Still, my heart swells with pride. I love this little boutique.

To the outside world, the boutique might not seem like much but each and every day, I wake up at the crack of dawn and pour all of my heart and soul into making my shop the best it can be.

I installed the up-cycled crystal chandelier all by myself. The tufted velvet armchairs, I found on the curb and reupholstered. I hand-painted the gold accents to the crown-molding. Bringing this place to life has been messy and it's been bloody at times and some nights, my friends held me while I cried buckets of tears. But every second of it has been a labor of love. I hold onto the belief that my efforts will pay off. One day.

Somehow, my mind moves back to the jerk from Jittery Joe's. I usually don't give a porcupine's ass what anyone thinks of me and my business but I find myself wondering how he'd feel about my humble little shop. I can't brag about billion dollar bank accounts, but I've kept this business afloat through some pretty tough times and I'm proud, dammit.

I'm a freaking business owner.

Not bad for a twenty-six-year-old from the wrong side of the tracks. That sort of thing is unheard of where I come from. My blood, sweat and tears put food on the table every single day. That's more than I can say for the people who raised me.

I position myself in front of the mirror and grin. "You really did good for yourself, Lexi." I glance down at my blouse and realize that it's been misbuttoned all day. Well shit. "Okay, the packaging still needs a little work but aside from that, I'm doing good for myself."

What I need is to figure out a way to usher more customers through the door. My marketing budget is virtually non-existent so I need some ideas that will draw buyers to my shop without costing me an arm and a leg. Worrying about that is what keeps me up at night.

The metal bell above my door dings, announcing another customer. I scramble to slip back into my shoes as I'm re-buttoning my shirt.

"Just me," sings a voice I recognize. Iris ducks in through the front door, still decked out in a boxy yellow Merlini's Sandwich Shop T-shirt and unflattering khakis from her day at the sandwich shop. The fact that my petite, curvy friend gets hit on nonstop in that outfit is a testament to how deep her good looks run. Because I could *not* pull that shit off.

I meet her halfway and yank her into a hug. "Hey, you!" She whips a small bouquet of flowers from behind her back and thrusts it at my face. "For me?!"

I love it whenever my friend surprises me with an artful arrangement from her garden. The flowers always make Renewed Gowns come alive.

Iris shrugs as I take the fiery multi-colored dahlias. "I just wanted to drop in and say thank you for having my back this past weekend. Friday was literally the worst day of my life, and it meant a lot that you were there for me."

"I've always got your back, girl. Always." I gush at the flowers as I speak. "Gosh, these are beautiful. You really do have a green thumb."

She peels off her hideous red visor and shakes out her blonde hair. "Gardening is my coping mechanism. I would have probably tracked down my husband and punched that fool in the throat by now if I didn't have an excuse to get my hands covered in dirt." We both laugh. "Anyway, I also want to thank you for, y'know, returning those, y'know...*things* to the post office the other day."

"By *things*, do you mean those big, hard, girthy, vibrating—"

"Stop that." Iris nudges my arm, her face turning beet red. She's such a damn prude.

Laughing, I flit around my shop, putting the dresses from Kayla's reject pile back on their racks. Iris grabs the broom to help me close up.

This is our unofficial late afternoon routine. On the days when my friend ends her day down the block at the sandwich shop early, she pops in to say hello. Whenever I close up before she does, I swing by her shop instead. I hope none of that changes now that her dirtbag husband has turned her world upside down.

"Don't worry your pretty head about that." I wave her away. "I'm just excited to see you up and out of bed today. You look good." Her eyes are still puffy, but the redness from all the crying has subsided.

A hint of a smile lingers on her face. "I don't *feel* good."

"Trust me. You, Iris Merlini, are going to be fine. More than fine. You are going to find your happily ever after. A kind, gorgeous, romantic Adonis who's going to make Kirk look like the sewage sludge that he is." The way she looks at me, I know she's doubtful. But I truly believe that. In the meantime, however... "I know what will make you feel better. Let's get all dolled up tonight and go clubbing."

"Nuh-uh. No way. Isn't today *Tuesday*?" Iris crosses her arms tightly, effectively shutting down the idea.

"Why not?" I pout.

"Because today is *Tuesday*." She whispers the word like it's blasphemous, like she expects a stern-faced nun to burst around a corner and pop her on the wrist with a ruler.

I flutter my eyeballs up to the chandeliered ceiling. "I'm sure it's Saturday somewhere in the world."

That gets my friend to chuckle. "Jeez, Lexi. Clubbing isn't always the answer, y'know."

What can I say? I love to let loose. I spend so much time putting up a front, trying to come across as professional, trying to get taken seriously. It's exhausting. At the end of the day, I just want to party. That ain't a crime!

"Plus, you might meet a guy and we both know you desperately need a fling." I wink.

Not surprisingly, my friend disagrees. "A fling is precisely the last thing on my mind right now. I have to figure out how in the world I'm going to afford my house, my shop, my life."

I frown as I empty the register and bury the cash at the bottom of my purse. "What do you mean? Isn't Kirk going to have to pay alimony?"

"Doubt it," she mumbles. "Our prenup was tighter than a virgin with a kegel addiction." I snort at the vivid analogy. "I doubt I'm getting a penny out of him. I was already three months behind on my rent *before* my husband walked out on me, and I expect that things will only get worse now that I've been dumped."

I cringe. "Three months?"

She nods, her forehead pleated with worry. Merlini's is one of the busiest eateries around town in the summer but things slow way down as soon as the out-of-towners go home at the end of the season.

I pull on my happy-go-lucky grin, wanting to make my friend feel better. "We'll figure this out," I assure her. "I'm a few weeks behind on my rent, too. Actually, I need to go talk to Mr. Kingston and try to work out a deal with him. You should come with me."

Iris shakes her head, looking sick to her stomach. She's not great at having uncomfortable conversations. "I can't. I'm so far behind. I'm not ready to face him yet."

"You'll be fine. Mr. Kingston is great. For a rich guy, he's pretty understanding."

It's well known that most businesses around here struggle during the winter months. Bordering on Lake Michigan, Crescent Harbor is a small blip of a town in the northernmost part of Illinois. Its breathtaking shoreline, quirky shops and lively nightspots draw throngs of visitors once the temperature starts rising but for the rest of the year, its five thousand residents are definitely not enough to keep the coffers of the local businesses overflowing.

Money gets tight for everybody when the snow falls and the out-of-towners retreat inland. Mr. Kingston knows that.

Things *will* get better. At least I hope so.

I flick off the lights and Iris follows me to the door.

"I almost forgot," she says, and without looking at her, I can sense the smile in her voice. "I heard from Jessa that you were totally flirting with a hot guy at the coffee shop the other day."

I groan out loud as I lock up. "Damn, my sister is such a gossip. I thought you had bigger things to worry about than my non-existent sex life."

My relationship track record isn't great. Yeah, guys try to hook up with me now and then. They want to mess around 'cause that's just the way guys are. But the minute they realize that I'm a handful, that I'm more than they bargained for, they tend to bolt.

I'm far from a virgin but I've never been in a real relationship. At least, nothing worth getting into specifics about.

But it's whatever. I'm focused on building my business and the less distractions the better.

Iris buries her face in my shoulder, suppressing a weak laugh. "Bear with me. I just need a break from all the drama in my own life."

I sigh. "Well, the guy at the coffee shop was a complete asshole, so I was definitely not flirting with him."

She hooks her arm through mine. "Sometimes arguing is foreplay," she quips as we stroll down the street arm in arm.

I roll my eyes. She couldn't be more wrong. "I can assure you that it was not foreplay. In any form."

When we reach the intersection, I turn to give her a

quick hug. But as we're about to part ways, I realize that her sad eyes are back. As her friend, I just want to make her smile again.

"Fine," I spit out grudgingly. "I'll admit it. The guy was kind of good-looking. Are you happy now?"

She breaks into a face-wide grin that looks extra-ridiculous under her stupid hat. "Tell me more..." She rubs her hands together like a comic book villain.

I fight a smile and turn in the direction of my landlord's office building. "You're a weirdo," I call out as I go.

Sure, I can admit that the jerkface was good-looking. But what I can't admit is that his gorgeous face played in my mind last night as I fingered myself to sleep.

6

CANNON

With bleary eyes, I blink at the mess of documents fanned out across the conference room table. I went back to my estate to catch a few hours of much-needed shuteye last night but not nearly enough. And now I've barricaded myself in Kingston Realties's top floor conference room. I'd be concerned about taking over so much space in an office that isn't mine, but it's become abundantly clear that no one cares. I could paint the space in a yellow and green zebra motif, and no one would even notice.

On the side wall of the room, I've begun mapping out my *Fuck Carl* plan, taking full liberties with the office supply of paper and tape. I think my strategies are playing out quite nicely.

Pinned in the center of the wall is a grainy photo of Carl's ugly mug. His assets and liabilities are detailed there in black and white, with colorful post-its and newspaper clippings and receipts thrown in, too. From his shares in various failing startups to the savings bonds his aunt Edna gave him for his bar mitzvah and his fishing boat in Tortola.

I have graphs and flowcharts branching off to the sides with notes mapping out the systematic demise of the asshat's wobbly empire.

Yup, I plan to wreck it all.

"Are you sure this is everything?" I ask my lawyer.

"My law firm used every means at its disposal—legal and not so legal—and these are the last assets we were able to uncover," Frank assures me.

Good, very good. I barely resist the urge to rub my hands together. I cannot wait to destroy Carl, to show him exactly what he's worth. Utterly nothing. That's what he's worth.

The backstabbing asshole won't even be able to go fishing when I'm through with him.

This is going to be way too much fun.

I'll admit to having a little hop in my step as I grab a file off the table and head out toward the photocopy room. My balls are practically aching to add these documents to my wall of doom. But right as I pass by the elevator, the door slides open.

My neck snaps back at the sight of the woman traipsing off the lift. She stops in her tracks with a hard blink.

Wild hair. Baby doll eyes. Outfit a mess.

"You..." she seethes under her breath.

At the sight of her, I feel like someone kicked out the chair from under me. I make a mental note to figure out what the fuck is up with this tight feeling in my chest. In the meantime, I manage to pull off a smirk.

"Good morning to you, too, Stormy. Look at you, beaming as always. Sunshine follows you everywhere you go, doesn't it?"

Tone light. Gaze aloof. Cock hard. She doesn't need to know that last part, though.

. . .

SHE RESPONDS, words bathed in fire. "Oh, vampires aren't supposed to be out in the sunlight. You really ought to stop taking those kinds of risks with your wellbeing, Mr. Billions."

A chuckle shoots past my lips. Christ, she's fiery.

She narrows her bright, inquisitive eyes on me. "And what are you doing here anyway?" Then she glances around the rental office and her expression shifts with panic. "Is Mr. Kingston your landlord, too? Please don't tell me you're opening a business in Crescent Harbor."

Her face is so expressive. Her eyes broadcast every little thought that flits through her mind, every fleeting feeling that moves through her body. I find that so endearing.

Yes, she may be a handful but I come from a world where every woman is putting on an act. It's refreshing to meet someone sincere, blunt, *real*. It makes me feel something.

I pluck my phone from my pocket and boredly scroll across the screen so I don't have to face these unsettling desires. "*Me*? Open a business in *Crescent Harbor*? That's cute." I spit out a laugh.

A hand leaps to her chest. "Oh, thank god. The idea of having to deal with you at merchant's association meetings was almost enough to make me close up shop."

When I step forward, the sweetness of her wild hair crawls into my lungs. Girly and crisp. Grapefruit juice. That's what she smells like. Grapefruit juice on a hot-as-hell summer day.

I lower my voice by her ear. "I'm not opening up shop in town but let me give you some business advice; it's not a good business practice to go around insulting your landlord's son."

I pull back just in time to witness her expression crumple. She examines my face. "You're..."

"Cannon Kingston." With a smirk, I extend a hand.

She freezes. She blinks. Her chest expands and her nostrils flare. Then she marches right past me. "Didn't ask."

I drop my head and shake it. God. This girl is fire.

I'm too intrigued to go off on my photocopying mission, so I hover nearby as she approaches the secretary. "Morning Sally. Can I speak with Mr. Kingston?" Stormy asks.

The bored-looking woman glances up from the sudoku puzzle she's hunched over. "Sorry, Ms. Robson. He hasn't come in yet today. What is this with regards to?"

Stormy recoils, appalled. "Hey, now. None of that. Call me Alexia. Hell, call me Lexi." She takes a glimpse of me over her shoulder like she's making sure I heard her name.

Yeah, I heard it, honey. Loud and clear.

Alexia. Alexia Robson. I like it. For some reason, it suits her.

And it appears that Alexia Robson happens to be a business owner *and* a tenant of Kingston Realties. I wasn't expecting that, but then again, I should know by now that half the townies I run into will have some sort of tie to one of our many assets. Ms. Stormy continues to catch me off guard.

She shoots me another glare over her shoulder. This one is less defiant, more self-conscious. I don't avert my eyes to give her the privacy she seems to be seeking. Instead, I smirk and lean a shoulder on the doorframe, feet crossed at the ankles.

She cuts her eyes at me and bends over the desk. And oh, what a glorious view. Tight waist, firm ass, legs for days and weeks and months. "I'd rather just speak to Mr. Kingston directly, if that's okay?" She talks in a hushed voice.

Sally smiles a motherly smile. "Of course, Lexi. Does next week work?" Stormy nods. "Great, I'll get you on his calendar then."

My phone buzzes in my pocket. A string of new text messages. I pull it out to check.

Carl: Hey buddy

Carl: How's it going?

Carl: DataCo's credit cards are frozen. You happen to know anything about that?

My mood sours instantly. *Well, thanks for killing my vibe, asshat.*

At the unpleasant interruption, I realize that I'm *way* too invested in Alexia and her secrets. I have enough shit of my own to deal with. Plus, I don't want to give her the satisfaction of knowing how very intriguing I find her.

Hell, I don't even want to admit to myself how very intriguing I find her.

I peel myself away from the doorframe and wander down the hall to the copy room. I force myself to think business-thoughts, billionaire-thoughts, world-domination-thoughts as I arrange my file in one of the feeder trays and prep the ancient machine to copy my documents.

The stack of papers lying abandoned in the print tray catches my attention and that makes me irrationally angry. Good god, not only is the staff here incompetent, they are also disgustingly lazy. How hard is it to take a break from eating Cheez-Its and playing sudoku to run some papers through the damn shredder?

Lucky for them, I've decided not to meddle in the way my Dad is running this business or else they'd all be in the unemployment line by the end of the day.

I move to grab the sheets to dump them in the recycling bin. But when my eyes graze the top sheet, my steps falter.

I read the first page. And then the next. And then the next.

"What the fuck am I looking at...?" I put on my glasses and drop into the folding chair beside the fax machine.

My eyes scan the list of Kingston Realties's assets and corresponding balance sheets. There's a hell of a lot more red ink on this page than black. All along I thought that Kingston Realty Holdings' biggest problem was employees eating junk food and playing puzzles on the company dime.

I was wrong.

No, the company's biggest problem is in the negative cash flow, the shrinking asset list, the outrageous debt value.

The truth is staring me straight in my face. My grandfather's company—his legacy—it's dying a fast and painful death.

My entire world tips off its axis. And suddenly, plotting revenge on Carl and Margot isn't the center of the universe anymore.

7

LEXI

"Who'd you rather?" Jessa holds the magazine to her chest and aims an excited look at Iris. "An athlete or a rockstar?"

Iris rolls her eyes at my sister from where she's wiping down tables across the sandwich shop.

"I'm serious," Jessa insists with a giggle, tucking her legs beneath her in her creaky plastic chair.

"And so am I." Iris sweeps her arm up and down, gesturing to her petite, voluptuous body. "What kind of athlete or musician are we talking about here? A blind ping-pong player? A clarinet player with a beer gut and body odor?"

Iris's body image issues make me so mad. How can she not see how fabulous she is?

"You stop it," I chide. "You are a prize and you are gorgeous." I tip my cup and slurp soda through my straw.

Penny struts out of the back room and pauses to study her cousin's outfit. "You're a babe, Iris, but that frumpy uniform you're wearing really isn't helping the situation."

Iris scoffs despite the laughter in her eyes. "How dare you?"

Her cousin grins and shrugs. "I can get away with saying that because you're the boss of this sandwich shop, so honey, that ugly uniform is *a choice.*"

Jessa and I laugh as Iris defensively smooths her hands down the front of her work t-shirt before adjusting her matching visor. Both items have Merlini's Sandwich Shop screen-printed across the fabric. "Excuse me, Miss Hot Stuff, but not everybody gets to show up to work looking like Jessica Rabbit come-to-life."

Penny throws an arm around her cousin and gives her a squeeze. "You know I'm joking, Iris. I'm just trying to interrupt your perpetual pity party and make you smile."

"The nerve of her," Jessa leans across the table and grins. "She is a *monster.*"

Iris's eye roll is accompanied by a half-smile.

"Anyway, I love you all." Penny goes around the room, kissing us each on the forehead. Then she adjusts her cleavage inside her low-cut halter top. "I'm off to earn my livelihood. Drinks on me if you guys come by the bar later."

I yip excitedly. "I'm in!"

Iris's shoulders clam up immediately. She gives me an uneasy look before her eyes flash over to Penny. "I-I don't know if I'm ready for that yet."

"It's just an invitation, Iris. No pressure. Take all the time you need. The bar isn't going anywhere." The cousins share a smile.

We call out our goodbyes to Penny as she exits the building, on her way to her bartending job at the Frosty Pitcher.

I shift my attention back to Iris and speak in a soft voice. "Hey. Come sit with us. You've cleaned that table at least three times, and we're the only people here. Take a break."

Iris falls into the seat next to me. That defeated look clouds her face again. "It's easier when I'm busy..." she confesses softly.

It hurts my heart to see her like this. All the uncertainty in her eyes. The way her shoulders curl in like a visceral instinct to protect her fragile heart. I can't even imagine what she's going through.

Jessa seems to be thinking the same thing. She puts on a cheery smile and slides a glossy magazine in front of Iris. "Play along. Open it. Pick your new obsession. Just for fun."

My friend eyes me and I nod, silently encouraging her to loosen up, to have some harmless fun daydreaming about men we'll never meet in person. I hold up an open page and gush about some random actor's amazing abs. My Disney princess sister gets pulled in by an alphahole in a crisp business suit with tattoos crawling up from the collar of his button-down. As for Iris, she lingers on an article about a bad boy football player.

"I knew it. Athletes are totally your type," I joke. Iris smacks me over the head with her magazine but she doesn't deny it so I tease her a bit. "Y'know, Iowa has a pretty good-looking NFL team, and I'm always up for a road trip." I wink.

"Oh boy," Iris groans, but it's only to disguise her laughter.

Before I can download a travel app and start planning a girls' weekend, I notice a uniformed man lingering by the shop's door. I recognize him as the county bailiff.

"Hey, Mike," I call out and wave.

From the sidewalk right outside, he nods in our direction, but doesn't smile. I'm confused when he lingers by the door instead of coming in for a salami sub like he usually does. But then I see him grab a piece of paper and a strip of tape out of his file folder.

And my heart stops.

The bailiff holds the sheet to the glass of the door and seals it with tape on each of the four sides.

"No..." Iris whispers, her eyes widening as Mike finishes his task.

Gingerly, he steps inside and slips a copy of the document across the table in front of my shaking friend. "I'm real sorry, Iris. Only doing my job." He leaves the room in silence.

Jessa is the first to speak. "What? What is that?" She cranes her neck to read the paper. I shake my head at her to shut the heck up.

She's not a business owner like Iris and me. She doesn't know that a bailiff showing up with legal documents can be the kiss of death for a small enterprise like this sandwich shop.

"What?" Jessa asks again, shaking her head back at me, completely not getting it. She pulls the paper toward her then proceeds to read Iris's eviction notice out loud.

The words of the document send an icy feeling down my spine, digging up painful memories I buried deep into my subconscious a long damn time ago. *Now is not the time, Alexia.* I push them down and focus on my friend.

Iris's throat quivers when she swallows. Her gaze slowly lifts to my face. "Seven days...I have seven days to vacate the premises..."

8

CANNON

I'm set up in my usual conference room chair when my father marches off the elevator. I slip my broken watch out of my front pocket to note the time. Color me impressed. This is the earliest I've seen Dad at the office in the days that I've been here. Not even Cheez-Its guy is here yet.

He's lost that tired, dreary look. This morning, it's pure fire in his expression. In fact, my father looks downright pissed.

When he shoves open the conference room door, it ricochets off the wall. "What the hell did you do, Cannon?"

Whoa there. "Good morning to you, too, Dad." Feet crossed at the ankles, I lean back and lazily stretch my arms above my head.

He isn't amused. "Three of my tenants called me last night in tears, because the bailiff served them eviction notices. And since I know I didn't file the paperwork, this has *your* name written all over it."

I knew Dad wouldn't be happy with me taking matters

into my own hands yesterday. But I was also aware that nothing would change unless I intervened.

My dad is a good guy. He's got a big heart. But that shit has no place in business.

"Well, expect more tearful calls," I say unapologetically. "because I'm still working my way down the list."

Sally lingers outside the door, pretending to rummage through a filing cabinet. I catch the discreet scowl she sends in my direction. It's the same scowl she's been wearing since I tasked her with coordinating the remainder of the evictions with the bailiff yesterday afternoon.

I get up from my seat and shut the door in her face. She scoffs.

Sally doesn't like me. Sally thinks I'm an asshole...Sally might be right.

I can't bring myself to care.

I grab a sheet of paper out of the stack in front of me, shaking it. There are at least two dozen names on this list. "Dad, how could you let all these people get away with not paying rent? For months on end?!"

Dad trudges past me and collapses into a chair across from me. "Cannon. Don't." Suddenly, he sounds like his tired self again.

"The company's cash flow is shit. And you're selling off inventory like crazy. Two properties on Elgin Street. One at Town Square. Half of the buildings on Promenade Boulevard are up for sale. The acquisitions department is practically inactive..." I stand and plant both fists on the table because I'm tired of him beating around the bushes. "What the fuck is going on here, Dad?"

My cellphone dings and I steal a peak down at the screen.

Carl: My savings bonds from Aunt Edna? Really???

Carl: Those were a gift for my bar mitzvah! You know how much they meant to me!

Carl: Me and Margot are TOGETHER Cannon and you have to accept that. Acting like a child is not the way to win her back. She loves me.

Margot? Really? The same Margot who has now resorted to sending me selfies of her genitals every chance she gets?

Congratulations to you, Carl. You've found a keeper.

My father wearily drags both hands down his face. "Cannon, I don't have time to chase down tenants for rent payments, and if I'm going to keep paying the few employees we have left, I need to unload some properties as soon as possible." He pins me with hard eyes. "This family is falling apart, so I could care less about running after a few dollars."

His words punch me in the gut. "What do you mean the family is falling apart?"

"Ever since your brother was convicted, everything has been shit. And not just here around the office. At home, too. Eli's wife dumped their daughter at the house and then she just took off. Your mother has been worried sick. She's having fainting spells. And I'm struggling to balance that drama with running a business that I practically retired from two years ago." Dad pinches the bridge of his nose and I recognize the gesture as pure frustration, a mannerism I inherited from him. "I'm sorry if this is a surprise, but when it comes to family, the business doesn't even come in a close second."

Silence settles in the room, crushing my chest. I collapse into my chair. "Why didn't you say something to me?"

He shakes his head and sighs. "Son, I tried talking to you. More than once. But I gave up because every word I say to you goes right over your head. You're so busy doing whatever the hell you're doing with your life..."

"That's not fair!"

"You've been in town for how many days now, and you *still* haven't come to see your mother."

Shit. I haven't forgotten. I've just been...distracted.

And in all honesty, I've been delaying the avalanche of worry that will sweep her up when I have to come clean to her about my failed relationship. Mom wants me to settle down and it always bothered her that my conjugal shit-show with Margot didn't seem to be headed in that direction.

Back to the issue at hand, my parents shouldn't have to handle this all by themselves. My drama with Carl and Margot should come second to this. To them. "Let me take some stuff off your plate, Dad. Let me get some managers in place to run the business—"

"I'm closing the business," he says abruptly, cutting me off.

What?! How? I think my jaw is hanging open.

"You can't close the business."

"I have to."

"You can't!" I slam my palm down on the tabletop. "This is Gramps's legacy. He built it with his bare hands, from the ground up."

My grandfather could barely put food on the table when a rundown guesthouse and the surrounding farmland went up for sale on the edge of the Parkroad River. My grandmother instantly fell in love with the place and Gramps knew he couldn't pass it up. He had to find a way to buy it for the love of his life. The place was practically crumbling, but he bought it, using all of his savings. He fixed up the building by himself, working evenings and weekends, until the couple could finally open up the space to guests. It took him two years to finish.

Eventually, the inn began profiting. Then Gramps used that profit to invest in a couple more places around town. An old auditorium. An apartment complex. He slowly added new assets to his name.

But the man bit off more than he could chew. He was working all the time. My grandmother felt neglected. One day, she up and left him. Gramps couldn't take it when his wife walked away. He hit a rough patch and was on the edge of losing it all. That's when dad stepped in. After my parents got married, my father helped Gramps turn the business around. Together, they turned Kingston Realties into a multimillion-dollar small town real estate dynasty. The dynasty that inspired me to build my own fortune and become the man I am today.

And now it's crumbling before my eyes.

I can't let this happen.

"Cannon, this is what I agreed to when I took over the business from your grandfather. I promised him that the company would always be run as a family venture, and that if I couldn't keep that promise, I'd shut it all down and distribute the proceeds amongst you and your brothers."

I don't believe this crap. Gramps would never agree to something so stupid. "That's bullshit. Let me see the acquisition documents," I demand. "I'll send them to my lawyer. I'm sure Frank can find a loophole."

Dad shakes his head. "It's not in the acquisition documents, son. But I gave him my word."

Popping up out of my chair, I start pacing the dirty low-pile carpet. I grate my fingernails across my scalp. "I can't even process what you're saying right now."

"This business tore your grandparents' marriage apart,"

Dad says, speaking slowly. "Your grandfather worked too much. He neglected his wife, and she left him. Losing her almost drove your Gramps crazy. So when he handed the company to me, the deal was that I would never let the business tear the family apart again. We would run it as a unit and if we couldn't, we would let it go. That was his one condition."

I laugh, but the sound is bitter and hollow. "This is insanity."

"My intention was always to leave it in the hands of Eli and his wife. But he went and got himself in trouble. Then Gabby dumped your niece and ran off. The rest of you boys aren't married so..." His shoulders heave when he exhales. "I have an outside investor coming in thirty days. I'll keep the guesthouse and Walker's farm but the investor is willing to buy up the rest of Kingston Realties's portfolio in one quick deal."

I scoff. "For pennies on the dollar, I'm sure."

Dad's haggard expression tells me he doesn't even care anymore. "It would be good for the family. It will allow me the time to take care of your mother and your niece. They're my number one priority. Not this place."

I still can't believe what I'm hearing. It's like I woke up in a bad network dramedy two weeks ago, and now I'm the butt of everyone's shitty jokes. What the fuck is going on?

But I can't let this happen. I can't let my father just sell off the business and hand me a check. Saving Gramps's legacy is far more important than money, and I will do whatever it takes to protect my grandfather's decades of hard work.

The old man taught me so much. Every life lesson I learned, I can tie back to him. The biggest one was loyalty, and my loyalty to my grandfather is unwavering.

The second lesson he taught me was resourcefulness.

No problem is born that doesn't possess a satisfying solution.

I flop back in my chair, silently seeking out a way to untangle Kingston Realties from this dilemma because I'm not going down without a fight. My eyes distractedly scan the list of non-paying tenants in my hand.

My gaze hooks on Alexia Robson's name, and instantly, the wheels start churning. The scheme slams into my brain so fast I almost need a neck brace for the whiplash.

"Well, Dad, as a matter of fact, I'm about to be a family man myself." My father looks up, confusion in his face when I make the announcement. "I am getting married."

Alexia Robson is about to be my satisfying solution.

Whether she likes it or not.

9

LEXI

When I yawn and stretch out across the front counter, I feel the back of my blouse pop out the waistband of my skirt. I groan. So not in the mood to adult today.

I only managed to squeeze in a few hours of sleep early this morning before throwing myself into a hot shower and getting my butt to the boutique.

I spent most of the night at Iris's sandwich shop, helping her pack up everything that wasn't bolted down. Who knew you needed so much shit to make deli sandwiches?

Iris did a good job of keeping herself together for the first few hours of packing but eventually she broke down into violent sobs. Penny took her home. Who could blame the girl for cracking? She's still coming to terms with the reality of her crumbling marriage. Now she has to deal with losing her business, too?

I couldn't walk away and leave all her supplies to be forcibly removed and auctioned off. Not when she's in such desperate need of money. Jessa stuck around and helped me for a bit but she took off when she thought I was almost done. Then I discovered a surprise supply closet that added two extra hours to my night. Now, I'm exhausted.

I can't decide who I hate more. Iris's two-timing bastard husband or Mr. Kingston, our scoundrel of a landlord. The man's timing couldn't be shittier. Hasn't he heard the rumors floating around town about Iris and Kirk's divorce? Why would he pull the rug out from under her when she's already struggling to get her footing?

Mr. Kingston always seemed so understanding. Apparently I pegged him all wrong. Hell, I better come up with my own rent—and quickly—or I'll be packing my own shit up next.

Anyway, now I'm sipping on my third latte of the morning, but the caffeine isn't even making a dent in my exhaustion. Instead, I just feel jittery. And I have to frigging pee again.

I should be stitching up the bodice of the lacy empire-style gown I got in stock this morning. But I just want to curl up under the cash register and take a nap.

I drop into the swivelling chair behind my desk and thumb through a personal development book I borrowed from the library.

After a few moments, I close my heavy eyes. Why not? I don't have any bridal appointments until this afternoon anyway and it's not like I'd actually fall asleep here. I just need a few seconds to rest my sore feet and my burning eyes.

But before long, I'm suspended in a state between sleep and wakefulness. I register the sound of the bell above the door. Faintly.

The heavy shadow stretching over me a second later wakes me the hell up, though. My eyes flick open.

Cannon Kingston.

My spine snaps straight and I wipe drool from my mouth with my forearm. Icy dread washes over me. "Why are you...? What are you doing here?" I slide my book into a desk drawer.

It feels like I'm trapped inside a nightmare. He looms above the front desk, staring down at me with a predatory smirk. "Napping on the job? You should write a handbook on your groundbreaking business practices, Stormy. It would revolutionize the industry."

I grab the edge of the counter and pop up to my feet. This is the asshole who insulted my little sister the first time he met her. He's part of the rich, apathetic family who evicted my best friend. And now he's mocking me straight to my face. I'm really in no mood to play.

But god—he *does* look good. In that rumpled, rebellious way of his. His button-up's sleeves are pushed back to his elbows to show off his tattooed forearms. His narrow tie is the slightest bit off-center. I want to reach up, wrap my hand around the fabric.

And pull.

"Wow," I start, my voice dripping with disgust. "I was expecting the bailiff to walk through my door. But I guess you showing up in person makes sense, too, Mr. Billions. Did you convince your dad to send you down here to evict me now? Are you here to do the honor yourself, just so you can enjoy the look on my face when you hand me my notice?"

I struggle to keep my true emotions clear of my face. I won't let him see how terrified I am by the idea of losing this business. My bridal boutique is practically all I have. I don't have a husband. I don't own my house. This shop means everything to me. It was my ticket to independence, my one-way voucher out of the life I grew up in. And I refuse to give up on it now.

Cannon's nostrils flare when he speaks. "My father has nothing to do with the eviction notices."

Is this guy for real? He's going to try and paint his dad as an innocent party here? "What are you talking about? I think I would know if Mr. Kingston sold the building. There are laws in this state that—"

"*I* sent those eviction notices."

Fuck. I should have suspected his hand in this from the beginning. Sadism definitely seems like this man's style.

"You are a *bastard*, Cannon Kingston." I seethe, shaking my head in disappointment. "There's a name for assholes who find pleasure in watching other people suffer. You're a frigging sociopath."

There's this half smirk on Cannon's face. It's dirty and it's evil.

And a dirty, evil part of me kind of wants to lick it clean.

"Let's cut the dramatic rhetoric, shall we? Yes, quite a few of your business neighbors will be getting evicted. They broke the terms of their leases by defaulting on their rent. Period. It's nothing personal. It's business."

He plants an elbow near my cash register and his musky, testosterone-heavy scent fills my head.

I hate that I'm getting a little hot and bothered for the son of a bitch.

My anger wars between wanting to hate myself and needing to lash out at him.

The latter wins out as I snarl at the man leaning against my shop counter.

"But *you* have a choice, Stormy. I have a very reasonable alternative for you. Maybe you don't have to lose your place…" I want to ask what the hell he's playing at, but I can tell he's baiting me.

"I feel so special," I deadpan. I wait for his next words with a thudding heart. My knees feel like they're packed with cotton. It's getting harder and harder to play it cool.

"You should." His fingers curl around the edge of the counter and they go white. "You just have to marry me. Be my wife and I'll save your shop."

10

LEXI

Cannon Kingston.

Rich. Gorgeous. *Clearly* out of his mind.

Wild laughter bursts from the back of my throat at his ludicrous statement. "Marry you? What makes you think I'd marry you? You, my friend, are certifiable."

He smiles, too. It's an abrupt smile. Almost patronizing. "This is serious, Alexia."

"Well, then you can seriously take a hike. I'd never marry you."

His voice brims with frustration. "I admit, this situation isn't...typical. But this will be a mutually-beneficial arrangement. Because if I don't find a wife—like yesterday—my father will shut down Kingston Realties. The whole business, gone." He presses his fingertips together then pops them apart, making an explosion gesture.

I almost roll my eyes at the dramatics. "How is that my problem?" A billionaire losing a few rundown buildings in a backwoods town? Hold on. Let me grab my tiny violin.

"I'll explain something to you, Stormy. If some outside

investor buys up the Kingston Realties portfolio, we are *all* in trouble. You included."

"Oh, I'm already in trouble. You're the one standing in front of me, waving eviction threats in my face. You've already kicked some of my friends out of their businesses, torn their livelihoods away from them."

He shrugs, like none of those people matter to him. "Kingston Realties is not a charity. If a tenant wants to keep their unit, they have to pay the rent. Simple as that."

"So, how would you be any different than an outsider buying the buildings?"

He sighs like I'm an exasperating little girl. "I'm willing to keep all the buildings in tact. Hell, I'm willing to repair them. I'm not trying to rip the whole of Crescent Harbor down to the ground. But an outside investor? There's no way they'd pour in the funds necessary to rehabilitate all these crumbling buildings around town. They will systematically demolish each and every building in Crescent Harbor. Then, they'll put up a big-box chain store on Elgin Street and a factory to dump pollution into the river. Hell, they'll probably flatten Town Square and put in a golf course just for the fuck of it. Anything to turn a profit." His voice goes soft and I think I hear a flicker of compassion woven into his tone. "If an outsider comes in, you and *all* your friends will lose your businesses. This town will never be the same."

His words sink in and cold bumps prickle the surface of my skin. I hate to even consider it, but what if he's right? What if some outsider strips this town to its bones? I didn't grow up here but this place has become home and the idea of it being taken over by some big, ruthless corporation...I don't even want to imagine what that would mean.

Still, I'm not jumping at the idea of selling my soul to this cold-hearted stranger. "Why do you need a wife to get your plan in motion? I don't understand that." I take a shaky step back from the counter.

His thumb and forefinger glide down the bridge of his nose, betraying his frustration. "Because my father won't give me control of the company unless I'm a family man, deeply devoted to my wife. He and my grandfather made this pact—Kingston Realties will always be run by the family or it will be dissolved. None of my brothers or I are in relationships and my Dad is one step away from throwing away my grandfather's goddamned legacy. That's why!" His tone of voice rises with each word he spits out.

His body language says more than he does with his words. I could be reading the man all wrong but I think that this company *means something* to him. Saving the family business isn't just about money.

Okay, fine—Cannon Kingston might have a soft side under his thorny exterior. Still, I'm really not sure I'd want his conceited ass for my new landlord. Let alone, my husband.

He watches me for a minute before speaking again. "This arrangement will work out for all of us, Alexia. You and I get married, I take over the company from my father and the town of Crescent Harbor stays standing." He thinks my acceptance is a foregone conclusion. His caramel eyes tell me that. "Let's just hurry up and hammer out the details so this doesn't have to be painful."

The brittle truce between us snaps.

I can't believe I almost fell for that act. Putting up with his spoiled ass will never be worth my freedom. He doesn't deserve to take over Kingston Realties. And he's probably lying about this whole thing through his teeth to fool me. He just strolled into town and he has *ulterior motive* written all over him. I'm not buying it.

"It's a hell no, Cannon," I grit out. "I would never marry you."

His eyes narrow down to caramel slits of indignation. "You're kidding, right?"

"I'M VERY SERIOUS."

His neck goes red and his throat muscles tense with anger. "You're not even going to consider this?"

"This isn't a negotiation, King. It's a 'no'."

His lips press into a thin line, and I can see he's struggling to keep his temper in check.

I'm tired and grumpy myself, and I have zero energy to continue this ridiculous conversation. "You need to go," I say, my voice shaking.

Cannon nods once and places an eviction notice on the counter next to my cash register. Just the sight of it makes it hard to breathe. "I'll give you some time to think about it. Twenty-four hours." On top of the legal document, he slaps down a crisp business card bearing his name in big, embossed letters.

I stretch the business card back to him and lock my eyes on his hardened face. "There's nothing to think about." I swallow. No hesitation in my next words. "I'll take my chances with the eviction."

I wait for him to react but he doesn't budge. He just stands there, staring at me. His body is a giant pillar of muscle and testosterone. And anger.

Well guess what? I'm pissed off, too.

FRUSTRATED AFTER A LONG STANDOFF, I reach up and slide the card into the chest pocket of his shirt. My hand lingers on his chest. I stubbornly refuse to acknowledge the way his solid pectoral flexes under my fingertips. I turn to walk away.

With a brisk movement, he grabs my elbow. He spins me around so fast my body crashes into his.

A startled breath catches in my throat. My hand rushes up and curls in the expensive fabric of his shirt for balance. Cannon's body is warm. It smells clean and male and wild.

Deftly, he slips the business card into the back pocket of my jeans, his expert fingers barely skimming the curve of my ass. His cock lays heavy against my gut. He's hard as fuck.

Y'know what? I'm not surprised. He's a sadist. Of course he'd get off on this shit.

My pussy clenches when his mouth comes near my ear. "Twenty-four hours to think about it, sweetheart. Before I take your precious business away." His voice is low, warning, bordering on a threat.

When he releases me, I stumble on my own feet.

Then he turns and walks out of my bridal shop.

11

LEXI

I'm sitting on the floor of Miss Lucille's hair salon, pouring all of my attention into figuring out the inner workings of this high-dollar blow dryer. The mechanics of it are much more complicated than the twelve-dollar hair dryer I have at home but honestly, with everything going on in my world right now, I welcome the distraction.

"Scoot!" Penny smacks my hip with the shop broom and when I glance up, she grins.

I slide out of her way, so she can finish sweeping up her aunt's salon. It's near closing time and this business is just as empty as the rest on Promenade Street, so the girls and I are all here helping out Iris's mom.

"The timing of this eviction couldn't be worse," Miss Lucille comments for the third time, falling into a styling chair and toeing off her shoes. The weight of her daughter's struggles are clearly beating her down.

"Do you think Mr. Kingston even knows about your divorce?" Jessa addresses the question to Iris. "Maybe he'd work something out with you if someone talked to him." She wears a hopeful look as she sprays down each styling station.

"How could he *not* know?" Penny cringes.

"This is Crescent Harbor. Everyone knows," Iris mutters, face pinkening as she gathers up a fistful of combs and tools to disinfect them.

Jessa sighs. "This really isn't fair..."

The girls continue to moan but I don't lift my eyes from the broken dryer. It's all I can do to keep from crying. Facing reality means I'll have to make a choice. And if I make the wrong choice, I could blow up my whole life—and everyone else in the blast radius.

"Hey. *Hey.*" Jessa pokes me in the shoulder with her spray bottle. That's when I realize it's gone quiet in the salon. I look up, tuning back into the girls' conversation. "You okay? You zoned *way* out there." My sister gives me a concerned look.

Everyone is eyeballing me. "Yeah. Yeah, I'm good," I lie.

"So what do you think?" Penny's expression is skeptical. "Is there anything we can do to help Iris get her shop back, or is Mr. Kingston a lost cause?"

Iris glances at me from over by the sink where she's washing the combs. "Did he work out a deal with you when you went to talk to him about your rent?"

Shit. I never told her—or any of the ladies—what happened that day. Or afterward. But it's clear I need to come clean now.

"I—I never got to talk to Mr. Kingston," I admit. "I ran into his son instead."

"Walker?" Penny chirps.

"Um, no. Remember the asshole from the coffeeshop that I did *not* flirt with?...That was Cannon Kingston."

Penny nods slowly, her face broadcasting surprise. "Oh...

Walker *did* mention that his younger brother was back in town."

"I don't know who he thinks he is, but he just showed up, and suddenly he's the one who's orchestrating all the Kingston Realties evictions. I...I don't think any of us are safe," I add quietly, hating to drop this on everyone.

"Oh, lord," Iris's mom croons.

Jessa whispers. "Are you serious?" Her skin goes pale. "He can't do that, can he? He doesn't even live in Crescent Harbor!"

"There's...more," I admit and the room goes silent. "Cannon says the whole company is going under, and Mr. Kingston is looking to sell it."

"So, maybe future evictions will be off the table, while they deal with all that?" Penny suggests hopefully.

"Not exactly. Cannon said they'll be selling to an outside investor. You know, some big corporation that will buy everything up, demolish it, and rebuild factories and warehouses and shit."

The salon is so quiet, I can hear my own heart beating. This is bad. Really bad.

"Cannon mentioned one option to prevent all that from happening." Every eye swings to me. "If he's married, he'll get control of the company. He said he'd stall the evictions...if I marry him."

There are wide eyes and then a ripple of hysterical laughter sweeps the room as the girls come to grips with the ridiculousness of our very serious situation.

"He wants you to *marry* him?" Jessa's jaw drops in disbelief.

"Oh, girl. I'd be all over that." Penny fans herself. "Jessa said the chemistry between you two was on-freaking-fire."

"Are you kidding?" I blink, incredulous. "I don't even know the guy. And I'd put money on him being a sociopath."

"He's not, I promise," Penny provides with a laugh. "He's my best friend's brother. He grew up in Crescent Harbor before making it big in the tech industry in New York." Of course Penny would throw her weight behind him. She's got the biggest crush on one of the other Kingston brothers. Too bad Walker had zero aspirations to be part of the family business. Then maybe *she'd* be on the hook here, instead of me.

"What about you? You know him, too?" I ask Iris. She grew up in Crescent Harbor. If she can vouch for the asshole brother, maybe I should give this some serious consideration.

"What?" Iris questions, suddenly very interested in cleaning one of her mom's brushes. She's acting strange. Instantly, I know that she's withholding information. Juicy information.

"What do you know about Cannon Kingston? Is he really the heartless bastard I think he is? Or did we just get off on the wrong foot?" The tiniest piece of me might be holding out hope that I'm wrong about him. Deep down, maybe I want him to be an upstanding guy.

"Nope, don't know him..." she spits out, earning more than one unconvinced look in her direction. The way Penny eyes her cousin, I know for sure that there's more to the story. But Iris is too sensitive for intense questioning at the moment so I let it go. For now. I drop my attention back to the hair dryer.

More than anything, I think each woman here is a little on edge, lost in her own fears. Business in Crescent Harbor always slows this time of year, but this is our home. Kingston Realties legit owns most of the town, and nearly all of the commercial properties. If they go under—or if Cannon continues his eviction crusade—we're all impacted. It's not like Crescent Harbor, Illinois is booming with available jobs either. If we're shut down, we won't be the only ones who are unemployed.

Penny earns her living at the bar in town. Jessa's getting her start at the coffee shop while she looks for stable work as a teacher. Everything Iris's mom owns is wrapped up in this beauty salon.

The buildings housing every single one of those establishments is owned by Kingston Realty Holdings.

And given how quickly they dumped Iris on the street, we all can see they mean business. Serious business. It's just a matter of time before we all follow Iris's demise.

It terrifies me. I've been in this situation before. I know what it means to have the rug pulled out from under you, to have to worry about whether you'll have food to eat or if this month will be your last with a roof over your head.

I can't live like that again.

"What are you going to do?" Jessa asks me softly.

I stop fiddling with the dryer and look up. I can read the terror on the faces of my favorite people. It takes my breath away. I essentially possess the power to save each and every one of them from having their lives upended.

But can I save them if it means selling my soul to a ruthless handsome devil?

12

CANNON

The turrets of my Tudor-style mini mansion cast long shadows across the wet black-brick driveway as my Tesla emerges from the garage. Rain beats down on my windshield and my lawyer's voice fills the cabin of the car. "Cannon, I'm afraid I have some bad news."

Stalled at the foot of my driveway, I brace myself for whatever bullshit he's about to throw my way.

My estate sprawls for acres, contouring the south bank of the river. The view from up here is fucking breathtaking, even in the rain.

The property is badass and I paid Kingston Realties a fortune for it a few years ago. But really, it's this view that makes it priceless. The way sunbeams crash off the surface of the water at the height of summer. The way the leaves shatter into a prism of reds and purples and yellows across the lawn in the fall. It's fucking phenomenal and it kind of sucks not having anyone to share it with.

When Margot would come out here, all she did was complain about the mosquitos. So, I decided to keep her presence in Crescent Harbor to a minimum. I didn't need all that negativity fucking up my feng shui.

Because of that, I haven't spent as much time out here as I would have liked to over the past few years. Every visit was just a day or two to check in with family before heading back to my penthouse in New York or my condo in L.A. or my flat in London.

As I'm sitting here, admiring this piece of architectural brilliance, I wonder if it might be time for me to slow down. Lay some roots. Stop and smell the roses—or whatever the hell that bush is jutting out of my overgrown parterre garden.

Damn. I need a landscaper. And nothing says 'I'm laying down roots' like hiring a landscaper.

With the flick of a switch, my windshield wipers kick up to full speed, scattering the torrents of rain clobbering my front window. I merge onto the narrow road leading into town. Through a tight jaw, I grit out. "Tear off the Band-Aid, Frank. What's the bad news?"

"Unfortunately, I can't, in good conscience, proceed with some of the requests you made." Frank's voice rasps. "We're straddling a thin line, Cannon. Bordering on illegal territory. I need to go at this from a different angle to strip Carl of the aforementioned assets without breaking the law."

I sigh, taking three full breaths to control myself before responding. "Make it happen, Frank. The plan I gave you is foolproof."

"But not necessarily legal."

I respect the old guy. He and his firm have gotten me out of a lot of shit over the years. But lately, he's been pissing me off. Frank used to be hardcore. That's what I liked about him. But ever since last year when his latest wife pawned off her wedding ring and left him to join a topless traveling folk band, he's gone soft on me.

"If you have a better solution, then do it. Otherwise, stick to Plan A. Consequences be damned."

He sighs wearily. "Cannon, this revenge thing has gone on long enough. You need to be here in New York, managing DataCo. You left a billion-dollar ship without a captain and Carl is driving it into a ditch."

I massage the line of my nose. I know he's right. But it's too early in the morning for melodrama and mixed metaphors. I won't let him dictate my decisions.

"I'm not changing my mind, Frank," I state tersely then change the conversation while switching lanes. "And one more thing—I'll be getting married."

"Oh?"

I choose to ignore his veiled surprise. I know the old man would appreciate more details, but I'm not willing to divulge too much. Not just yet. I mean, Stormy hasn't exactly agreed to our arrangement, but I know she will. And, soon. She's running out of time.

"Yes, and it'll happen quickly. Can you pull whatever applications and documents that are needed?"

"I'm on it as we speak."

"Perfect. Thank you," I clip before hanging up.

This marriage cannot happen fast enough. I will not allow everything Gramps built to fall into the hands of the highest bidder. I'm proud of the legacy my grandfather built. He worked his ass off to make sure his family was taken care of. But he didn't make all those sacrifices for us to just fuck it all up. He ensured the company was in good hands—in a position to grow—when he passed it along to my father. I'm more desperate than ever to save Gramps' legacy.

My desperation brings me full circle to a crazy woman I barely know.

That damn sassy girl keeps popping into my thoughts, obstructing my peace of mind with her long legs and her thick hair and her pushy attitude. As I roll up to a stop sign, I make a conscious effort to block out the memory of the way I fisted my cock last night in the shower, imagining her on her knees in front of me. Or the fact that I did it all over again this morning.

That's so not like me.

I've never had a problem controlling my thoughts so to have this stranger barge into my head and start changing the drapes and moving the furniture around is really pissing me off.

I don't possess the time or energy to put together the jigsaw puzzle that is Alexia Robson. I have just two targets right now. Save my family's company and destroy the two backstabbing cheats in my circle. I need to stop letting my libido run amok with Lexi and just focus on getting her to be my on-paper wife.

Because that's all this can ever be. An on-paper arrangement for mutual gain. Nothing more. I just need my subconscious to accept that.

With no warning, an old pick-up truck swerves off the shoulder of the road and bumps into the lane ahead of me. A broken television set with the wires hanging out is wedged between a doorless refrigerator and a cracked microwave oven. The lot of it balances precariously on top of an ancient washer/dryer set and is bound together by a fraying rope.

The fuck is wrong with people?!

As a precaution, I pump on my brakes and allow a careful distance to grow between our vehicles.

The truck veers abruptly. It comes to a reckless stop beside a discarded sofa and a pile of other garbage on the curb. I swerve just in time and lay hard on my horn. "Pick a lane, you little fucker!"

An old man in a faded red baseball cap and overalls hops from the driver's seat. He throws me a friendly wave as I zip by.

"Indicate, Dipshit!" In my rearview mirror, I see his frail body hauling the dirty couch toward his truck.

A right turn onto Hart Road brings me away from the waterfront and down the narrow tree-lined strip that runs past my old high school. Huddled figures move along the sidewalks, cowering under shared umbrellas. There's not a streak of sunlight in sight to soothe the uneasiness digging a path under my skin because I don't know what's awaiting me when I reach my destination.

I pull onto the semi-circle stone driveway. I cut my engine under a maple tree at the curb before darting out into the rain. The three tiny women crammed hip to hip on the porch swing halt their lively chattering to observe me with curious eyes. I throw them a quick greeting, refusing to stop for idle chat.

Water clings to my brow as I push through the door. My footsteps leave big wet prints all across the lobby tiles. I avoid eye contact with the blushing nurse who gives me an interested onceover on the narrow staircase.

Tension tightens around my ribcage. My heart thumps in my throat. I've been coming here every day since Dad announced his plan to sell the business. With each visit, the eager little boy somewhere inside of me brims with hope that things will be a little bit better than the previous time. But it's always more of the same.

I slow my pace as I move through the hallways, making

sure not to knock over the hoards of slow-moving occupants wandering around. I pause right outside the door.

"You can do this," I mutter to myself before entering. "You can fucking do this."

The room is small and smells like boiled foot ointment and floor cleaner. I hold my breath.

The soles of my shoes scuff against the linoleum floor. The sound catches the attention of the old man in the wheelchair by the window. He looks me up and down with furrowed brows.

Digging my hands into the front pockets of my pants, I take a step closer. "Hey, Gramps."

When he scowls, that ever-present line between his gray bushy brows goes deeper.

Just like my last visit, he puffs up his narrow chest. Just like my last visit, he asks, "Who the heck are you?"

13

LEXI

"Come on, Iris. Let's Saturday it up!" I shamelessly twerk my way into her personal space. An obnoxious effort to coerce her into loosening up.

She glares peevishly into her shot glass and shakes her head. "Saturday is not a verb, Lexi," she says dryly. "You can't just make Saturday a verb."

Eye. Roll.

I'll give her a pass for being a grouch. It's been another rough week for my bestie. Her marriage wasn't ever anything to build a #CouplesGoals Pinterest board about but at least, it had offered her a sense of stability. She was moored in its familiarity with the man she'd been in love with since childhood. Now, she's been tossed back into the wild without a compass. Plus, the business she devoted her life to has just been yanked out of her hands. She feels unsteady and as her friend, all I want to do is prop her up as best I can.

And fuck me up some Kirk Bunting ass. But that's a whole other story.

Anyway, I've finally—*finally*—managed to get this girl

cleaned up and out of the house. Now, we're at the Frosty Pitcher and it's time to cause some trouble.

The room explodes into cheers at the opening notes of the new Ed Sheeran song. Iris slides lower on her stool like she's trying to disappear.

"You should be drunk by now." I give her shoulder a little shake then turn my attention to the other end of the counter. Penny is doing her best to gently deflect the flirtations of a brawny out-of-towner without compromising her tip jar. She wears red pleather leggings and a tight, patronizing smile as she pops the caps off of the beers in front of her. Sliding onto a stool, I wave an arm to grab her attention. "Penny! This tequila is broken. We're gonna need something stronger."

One glance at her woeful-looking cousin and compassion rises to the bartender's face. "Oh, honey." Penny turns her back on her frisky customer and, with a confident strut, moves along the counter to where we're stationed. She snatches the shot glass from Iris's fingers and tosses it back herself. "Do you want something sweet instead? A daiquiri, maybe?"

Gathering up her purse and coat, Iris shakes her head. "Um, no. I think I'm just gonna go home. Get some sleep. I-I don't think I'm ready to, y'know, be outdoors, peopling and stuff."

What is this nonsense?!

Iris is a hot chick. She's a total blonde bombshell with an enviable C-cup and a figure that has hourglasses from here to Honolulu wondering what the heck they've been doing with their lives. She does *not* need to be at home in her sweats on a Saturday night, pining away over her cheating husband.

"Oh, come on!" I clasp my hands in a prayer pose, ready

to beg shamelessly. "Just stay. You don't have to talk to anybody. You don't even have to dance. And I promise, if *Single Ladies* comes on, we totally don't have to do the choreography I made you practice before we left the house."

Iris looks at me with the smallest hint of the saddest smile I've ever seen. Her big blue eyes swim in unshed tears. It gives me pause.

My shoulders slump as I realize that a real friend wouldn't force her to stay. Not when she feels like this. "Okay, fine. Let's go." I stand and grab my sweater off the back of my stool.

"No." Iris pats my cheek. "You stay. Have fun for me. I'll walk home. I could use the fresh air and a few minutes to clear my head." I open my mouth to protest but she levels me with a stern glare.

She's right. I'm being over-protective. Her house is just around the corner and half a block down. Besides, Crescent Harbor isn't a dangerous town by any stretch of the imagination. She doesn't need a chaperone.

"Fine," I mutter and she gathers me into a quick hug. "I love you."

"Love you," she says back and braves a smile when Penny blows her a feisty kiss across the bar. "Love you, cous'."

I drop into my chair and I watch her, bowed head and curled-in shoulders, as she moves briskly toward the exit of the Frosty Pitcher, snaking through the drunken masses clogging up the dance floor.

As her hand reaches for the door, it swings and Iris falters, startled. I see thick, long fingers slide against the frosted glass pane to hold the door open for her. My friend regains her footing and nods in appreciation then slinks out into the night.

The air in the bar shifts so fast I nearly lose my center of gravity.

Cannon Kingston's broad shoulders edge through the doorway, that pissed-off, jaded, always-impatient expression etched on his way-too-perfect face.

And immediately, I'm sober and I'm edgy and I'm ready for a fight.

14

CANNON

My mind is unsettled and my thoughts are racing as I throw my car into park on the curb outside of the Frosty Pitcher.

I *seriously* need to unwind.

I need to slip into a dark booth at the back of a half-lit bar, order a whiskey neat and chill the fuck out.

Maybe a pretty girl might catch my eye. Someone who'll wrap her hand around my cock under the table and not give a fuck that I can't remember her name. Or that I never bothered to ask. I just need a distraction.

Because my entire life has gone off the rails. It's a speeding train heading toward a ditch: I don't have the time to focus on my revenge plot; my grandfather battles Alzheimer's Disease as his company totters on the edge of complete ruin; and, no matter what I do, I can't get that enchanting, little lunatic off my mind.

Lexi Robson.

Grit and grace.

Half goddess. Half gangster.

She's a hurdle I didn't see coming. Stubborn, feisty,

temper as wild as the untamed forest of hair tumbling around her narrow shoulders. I want to get my hands on the long, trim lines of her body. I want to sink my tongue into that sassy mouth to see if it tastes as sweet as it looks.

She's fucking with my plans and it's pissing me off. I need her to become my wife so I can save my family empire and get back to the business of fucking up Carl's life. I hate that she's putting up a fight.

Normally, I wouldn't hesitate to manipulate, exploit, destroy any obstacle standing between me and my goal. Under any other circumstances, a bailiff would be flinging her shit onto the street and nailing that bridal boutique shut as we speak.

But this girl makes me hesitate.

She makes me second-guess myself. She makes me want to take a step back and reevaluate the consequences of what I'm about to do.

If I go through with my plan, I'll hurt her...And I don't want to hurt her.

The truth is, I'd much rather bend her over the table and screw her literally than screw her over figuratively-speaking. I'm trying to figure out if that's just my cock talking or if it's something...*more.*

It's a feeling I'm not used to. A feeling I don't like. It has me out of sorts because I'm usually a man who goes after what I want with absolute certainty. I'm frustrated as hell because this whatever-it-is she makes me feel is getting in the way.

As I'm shutting my car door, my phone bleats. I pull it out of my pocket and check the newest text message from my ex-business partner.

Carl: My fucking fishing boat just got seized for not having a license. I know ur behind it.

Carl: Are you really gonna stoop that low, man?
I am, jackass. Thanks for asking.

When I pull open the heavy wooden door to the Frosty Pitcher, a clumsy blonde stumbles out, one misstep away from flying headfirst onto the sidewalk. I think I recognize her. I'm not sure. But as she thanks me and ambles off into the night, I don't bother overanalyze it. I'm not feeling very sociable right now anyway.

I just need a drink.

And a hand job. Maybe.

Shouldering through the mass of rowdy partygoers, I barely make it across the room without having to punch a fool in the throat. Coming out in public tonight may not have been such a great idea after all. With the mood I'm in. I momentarily consider turning around and going home but dismiss the thought. This storm of a girl has already tipped my mind off balance. I won't let her ruin my night, too.

There's an empty table in the corner. No harm in taking a seat and having a damn drink on a Saturday night. It beats sitting at home, thinking about her and jerking off, having a meltdown like a teenager who doesn't know how to control his fucking hormones.

The DJ stands on a platform at the back. Clunky headphones over his ears, one fist pumping to the sky as he drives a screeching synthesizer beat through the room. I can feel the jarring vibrations of the music all the way to the nerve endings in my teeth.

A waitress in a low-cut top and a leather skirt shimmies up to my table. Her hair is an electrifying shade of blue and tattoos blossom like ivy vines down the length of her arms. She flashes a toothy smile and takes my drink order.

As she sashays away I wonder if she'll be the one to end the night with her fingers around my cock.

Or maybe the petite brunette leaning against the jukebox, sucking seductively on her plastic straw and giving me the come-get-it eyes.

Or the leggy one curled over the pool table. She grins at me and her cleavage tries to burst through the laces of her leather corset when she bends lower and aims the cue stick.

For some reason, I'm not feeling any of them, though. I just can't get into the vibe.

Sighing, I lean back in my seat and push back the sleeves of my sweater. As if that will somehow telegraph the message to my brain that I'm here to relax. Not to obsess about a girl who is intent on driving me insane.

The harder I try to get her off my brain, the harder she insists on dominating my thoughts.

There's vulnerability that peeks through the cracks in her fierce facade. She's sort of a mess but she owns it in a way I've never seen any woman own any*thing*.

Grit and grace.

You don't just forget a woman like that.

And now, I'm so invested in trying to figure her out that it's messing with every goal and plan and objective I've set for myself since the day I cruised back into Crescent Harbor.

I'm about to turn her life upside down. And I just don't know how to *not* feel guilty about that.

At first, I'm convinced it's a mirage when my eyes move to the dance floor and I spot that sweet body, clad in nothing more than a shimmery pink top and a tiny excuse for a skirt. Making sensual lines under the dim light. Not even bothering to keep time with the music. And that crazy, crazy hair.

They'll need a search party to find my fingers when I finally get my hands lost in that hair.

Alexia Robson.

She catches my attention the way no other woman in this bar has all night. She catches my attention and she holds it in a death grip. I'm practically spellbound as I watch her dance. A smile moves my lips and very unwelcome feelings sprout up beneath my ribs as I watch her engineer her choreography on the fly. My need for her swells into a raw, pounding ache in my dick. I can't stop the lust hammering in my veins.

Out of nowhere, my mind is invaded by the craziest thought I've ever had. *Maybe I can have her. Just once.*

Maybe it won't mean anything in the end. Maybe I can get this craving out of my system and go back to business as usual.

Maybe if I get her in my bed then I'll finally get her off my brain.

Deep down I know that line of reasoning makes no logical sense. I'm trying to get her to marry me for money. Sex will only complicate things more. But my primal brain is obviously not a fan of logic.

All I want to do is pin her to the wall and kiss her until her head goes light, kiss her until her panties soak through, kiss her until I break through all the reasons she refuses to be my bride.

I toss back my drink in a gulp. My empty glass hits the tabletop with a clank. Next thing I know, my feet are taking me in her direction. My cock throbs.

I just want to kiss her...

As a matter of fact, I think I might.

15

LEXI

I smell his musky scent even before his large hand lightly grasps my side, in that sensitive space right above my hip. I turn around, unsurprised to find Cannon staring down at me. By this point, my nerve endings are so in tune with the bastard, I can sense his presence with my eyes closed. It's disturbing.

He looks *delicious* tonight. He's wearing a casual black crewneck sweater with dark jeans. His man-bun is a sinful mess and when he swallows, I can barely restrain myself from inching my tongue along that sensual Adam's apple.

The crowd around us pushes us together, and I don't stop dancing. He can stay. He can leave. I don't care.

But then his hands find my elbows, and his hard body begins gyrating in beat with mine...Holy hell. The jerk knows how to move.

Part of me wants to grind all over his muscled thigh. And another part wants to tell him to get lost. But deep down, I feel I have something to prove. I need to prove I can do this. I can dance with this hot bastard without succumbing to his charm.

In the few short days this man has been in town, he has bullied my little sister, evicted my best friend and tried to blackmail me into marrying him. He has earned his place on my shit list. I'm justified in hating him. So why do I find myself attracted to him?

His twinkling eyes look deep into mine, shamelessly unearthing all my poorly-buried secrets. He can see through me, right into that space where my conflicting thoughts collide into each other. Like my confusion must be echoing on my face, playing like a video, flashing in my eyes like subtitles.

A self-satisfied grin unfolds across his mouth.

Argh! What a smug asshole.

I want to slap him across the cheek. And hump his leg, too.

I growl and the sound rises above the tail end of the fading techno song.

"What?" he demands, his voice low and hypnotizing, his eyes glinting brighter under the effect of the whiskey in his blood.

I narrow my gaze on his pretty, pretty face. "Y'know—you're not as impressive as you think you are."

His brow twitches, almost imperceptibly. "I'm not?" His grip tightens on my waist. His pelvis presses closer to my knotted gut.

A wispy breath quivers its way up my throat. I inch a half-step closer, aching to feel the thick length of his erection brush against me again. "No, You're not."

"Hmm..." The very tip of his tongue peeks out from between his perfect lips and whisks across the seam. "I'm not impressive at all, huh?" His fingers sift through the ends of my hair. Miss Lucille spent an hour brushing it and flat-ironing it and wrangling it under control. But none of that matters now that Cannon's got his hand tangled in it.

I shake my lying-ass head and fall deeper into the trance of his eyes. "Not impressive at all."

Another bold sweep of his fingers across my skin, another subtle rotation of his hips against my body as a new song starts up.

Violent palpitations hammer between my thighs. My pussy is such a melodramatic fool. I think I'm about to pass out from arousal.

"Is that why your breathing is so erratic, Alexia?" He presses two thick fingers to the base of my throat. "Is that why your pulse is throbbing like crazy?" Those fingers travel lower, tracing the lacy neckline of my blouse to settle over the left side of my goosebump-coated chest. "Is that why your heart is roaring in your chest?" I swallow and my ribs shake just a little bit. "Is that why your panties are so wet I can smell it?"

My gut contracts harshly and another river of wetness pulses out of my traitorous pussy.

God, I hate this man.

He bites into his bottom lip and his caramel eyes sparkle with humor and heat and determination.

I should head-butt him.

Or kick him in the groin.

Or, at the very least, stomp on his foot.

The point is, I have *options*. Yet, here I am, plastering my body to his, sliding my palms up the hard planes of his chest, fluttering my lashes with stars and cartoon hearts shooting from my eyes.

I groan and drop my forehead to his rock-hard chest. Realization hits me. I'm not strong enough to fight this.

Frustrated by my weakness and intoxicated by his scent, I bite at his chest through his shirt.

He hisses. "Watch it, Stormy." I hear the want in his voice.

Slowly, I lift my face. "I really can't stand you." I have to feed myself these lies so I can feel justified in the way I'm rubbing against his body right now.

He leans in. His stubbly cheek grazes my skin as he brings his mouth to my ear. There's soft laughter in his gritty voice. "I can see that."

His playfulness twists me up. I wasn't expecting it. I'm not sure how to react.

"Tell me, what date works best for you?" His mouth is in my ear.

"For what?"

His lips curve up into a dangerous smirk, following the rise of his eyebrow. He doesn't answer me with words, but his expression does. Damn him.

"I am *not* marrying you, Mr. Billions." This guy is a pigheaded, persistent asshole who only cares about himself.

He's also sexy as hell. But that's beside the point.

My refusal only makes him grin wider. "You're just scared to marry me because you know you'd fall head over heels in love with me."

I bark out a short puff of laughter. "You're delusional."

"Your body tells me otherwise, Stormy." His caramel eyes twinkle.

I try to give him my dirtiest hate glare, but who the hell am I kidding? He does things to my body without even physically touching me. *The alcohol and his mind-bending touch must be short-circuiting my brain.*

He trails his fingertips down my sides and lightly grips

my hips while we shift, rock and sway to the heavy beat. "I'd pay you for marrying me—y'know—for your trouble," he says, and I struggle to read his eyes under the dim lights. I think he absolutely means what he tells me, but I'm not sure he's one hundred percent comfortable with the idea.

I know I'm not.

"You can't just buy your way out of every problem, King. That's not the way life works."

His hands shift, sending icy heat down my forearms as his touch moves along them. Then he intertwines his fingers in mine. It's too much. It's too close. My focus is such a frigging mess, it's hard to concentrate on his next words. "I'm not asking you to throw your life away, Alexia. The marriage would just be short-term. Just a month or two. Three tops, for the lawyers to transfer the business into my name."

My pulse thuds. Well, that doesn't sound quite so horrible. A couple month's time to save my business? To save my friends? To save this town?

His breath tickles the top of my lip. "We'd have to live together after we get married, to hold up appearances, of course. But you could have your own separate bedroom. My estate is big enough that we'd hardly have to see each other..." He grinds against me. "...if that's what you wish."

My body throbs when he says that. I know his words should be sending up red flags. Big wavy, neon ones. Because this arrangement he's proposing is *not* purely business. Sex drips from every syllable that leaves his plush mouth. But none of what he's telling me sounds like torture.

Could I do all of that? Could I go through with a fake marriage and live in his big fancy 'estate' for a few weeks?

And could we maybe throw in a few orgasms for good measure?

Shut up, brain...

Narrowing my gaze on him, I speak the first thing that comes to mind. "If I agree to this, you have to immediately remove the threat of shutting down my bridal boutique."

He nods without hesitating. "That was the deal."

"And you have to give Iris her shop back, too."

"Who's Iris?"

I growl. "My best friend. The woman who ran the sandwich shop."

He hesitates. "She was months behind, Alexia."

"I don't care. Those are my terms. Wait." I hold a finger in his devastatingly beautiful face. "Actually, you have to 'un-evict' everyone you've kicked out so far."

Cannon's head rears back, and I already miss his closeness. "I don't know...You're asking a lot. We're talking thousands of dollars. Tens of thousands. Kingston Realties needs cashflow to survive."

I level him with a look that says I don't give a shit. Because I don't. He's a fucking billionaire. He can afford to bailout his family business. We're talking about people's lives here, their futures. "Do you even know the lives you ruined with those eviction notices?"

His lips form a tight line. He glares.

I carry on my tirade. "Let me give you a little background. The owner of the record shop you shut down was saving up to take his wife to Greece for their thirty-year wedding anniversary. The woman from the little craft store just got custody of her sister's three kids. And my friend Iris—the one from the sandwich shop—she got served with divorce papers just days before you hit her with the eviction." My stomach twists. My voice goes soft. "I care about those people. Deeply. Do you know what it's like to care about someone other than yourself?"

"Business can't be personal if you want to be successful." He says it like a stubborn child but the tension in his shoulders tells me I'm slowly winning him over to my side.

"Cannon..." I angle my head to the side. Somehow, I still have a little faith in him, in the idea that there's a heart beneath all his thorny layers of indifference.

"In my world, feelings just slow you down," he says roughly. "They get in your way." His tone of voice leaves me wondering if there's a story there. Did someone hurt him?

"Well, your world sounds miserable," I argue. "In *my* world, feelings are what make you human. They're what allow you to connect to the people you care about. They're the foundation of friendships..." I emphasize the word to convey its meaning. "...*relationships*."

He shakes his head.

"Take it or leave it, Mr. Billions. I'll agree to marry you, if you give everyone their places back."

His caramel eyes bore into mine for a long, intimidating beat. "Fine," Cannon grits out after an eternity. "Fine."

I feel a sweeping sense of relief. "We have a deal, then..." Saving my friends, saving this town, that's what matters to me.

Victory glints in his smug expression.

The music around us continues to thump, and from his grip on my body, I know he has no plans to end our dancing any time soon. And I'm okay with that. More than okay. I really shouldn't be so blindly attracted to this man.

From the way he's looking at me, I may not be alone in that attraction. His scrutinizing stare is fixed on my mouth, and somehow, it's sucking all the oxygen out of the room.

"Don't!" My fingernails bite into his flesh through his shirt as I hiss the warning.

He licks his lips. His gaze snaps back to mine. "Don't what?"

I swallow shakily. "You really, really look like you want to kiss me right now. And I swear to god, if you do, I will headbutt you right into a coma."

A slow, vulpine smile unwraps across his mouth. Those lips are succulent, plump, downright chewable. Lips made for ravishing. And for being ravished. I'm so mad at myself for noticing.

"Enforcing the 'honor and obey' part of our vows is gonna be so much fun." He growls.

With one fingertip, I poke him in the chest, forcing him to take a step back. Then I pivot on shaky feet and sashay away. When I'm a safe distance from him, I glance back. The hungry look on his face makes me fluttery in the belly.

I'm gonna need a game plan to survive this man.

16

CANNON

"You're engaged?" Walker is crouched down beside a mammoth of a tractor. He stares up at me.

I toss a sharp glare at my oldest brother. "Yes," I declare, my tone as crisp and frosty as the beer in my hand. "I'm engaged."

Silence follows for a long beat. I already know where this is going.

A thick, judgmental eyebrow gets lost beneath the brim of his straw hat. It looks goofy as hell, if you ask me. But that's always been Walker...

"*You*—" he points a big greasy wrench at my face. "—are engaged?"

"Yes. *I* am engaged. Why's that so hard to believe?" I lean my weight against the thick wooden beam behind me and cross one ankle over the other. I hold eye contact, silently daring him to say what's on his damn mind. At this point, I wish he'd just get on with it already.

My brother leaves my question hanging in the air, taking his time to settle a five-gallon bucket beneath the vehicle's engine. Slowly, he fiddles with a network of valves and plugs

I won't even pretend to understand, and thick, dark oil begins to spill out of the tank. Finally, he rises and turns to me, the faintest smirk on his ever-brooding face.

"You gonna say something?" I prod, my impatience flaring, my need-to-know pushing to the surface.

Walker and I are both pretty much the same height with dark blond hair, light brown eyes and sturdy, muscular build. But Mom would always say we're polar opposites in terms of temperament. He's guarded and introspective. A former military man who is fiercely protective with an impenetrable resolve when he sets his mind to something.

Where I resort to ripping sarcasm and merciless jabs, my brother wields his silence as a weapon. Sometimes deliberately, sometimes not. It's annoying as fuck.

Needless to say, he drives the women he dates absolutely insane, and most days the only person who'll even try to figure him out is his childhood best friend, Penny. She's gorgeous and funny and as patient as a saint. Walker has had her in the friend zone since preschool.

I think my brother might be afraid of his own dick. That's the only explanation I can come up with. But I digress.

He marches ahead of me across the farm's cluttered workshop, checking gauges and dials on the various vehicles as we go. He half-glances at me over his back. "You were dating Maria for—what?—ten years?"

"Margot. On and off. So?" I take another sip from my beer.

"And marriage never came up?"

"It did not."

"And now, out-of-the-blue, you're head over heels in love with Lexi? Some woman you just met? You haven't even been in town long enough to visit Mom, but you've fallen in love? There's something hairy there, brother."

Feeling defensive, I ball up my fists and spit lies. Pure lies. "We met online. A while ago. And yes, we're in love." I rehearsed this line more than a few times.

He doesn't answer. He just keeps walking. Christ, Walker drives me mad.

I press him. "What are you trying to say?"

His muscle-bound shoulder juts up beneath his checkered flannel shirt. "Nothing...I mean, it just seems a little out-of-character for you. That's all."

Getting hitched had never been part of my life plan. With Margot, I dodged the topic for years. But now it's something I need to do. A means to an end. I have to save my grandfather's company because I'm quickly realizing that getting revenge on Carl and Margot isn't enough. The idea of them flailing and squirming as I wreck their lives won't be enough to fill the hollow ache inside my chest.

I'm still grasping for...*something.* A sense of fulfillment to plug the throbbing hole beneath my ribs. Saving my grandfather's legacy will give me the satisfaction I'm searching for. I'm sure of that.

To be honest, all this revenge shit is fucking exhausting. I'm starting to wonder if maybe there's more to life than money and retaliation and teaching assholes a lesson. What if life is supposed to be on the opposite end of the spectrum? Looking out for the people you love—the way Lexi does—might just be more important than sabotaging others.

The woman is so damn loyal. And after the betrayal I just suffered with Margot, loyalty means more than ever in my book.

There's a worktable in the front room. I settle on a

bench, and Walker snatches my empty beer can from me. I'm not a big beer drinker but when he offers me another, I grunt and accept it from his greasy hand.

God knows I need it. Because obviously, I'm losing my mind.

"You're out here on the edge of the woods, dressed in a lumberjack shirt, like a frigging mountain man. I don't see anybody judging you for *your* life choices."

My brother stops with his own beer halfway to his mouth and glances down at his shirt. A rare laugh shoots from his chest. "What's wrong with my shirt?"

I grin mockingly. "I'll let you figure that one out on your own."

He continues to stare at his checkered flannel atrocity, with a perplexed look on his face. The poor guy was always clueless in the fashion department. Finally, he gives up, shaking his head and continuing his stroll through the barn.

"You're the most random fucker I've ever met," he tells me, his tone bewildered but amused.

I chuckle and take a drink. "I prefer *spontaneous*, actually. Plus, I follow my instincts when I see an opportunity. That's what makes me a rockstar business man."

I'm not surprised he'd find me reckless. Unlike the rest of us Kingston boys, Walker never takes a step without careful consideration. Sometimes he goes overboard, in my opinion.

He tosses his beer can onto a recycling heap, analyzing me in that careful, skeptical way he analyzes everything.

"That's exactly what I thought," Walker clips. "You, getting married? Just business as usual. Just another means to get ahead somehow."

I plunk my can down on the counter, spring out of my seat and head for the door. I'm over this.

Walker calls out from behind me, and I hear some tools clatter against the floor. "Oh, come on!"

I grind to a halt at the door and face him. "Carl fucked my girlfriend. In my own bed." I remind him. "What was I supposed to do? Tuck them in and offer them a bucket of fried chicken and the TV remote? I moved on. Moving on is not a fucking crime."

I'll tolerate a lot of things in a relationship—constant tardiness, post-argument vaguebooking, even halitosis—but disloyalty will never, *ever* be one of those things I overlook.

"That's not the point, Cannon."

"What *is* your point, then?" I challenge.

"My point is that you're impulsive." His finger jabs me in the shoulder. Hard. "You're ruthless. And you make everything about money."

"And what the fuck does *that* mean?" I demand. Christ, kick a man when he's down, why don't you?

"Cannon, do I look like a moron to you?"

I glance at his stupid shirt. "That's a rhetorical question, right?"

His gaze narrows with annoyance. "Tell me what's really going on here. Why are you suddenly engaged to the woman from the local bridal shop?"

Crap. I *might* be able to bullshit the rest of the family, but I certainly can't bullshit Walker. I might as well tell him the truth. Who knows? Maybe I'll gain an ally in this crazy plot.

Hell, Dad clearly doesn't buy my story, but oddly enough, he seems willing to play along. Maybe Walker will, too. He deserves to know what's going on with the company in any case. His future is tied up in Kingston Realties, too.

We walk up the farm's dirt pathway. I break down and tell him everything. I tell him that our dad is planning to sell our family business and that I plan to fake-marry Lexi to save Gramps' company. He listens quietly, letting me spill my guts.

My rambling cuts off when a streak of a miniature person runs by, her long blonde hair and bright pink dress practically blurring behind her. "Is that Callie?" I ask.

Walker nods.

"Shit, she's grown." I feel a twinge of guilt for being away so long.

The cute, tiny girl sprints toward us. Eli's four-year-old giggles and grabs onto my brother's leg, hugging him tight. "Uncle Walker!"

He whisks her off her feet and plants her on his side. "Hey there, Pumpkin."

"It's not Pumpkin," she chides. "It's Princess Callie!"

Walker smacks his forehead playfully. "Oh sorry. I keep forgetting."

"Hey, Princess Callie." Hands stuffed into my pockets, I drop my trademark intimidating scowl. My mouth curls into a welcoming smile for the child's benefit.

She says nothing to me, but eyes me with more skepticism than I've ever seen in one person's face. Big or small. "Who's *that* guy?" she asks my brother, jerking a narrow shoulder my way.

"That's your Uncle Cannon." Walker clearly finds it amusing that my niece can't tell me apart from any other random asshole to stroll onto the family farm. He pokes her in the ribs. "You wanna say hi?"

"No," she deadpans. I swear she glares at me before she squirms out of my brother's arms and takes off again.

"Damn, that kid is savage," I say in disbelief as we continue our trek up the path toward my parents' guesthouse.

Walker shrugs. "You never come back home to visit so that's what you get..."

I toss back my head, frustrated. This guy is always busting my balls. "Can we not get into that right now?"

Our mother spots us through the kitchen window as we walk past the house. She sticks her head out the backdoor and waves. "What are you boys up to?"

"Just taking a walk, Ma," I say, forcing a smile to the surface. I slide my aviators over my eyes. I don't want Mom to pick up on any tension between my brother and me or she'll open an FBI-level investigation to get the whole story. I'm not in the headspace for an interrogation today.

Her eyes move between us, anyway. Mom takes that maternal instinct thing to a whole new level. "Everything okay with you two?"

Walker flashes a tight half-smile. "Everything's fine, Ma." Shit, he lies just about as good as he dresses.

The suspicious slash between her brows deepens. "Cut the crap. What are you two arguing about?"

My brother and I share a knowing look. We've got to shut this down before she makes us sit on the tiny bench in the corner together. If any of us boys fought as kids, she'd force us to sit side-by-side until we made up.

Forget the FBI. That was some CIA-level shit.

Walker speaks up. "Cannon said my shirt was ugly, Ma. You wanna tell him he's wrong?"

Mom shoots a glare my way. Christ, thank you, Walker. "Get in here. Both of you," she demands.

I elbow my brother, as we head inside. The door hasn't even slammed shut before I hear her holler, "Cannon William Kingston, why do I have to hear about your engagement from your father?!"

I reach down, wrapping my arms around my mom

before she can break down. I know she's a sucker for hugs. "I'm sorry, Ma. You'll love Lexi, I promise."

"Good. Bring her to dinner this week. Friday?"

Dammit. "Oh, I don't —"

"Grandma!" Callie interrupts, running up to tug on Mom's dress. "Can we make chilli for dinner Friday? I'm gonna help you make chilli!"

I narrow my eyes on this tiny girl. Sneaky little thing. She may be shy, but she's a mischievous little booger.

My mother wraps an arm around her only grandchild, wearing a toothy grin. "That sounds like a wonderful idea, sweetie. Doesn't it, Uncle Cannon?" Both of them look at me expectantly. They've backed me into a corner I can't elbow my way out of.

Defeated, I grouse. "Fine."

I've just agreed to bring my reluctant fake fiancée to dinner with my meddling mother, and my sneaky-ass niece will be helping in the kitchen.

God, help me. The women of Crescent Harbor are going to be the death of me.

17

LEXI

"Try this," Jessa chirps. She hands me a plastic hanger holding a knee-length floral dress.

With a frown, I take the dress and hold it up against my body. My eyes scan it doubtfully in the mirror. "It's pretty but it's not...*me*."

My little sister twists her lips to the side and slowly nods in agreement. "Yeah, you're right. The 'wholesome homemaker' vibe isn't really your style." She giggles and ducks back into her closet.

I massage my temples, not sure what I've gotten myself into. Nothing in my own wardrobe seemed good enough so I decided to rummage through Jessa's closet. I figured my sister's trademark demure kindergarten teacher look might be the more appropriate option for tonight. But now that I'm wading through her flamingo-patterned cap-sleeve dresses and vegetable-print drawstring capris, I'm having second thoughts. I lost all hope when she brandished a solar-system-themed collared dress in my face.

Jessa thrives in a world where finger-painting, afternoon naps and juice boxes are all the rage. Her wardrobe reflects that. I look like I'm about to hand out string cheese and read Dr. Seuss books to a group of high-strung preschoolers.

At this point, I'm strongly tempted to re-wear the outfit I wore the other night to the Frosty Pitcher. I know Cannon's eyes fully appreciated that look, but that Coyote Ugly-inspired outfit is a big, big no-no for a fancy pants restaurant like *Le Sous-Sol*.

The growly billionaire thought it would be a good idea for us to go for dinner together—*alone*—before meeting his family. It seems smart to learn a little basic info about each other if we're going to convince the Kingstons that we're really, truly engaged.

I want to appear classy because *Le Sous-Sol* is that kind of place, but I realize now that I want something on the sexier side...to impress Cannon.

My brain is broken.

Even when he's an asshole, I find myself wanting to gain his approval. I care about his opinion of me, and to my utter horror, it has nothing to do with saving my bridal boutique.

This is not good.

"The Kingstons are like Crescent Harbor royalty and I'm about to fake-marry into their family," I whine to my sister. "I need something classy. Something simple. Elegant."

What I don't say is that I need something that doesn't scream where I came from. I need something that convinces the world that I am on par—or at least hold the potential to be on par—with an upstanding family such as the Kingstons.

I don't need to voice my insecurities out loud for Jessa to recognize them. She remembers that period in time when we found ourselves surrounded by the rich. We didn't belong. We were out of their league and they never missed an opportunity to remind us of that. I never want to find myself in that space again.

She pokes her head out of the closet. She's wearing a frown. "Since when do you doubt yourself?! Alexia Robson does *not* doubt herself. You are more than good enough to be in the company of Cannon Kingston. So he's got money. Who cares? You're smart, beautiful, and hardworking. He'd be lucky to have you."

I drop to the edge of Jessa's bed. This is scarier than I thought. Not only do I have to convince Cannon's parents that we're a legitimate couple, I also have to win over a prospective—albeit fake—mother-in-law all while keeping my nagging insecurities in check. These colossal tasks didn't cross my mind when I agreed to this scheme.

Jessa's muffled voice comes from the back of the closet. "By the way, Dad says he's been trying to reach you. Why haven't you returned his calls?"

At the mention of our father, my gut goes tight and I struggle against the mass of guilt trying to push its way to the surface. "Every time I talk to Dad, he asks for money and I'm too much of a damn softie to say 'no' to him. *That's* why I stopped taking his calls."

Jessa pokes her head through the door to look at me. "Maybe he just wants to check in with you, Lex."

"Fat chance," I grumble under my breath.

My sister tosses another dress at me, smacking me squarely in the face. "Try on this one. I think it's closer to what you're after." It has polka dots and a bow at the neck. Gag.

I scrunch up my nose. "Do you know me at all?"

She rolls her eyes. "Just try it on."

I comply to appease my sister.

"Look, I know that Mom and Dad fucked up when we

were kids." She cocks her head. "But they're still our parents..."

"And I love them. But I refuse to let their irresponsibility drag me down into the ditch because if I'm down in the ditch together with them, then I can't help them *or* myself. Constantly skimming off the top of my rent money to make loans to Dad is what got me into this mess in the first place. Here I am about to marry myself off to an evil super villain with a questionable moral code just so I can save my business from eviction."

With a sigh, Jessa returns to her wardrobe. I know she doesn't like my position but Mom and Dad had their shot to make something of themselves. They squandered it. Now, it's my turn and I don't need the guilt trip.

I stand in front of her floor-length mirror and she comes up behind me, carefully assessing this option.

"This one won't do," she concedes. "You look a little bit like a pilgrim about to board the *Mayflower*." No shit.

Giggling, she dives into her closet again and pulls something out of the very back. "Okay. This is my break-glass-in-case-of-emergency dress but I think it'll look hot on you."

It's short, it's sexy, it's ruby red. And it absolutely steals my breath away.

I grab the shroud of fabric from her hands. When I slide it on, I stand in front of the mirror, absolutely in love with how it flatters my body.

Mother Nature gave me the smallest titties possible—which if you ask me, was a total dick move on her part—but I never let that stop me from owning my body and my sexuality. I come from a world where you work with what you've got. It may not be perfect but this body is *mine*, dammit. And I'll claim every inch of it.

I spin to face my sister. "How do I look?"

She whistles under her breath. "Girl, you're gonna have to beat that man off of you with a stick tonight."

I grin, feeling like a woman who belongs on the arm of a devilishly sexy billionaire. "Well, that's the effect I was going for."

18

CANNON

Arms folded across my chest, I perch on the edge of the conference table, and I glare at the corkboard on the wall.

I'm debating just how much energy I'm willing to invest into this revenge plot. Honestly, the whole thing seems less appealing by the day.

Margot and Carl are together. That should be punishment enough for the both of them.

I'm re-considering some of my plans when I hear the elevator doors open. Who the hell could it be?

I ignore it, hoping it's not my father. I'm not exactly hiding my project here, but the less he knows, the better.

It's definitely not any of the remaining Kingston Realties employees. Dad wouldn't let me fire them so I had to come up with a clever alternative. I sent them all on an extended paid vacation just so I wouldn't have to look at their useless faces every day. None of them deserves vacation perks but on the bright side, at least now, I don't have to worry about Sally trying to sweeten my afternoon coffee with chloroform.

A short tap on the door has me grinding my molars. Christ. *Now what?* To say the disturbance is unwelcome would be an understatement. I don't have time for this.

"What?" I call out loudly.

No one responds. But before I can drag myself out of my chair, the conference room door swings open. Alexia stands in the doorway.

My gut contracts, like someone just sucker-punched me. She's backlit by the bright office lights, creating this angel effect around her. That's exactly what she looks like. A fallen angel with big blue eyes, unruly brunette hair and a tight red dress hand-selected by the devil.

And all of a sudden, I can't even remember what I'm supposed to be doing.

On instinct, I vault to my feet, bounding toward her. "What are you doing here?"

She eyes me skeptically, looking more guarded and unsure than ever. "We have dinner plans, don't we?" Her hesitant gaze shifts past my shoulder into the room.

"Oh, yeah...Um, dinner. Of course."

Dinner was my idea. The purpose of the meeting is to come up with a game plan to convince my mother that we're head-over-heels, can't-wait-another-minute-to-get-married in love. The men in my family already see through me, but I need to step up my game if this scheme is going to work on mom.

"So, dinner..." I'm staring at Alexia's legs. I can't help but lick my lips. I want this woman spread out on my plate.

Slowly, my eyes travel back up to her face. A slight smirk curves her mouth at my stupefied reaction.

Lexi tries stepping through the doorway and that's when I recall the war room I've created around me. I snap back to my senses, slyly using my body to block her entrance. She narrows her eyes and pouts her crimson painted lips. I want to suck on them.

"Cannon? You there?" My lawyer's voice fills my head.

That's when I remember my phone is pressed to my ear. Hell. "Frank, I'll have to call you back." I hit the red button to end the call.

Lexi uses my distraction to her advantage, ducking under my arm. She slips into the room, hips swinging, little red dress suctioned to her sexy frame.

Focus, idiot.

Her eyes immediately fly to the corkboard on the wall. Her jaw drops open in fascination. Or concern. Or suspicion. One of those. "Whoa! What are you planning? An assassination or something?"

I tilt my head to the side and stare at the back of her skull. "Can we just concentrate on the issue at hand? Going to dinner? Our reservation is for seven." I round the conference table, grabbing my jacket and briefcase. She ignores my request *and* my hand that's gesturing her toward the door.

Her eyes are wide. She's waving an arm at the corkboard. "Um, Cannon, this is the kind of shit that gets a girl subpoenaed. Or worse...If I'm about to get tackled by the FBI in the deli section of the grocery store, I think I have a right to know what I'm looking at here."

Annoyed, I growl at her. "I'm not planning an assassination."

She nails me to the wall with her demanding stare. "Okay...then, what is it?" This woman will not just let it go. But then again, this is Lexi Robson. I wouldn't expect anything less from her.

I give it to her straight, my voice as absent as a cloudy

weather forecast. "I walked in on my business partner banging my girlfriend. I'm figuring out what to do about it."

I dare to meet her eyes. I witness the shock swirling in those bright blue orbs, the compassion that swoops right in. It's like I can see right through her and I swear, this woman can see right through me. She holds a direct line to my soul.

Fuck this. There's too much tenderness in the room. If I'm not careful, she'll puncture my hard, ruthless facade. And right now, that's all I've got.

I end the moment, spitting out an impatient growl. "Are you done with the questions? Because I'd like to get this dinner over with."

The compassion snaps right off her face. Annoyance moves in to replace it. "Wow. I'm marrying the most romantic man in northern Illinois," she quips, stalking out of the conference room ahead of me.

I shake my head, closing the office door and trailing her to the elevator. She's such a sassy thing. But she doesn't intimidate me. If anything, she's a challenge. A girl like Alexia needs a real man. A boy wouldn't be able to handle her.

When the elevator doors slide open, I gesture for her to walk inside first. She gives me a surprised look.

I can't stop my eyes from wandering over her slim, fit body again. She catches me staring. I grin. "I may not be romantic, but baby, I'm a gentleman."

19

LEXI

Cannon brushes a spot of dust from his car door. He gives the vehicle an amorous look that makes me roll my eyes. The man is insufferable.

He catches me in the act and his lips curve into a boyish grin. I hate the fluttery feeling that moves through my belly.

His hand firmly encases mine as we stroll into the restaurant. I try to ignore the way my body feels with Cannon Kingston so close to me. I have to remind myself that it's all for show—a faux display of affection—to convince the people of Crescent Harbor that our 'love' is real. But combine this tingly warm feeling in my belly with Cannon's shocking admission that he walked in on his girlfriend in bed with another man? My head is a frigging mess.

I haven't had the best luck with dating, but even I haven't had it *that* bad. Cheating is one thing. But catching them in the act? No one should have to go through that.

Not even assholes like Cannon.

Maybe...maybe Mr. Billions isn't the cold, heartless man he pretends to be. Maybe his hard exterior is just a mask he wears to protect himself from the pain he's experienced? What if there's more under that tough shell?

Candle light flickers all around the room. Soft music twinkles in the air mingling with the hushed conversations of the patrons. The *maitre d'* seats us and we order drinks. I steal peeks at Cannon across the table, trying to visually peel back his layers and solve the sexy enigma sitting across from me. I want to be right about him. I do. Because then I won't have to hate my body for reacting so viscerally to this man.

As soon as we order dinner, and the waiter retrieves our menus, Cannon reaches into his briefcase and pulls out a slick black folder. Wordlessly, he hands it to me. Could this be the paperwork that gives everyone their businesses back? Is it a dossier on his life story, so we can get to know each other better?

No. Of *course* not. Because this is Cannon Kingston we're talking about. Asshole extraordinaire.

"A nondisclosure agreement?" Reality. Check.

"Yes, I had my lawyer prepare the NDA yesterday. Typically, I would have obtained your signature before our negotiations commenced. But I think we can both agree that these circumstances aren't typical." He speaks in a sterile, distant tone. He's going to have to work on that if he wants to convince anyone we're crazy in love. He stretches an expensive-looking pen across the table to me. "I need you to sign tonight. Preferably before we share anymore confidential information."

I ignore the damn pen. "Well, I prefer to read documentation before signing my life away. Considering this fifteen-page treaty here, signing isn't going to happen tonight," I state, sitting up a little taller. "Plus I need to have my lawyer review it."

I don't have a lawyer. I usually get my legal advice from Google Esquire, but Mr. Billions doesn't need to know that.

His tone drops menacingly. "This is urgent, Alexia."

"Also, I highly doubt there's anything too private in learning about each other's favorite color," I add dryly.

I can't believe I actually entertained the notion that Cannon's douchey behavior is just a coverup. His asshole nature is more consistent than my menstrual cycle. Clearly, I need to stop underestimating this guy.

His gorgeous face pinches for the briefest moment—I don't think he likes someone standing up to him—but then he sighs. "Fair enough. I definitely don't appreciate the delay, but seeking legal counsel is reasonable. And that way you won't be able to contest the terms of the agreement later on."

I can't help but laugh at his formalness. Even when he's being nice, he still has a stick up his ass.

Glaring, Cannon reaches back into his briefcase. "Good lord. What else do I have to sign?" I throw my hands in the air.

He seems put out. "Nothing. I just had my assistant compile a list of dating questions for us to review, so we can get to know the most important information about each other. Y'know, ensure this insta-marriage will be plausible to other people."

"Right." I would have loved to be a fly on the wall as he explained what he needed from his assistant.

After the server drops off our meals at the table, and we've taken a few quiet bites, he focuses on the dating questions. He holds the sheet in front of him. "Ready?"

I shrug. "Go for it." I shift my attention to my plate and dig into my Nicoise salad again. Oh my gosh. This is obscenely delicious. My taste buds are freaking out right now.

"What's something you want to learn or wish you were better at?" he reads before meeting my gaze. Okay, not a bad question.

"Yo-yoing." I take another bite and moan from behind my palm, a little self-conscious to be making sex noises in this fancy French restaurant.

He tilts his handsome head at me, annoyed. "Yo-yoing? This isn't going to work if you can't be serious," he declares in that bossy voice of his.

"I *am* serious. One hundred percent. I'm awful at yo-yoing, and it's always something I wanted to learn. The last time I tried to yo-yo, the string got all tangled around my arm. I had three feet of string wrapped around me so tight, Jessa had to cut it off."

"Huh," he says on an exhale, leaning back in his chair. "Okay. That's something." The corner of his mouth twitches. I can tell he's trying hard to keep a straight face. "And who's Jessa?"

"My younger sister. The barista you insulted," I sneer, holding tight to my grudge.

"The barista's your sister?" A smile pulls across my lips when he flinches subtly.

I nod. "She's the one who gets me out of trouble when I get carried away."

"I bet you keep her busy," he says under his breath. I want to act offended but hell, he's right.

Instead, I throw a question at him. "What about you? Tell me about your siblings."

"Three brothers. Walker's the oldest. Then, Eli. Then, me. Jude's the youngest." He runs a finger around the base of his glass. "And the rest of your family?"

I swallow. "Jessa's all the family I've got." I see the question marks rising in his eyes. He wants to ask about my parents. I veer the conversation back to the questionnaire before he manages to voice his interrogation. "Okay, back to your little quiz," I say chirpily. "What's something you want to learn or wish you were better at?"

Cannon chews on his bottom lip for several seconds before replying, "Mutual fund trading. I leave my portfolio in the hands of a team of professionals but I'd like to be better informed so I don't have to rely on third parties to understand the details of what's going on with my money." He casually digs into his meal like it isn't the most delicious thing he's ever eaten.

Ugh. "Boring. Why does it always have to come back to money with you?"

At that, he winks. "Because money makes the world go 'round." He attacks his *coq au vin* with knife and fork.

"If you say so, Mr. Billions." I pluck an olive out of my salad and pop it into my mouth.

He grins lopsidedly. "All right. Let's see what's next." He looks down at his printed list again. "What's something that bugs you? Okay, that's a dumb one."

"Nope, we're going to answer each one," I argue. Then I tap my jawline, thinking hard. "Snoring. It bugs the heck out of me. Do *you* snore? Because that's a dealbreaker for me. Snoring is basically you *bragging*—super loud—that you're asleep and I'm not."

Cannon's facade cracks when he bursts out laughing at my answer.

"Well, do you?" I repeat, licking salad dressing from my finger. "I'm not kidding here."

"I don't know if I snore," he answers lightly. His gaze

surfs down my body. "But you're welcome to join me in my bed if you're really that interested in my sleep habits."

I dramatically roll my eyes, feigning my annoyance despite the instant flash of lightning between my thighs. "Nice try."

"And as for what bugs me? Disloyal people." His expression goes sober. "Nothing disgusts me like a person who grins to your face and then stabs you in the back."

I lift my glass. "I feel that on every level of my soul, King. To me, nothing is more sacred than friendship and you can't build that on a foundation of disloyalty."

"Agreed. Wholeheartedly." He clinks his glass to mine.

He wears a strange expression as his gaze rakes over me again. I can't tell if he just appreciates my tiny dress, or if he's processing the fact that we actually just agreed on something. I'm feeling kind of strange, too.

He's doing the whole rumpled billionaire thing again tonight, but it works on Cannon. I'd never considered myself attracted to businessmen, but the way his button down shirt accentuates his muscled chest, and the way his slacks hug his ass, and the way his messy dark blond man bun highlights his chiselled features…I'm a big fan of this look on Cannon Kingston.

The man is hot as fuck.

As far as fake husbands go, I really could do a whole lot worse.

To break the tension, I grab the question sheet from his hands and ask. "What's your favorite place on earth?"

"Home, I guess. Right here in Crescent Harbor. I wouldn't have said that a month ago, but I'm realizing I don't want to be anywhere else." I shouldn't read anything into that, but my body can't help it. And the way he uses his voice makes my stomach go tight tight tight. "What about you? Favorite place?"

"My bed."

At that, he leans forward interestedly with a half-smile. It's only then that I realize how that sounded. I didn't mean it like *that*.

What I meant to say was, at the end of a long day when I get home, I just want to curl up beneath my sheets. I eat there. Read there. Watch movies there. It's my safe space. I should take it back, correct myself.

But hey, if he can play that innuendo game, so can I.

Cannon's gaze heats up. "I like that."

I grin lazily.

His eyes stay on me and when he leans across and wipes sauce from my lip with his knuckle, I swear I almost die.

"Sorry, the food is so good and I'm being such a slob." I grab my cloth napkin and self-consciously blot my mouth. His attention stays on my lips and the devil in me wishes he'd just lean closer.

Thankfully, right then, the waiter comes back to refill our drinks. Cannon shifts, tugging his collar from his neck. "What's your favorite movie?" he asks after clearing his throat.

"*Pride and Prejudice*. The one with Kiera Knightley." I take a sip of my wine.

"Huh. The movie? I thought most women loved the book."

"Yeah. I admit...I tried to read the book a million times. I just couldn't get through it. I kept thinking to myself, 'What the hell are these people talking about?'" I overshare, before giggling. The wine is obviously messing with my filter.

He laughs at me. "Can't say I've read that one."

"What's your favorite book?" I ask, switching up his

question a bit. He definitely strikes me more as a reader. The thought of him in a movie theater nearly makes me laugh out loud.

"*Lessons the Successful Man Must Never Forget.*"

"I don't think I've heard of that one. Good stuff?"

Cannon nods, getting this faraway look in his eyes. "The best. It was my grandfather's favorite. He loved business books, personal development stuff." His voice cracks, just a little.

His tone makes me brave enough to make my own confession. "I'm an absolute junkie for personal development books." The reading I did as a teenager planted seeds in my head, seeds that gave me the courage to leave my family's trailer, to open my own business, to break the toxic cycles I grew up in, to pave the way for a better life for Jessa and me.

He jerks an eyebrow and one corner of his mouth curls approvingly. "Gramps's entire collection is in my library. Maybe I can show it to you sometime..."

I bite down on my lip to tame my own smile. "Maybe..."

Our eyes linger for a while. Too long. I find myself blushing and looking away. Lexi Robson is *not* a blusher. Oh my gosh. What is this man doing to me?

"Okay. Subject change. Getting really deep here with this one. Who would you die to protect?" I ask finally without consulting the printout. I half-expect him to say something selfish, like himself.

He thinks for a while. "My niece, Callie. Her dad's in jail. Her mom fucked off. The kid's been through too much. She doesn't even like me but I'd do anything to shield her from more pain."

There have been rumors around town about Eli Kingston's imprisonment. It's hard separating truth from lies so I've avoided forming opinions. I also never took the time to consider the impact something like that would have on a child.

I giggle a little. "She doesn't like you?"

Cannon rubs the back of his neck and grins sheepishly. "Nah, she doesn't like me. But it's all good. I love her enough for the both of us."

My heart is in my stomach. Dammit. Why does he have to go and be so sweet sometimes? Ugh. It's hard to keep hating him when he starts acting like an actual human. When he goes and says things like that, I can't help but want to kiss him. His face tells me he feels it, too.

Our eyes hold again. He stretches across the table, and I think he's going to touch me. He's going to kiss me. My insides dance.

But instead, he drops a glittering engagement ring next to my plate. All emotion evaporates from his face. "You'll wear this."

My smile falls.

Oh, never mind. Mr. Billions is back.

20

CANNON

I stand near the antique liquor cart in the dining room, eyeing Lexi as she interacts with my mother. My chest swells at the sight. It's clear that Stormy is outside of her comfort zone here with my family. I thought nothing would faze that woman, but she's less than her usual feisty self at the moment. Still, she's charming. She's adorable.

She's exactly the woman I want to take to bed.

My brother Jude walks up to me, digging an elbow into my side as he sets his teacup into a delicate saucer. I know he doesn't drink during football season, but damn, the tea thing is kind of strange?

"How long are you staying?" I ask Jude.

"I'll be out in twenty four hours."

"Well, thanks for coming," I mumble, unable to take my eyes off of Lexi. She's wearing this loose-fitting plum-colored little number with a skinny belt at the waist, and she looks absolutely stunning. Those legs go on for-fucking-ever.

"I just flew in for the entertainment, bro. Your fake fiancée meeting the parents? You kidding me? I wouldn't miss that."

I level him with a look. "You need to keep your freaking voice down. And for a surly recluse, Walker really does gossip a lot." I head for the empty dinner table and my younger brother follows me.

Jude's not exactly the marrying type. He's more focused on sleeping his way through football groupies at the moment. So if he tries to embarrass me today, I wouldn't be the slightest bit shocked.

Callie is running around, helping the ladies set the table. Everything is prepared and we're already seated, as the little one carefully places the forks around our placemats. She drops her last fork off at the seat next to mine.

"Thank you, Callie," Lexi says from beside me. She and the child share a smile.

"You're welcome," my niece says, good-manneredly. Then she turns and gives me a weird look. "Grandma! There's no more forks!"

Well, that's messed up. I have a sneaking suspicion the girl planned for everyone to receive silverware except me.

"Yes, there are," my mother calls back. "You left one here on the counter, honey."

I eye my niece, and she grins. Christ, she's going to be too smart and too mischievous for her own good. She's going to be more like her father than I care to admit.

When my parents, niece, and two brothers join Alexia and me at the dining room table, I finally announce some of the wedding details.

"I apologize up front for the late notice, but the wedding will be happening this weekend."

"Wow. *This* weekend?" My mother sits back in her chair with a worried expression.

"Man," Jude speaks up, clearly disappointed to be missing out on further entertainment. "I've got a game this Sunday. I won't be able to make it."

I shrug. "So be it. I understand not everyone will be able to drop everything, and I don't expect you to. Honestly, I don't care who is there. Alexia and I just can't wait to begin our life together." I eyeball my fake fiancée sitting next to me. The way she smiles back at me makes me forget this is all a lie.

"I sure wasn't expecting this all to move so quickly, but I'm here to help in any way I can," my mother says with a smile.

I was with Margot for so long and that relationship was obviously going nowhere. So even though this engagement to Lexi is moving at lightning speed, I think Mom's just ecstatic I'm settling down. She'd be willing to marry me off tonight if that's the timeline I gave her.

"Where will the wedding take place?"

She looks at Stormy, but I answer for us both. "We expect it'll be a small ceremony, and we'll—"

"We're actually thinking of the rooftop above my bridal boutique," Lexi interrupts smoothly. "If that's all right with you." She glances at my father for his approval.

Huh. I didn't realize she was a step ahead of me. It's kind of hot.

Ma nods. "A rooftop wedding? That's so romantic. What about a guest list? Who and how many are we looking at right now?"

My gut twists as I answer her. "The one person I'd really like to be there is Gramps."

Dad clears his throat and winces. "I don't think that'll be possible, son. You know he's sick, and arranging for him to leave the nursing home will be a logistical nightmare."

My mother smiles softly and then places her hand on top of mine. She gives Dad the pleading look that would make him move heaven and earth for her. "Honey, we'll make it happen. I know how much this means to you."

I take both of Ma's hands in mine. "Thank you." My voice cracks. When I risk a glance at Lexi, I catch her watching me curiously. Our eyes lock, and the warmth I see in her gaze blankets my body.

"Dear, do you have a wedding dress yet?" Mom's working through her mental checklist.

"No, not yet," Alexia answers embarrassedly. "I think I may have too many gowns to choose from at the shop. It's overwhelming."

"Well, I don't want to put you on the spot, but you're welcome to wear *my* wedding dress. I promise, it's not awful," Ma laughs.

The bride-to-be gasps. "Oh, that's too generous, Mrs. Kingston. I couldn't accept."

"I just want you to consider it. I'll grab it, and you'll let me know what you think. No pressure," she promises, already halfway down the hall.

Stormy flashes me a nervous look as if she's waiting for my blessing to accept my mom's offer. I lift a shoulder and give her a half-smile. If she likes the dress, I see no good reason why she shouldn't wear it. Fake wedding notwithstanding.

When my mother comes back into the dining room, I watch Lexi's eyes light up. I can tell she was not expecting this. The gown may be over thirty years old, but it's simple and classic. It'd look amazing on my bride.

My bride...I like the way that sounds.

Christ, I'm starting to lose my grip on the line between real and fake.

"Oh, Mrs. Kingston. It's so gorgeous," Lexi gushes, rising to meet Ma. She delicately runs a finger over the material. "It's whimsical. It's perfect." She glances at my mother with wide eyes. "I-I'm a bit clumsy. Are you sure about me wearing it?"

"Absolutely, dear. I don't have any daughters of my own and by the time Callie is ready for marriage, brides will probably be traipsing down the aisle in skin-tight, silver-plated dystopian jumpsuits or something like that." The women share a laugh.

She holds the dress over Alexia's body and my fiancee touches it reverently, like she's scared it will fall apart in her hands.

My niece rises onto her knees and leans across the table with a mouth full of bread. "It looks like a princess dress." She eyes Lexi amorously.

"You like it, Callie?" my wife-to-be asks.

"Yes," the child says definitively. The two share a smile and I instantly know Lexi has just earned herself a friend.

Meanwhile, my brothers continue silently shoveling food into their faces, completely uninterested in the wedding plans. I should be gorging down right along with them. After all, this wedding isn't even for real. But I find myself invested in all the details.

"Is your mother helping with the wedding planning?" Mom asks Lexi as the women settle back at the table. "I don't want to step on anyone's toes."

"Oh, no," Lexi says, face reddening. "My mother and I aren't on speaking terms."

No one says anything for a minute. I can't fight the urge to reach over and drape my arm protectively around Alexia's chair because this turn of conversation is awkward as hell. Luckily, no one presses her on her family drama.

Silently, I wonder what happened with her family. Why are she and her mother estranged? Does she have a better relationship with her father? Does she have anyone other than her sister?

The Kingstons aren't exactly a model family. We live states apart, we don't always communicate what we're feeling and we don't see each other as much as we should. But we love each other, without a doubt, and I can't imagine not being on speaking terms with my parents.

"Well, you two don't need to worry at all," Ma finally says, wearing a reassuring smile. "I will help with every detail you need. I don't know if Cannon told you, but Lucas and I had very little time to plan our wedding, too." She reaches across to hold my father's hand. "I was pregnant with Walker at the time, and needed to fit into that tiny dress before I started showing!"

"Ma, overshare much?" Walker shifts uncomfortably in his seat. The way he does anytime one of us brings up the fact that his growly ass was conceived in sin.

"Is that what this is?" Jude speaks up with a smirk. "Is Lexi knocked up?"

"Jude!" Mom scolds.

My brother is such an ass. He knows the real reason Lexi and I are dashing to the altar. Yet he won't pass up the opportunity to get me in shit with mom.

I let it roll off my shoulders with a light laugh. "No, no babies in our near future," I assure the family. Though, the idea of getting Alexia in bed has been on replay in my head. I'm not itching to have kids anytime soon, but if procreation is the outcome of getting my hands on that beautiful woman, then so be it.

I have to shake out my arms. Seriously, though—am I the only one sweating right now?

Lexi's uneasy smile reminds me of the wicked threats she made the last time I tried kissing her on that dirty bar's dancefloor. She left very little room for ambiguity there. Clearly, physical contact is off the table between us.

That fucking blows, but I need to keep my eye on the bigger picture here. Saving the family business. At all costs.

Mom and Stormy continue to hash out details, and we're one step closer to my target. We get through the meal without any major hiccups, for which I'm incredibly grateful. It's nice to get a break from constantly having to put out fires.

But that doesn't stop my father from pulling me aside after dinner. "I'm holding off the outside investor for the time being," he explains once we're alone in his study.

I nod. "Thank you. You can tell him the company is no longer for sale," I add.

"We'll see about that," Dad says, narrowing his keen gaze on me. "My gut says this whole thing is a farce. You're brilliant with business strategy. I'll give you that. And I also know nothing matters more to you than money."

"Come on," I exhale, shaking my head. Because what else can I say?

"You will break your mother's heart if she finds out this whole thing is a sham. I won't bail you out when that happens."

Shit. I hadn't really considered the consequences of my fake marriage's dissolution. Stormy and I will just have to come up with something smart, and make our breakup look just as believable as our nuptials.

In my mind, I start formulating a plan. Planning the demise of my marriage before I've even said my vows? On every level of my being, it feels wrong.

21

LEXI

Cannon is extra touchy feely as we leave his parent's guesthouse.

I'm sure it's just because his mother is energetically waving at us from the doorway. One of his hands burns the small of my back as he dutifully helps me into his passenger seat. And then his other palm heavily grazes my thigh before he shuts me inside the car. That last one sure didn't seem like a show for Mom. And it lights my nerves on fire nonetheless.

The air crackles on the ride to my house. It can't just be me, can it?

My skin feels hot and flushed from head to toe. I wasn't prepared for the amount of touching tonight. That was the most physical contact between us since the night on the dancefloor. I'm completely on board with ensuring we make this relationship believable, but holy hell, is my *body* supposed to believe what we're selling, too?

I need to distract myself before I throw caution to the wind and jump his bones once and for all. "Can I ask you a question?"

His eyes briefly swing to mine from behind his aviators as he navigates the car down the winding road back into town. "Since when do you need permission to go running off at the mouth?"

I roll my eyes despite my small smile at his asshole comment. "I'm serious."

"Okay, go ahead."

I take a deep breath. I hope I'm not overstepping here, but I need to voice the question that has been plaguing my mind for days. "Why didn't you just take the money?"

"What do you mean?"

"When your dad offered to buy you out of Kingston Holdings, why didn't you just take the money and run? Y'know, instead of keeping those crumbling buildings?" I shift my body in my seat so that I'm facing him more fully. I stare at his handsome profile as he focuses on the road. "You're going to have to sink a ton of money into fixing those buildings...Don't get me wrong: I get to keep my business, and so do my friends, so I shouldn't complain. But as far as you're concerned, it was a poor business decision." I wiggle my glittering ring finger in his direction. "And you went to a lot of trouble to make this happen."

He's quiet for a long time, giving the road his undivided attention. I watch this faraway look shutter over his eyes. "All my life, I've been pursuing things that were shiny or things that just padded my bank account. Things that ultimately didn't matter." He exhales heavily. "For once, I want to do something that matters."

"What do you mean?"

"My grandfather was my best friend growing up. I spent more time with Gramps at the office than I did with my own brothers. He sacrificed everything for that business. His health, his happiness, his marriage. It would kill me if those sacrifices were all in vain."

"The business was important to him?"

A short laugh leaves Cannon's lips. "You could say that. My grandmother left Gramps because he was so committed to his work. Losing his marriage was his wakeup call. I think that's why he insisted that my parents run the business together and that their children run it as a family for generations to come. Gramps wanted Kingston Realties to be something that holds our family together, not something that tears us apart."

"So you're doing all this for him?"

His eyes meet mine as the car slows at a red light. He doesn't answer my question, but he doesn't have to.

Cannon reaches deep into his pocket. In his open hand, he shows me an old wrist watch. It is missing one of its black leather straps. The face of the watch is cloudy and heavily scratched. I can barely make out the numbers, but when I do, I see it's still running. The time is spot on.

He lets me pick it up from his hand as the street light turns green. "It was Gramps's watch. I snuck it out of his desk years ago."

"And he's in a nursing home?" I ask, squeezing the old watch and trying to piece together the various clues I picked up over dinner tonight. It sounds like the man is ill, and that breaks my heart.

Cannon nods. "Alzheimer's," he says softly, his voice cracking. "He doesn't even remember who I am." He quickly clears his throat, covering up the thick emotion that's weighing down his tone.

"But you remember him. That's what matters." I lay my hand over his as he pulls his car into my gravel driveway. He flashes a genuine smile my way and gently takes the watch from my hand, before climbing out of the car.

I'm lost in my head, mind whirling at this avalanche of new information about what makes this enigmatic man tick. I feel like I've peeled back a new layer of Mr. Billions.

Whether he likes it or not, I know now that there's a great deal more to him than his rough external shell.

He opens my door and I'm so overcome by my new discoveries that I don't even have a snarky comment for him. Instead, I meet his eyes as I rise to my feet.

I pause there, trying to read his expression. "Thank you for bringing me home," I whisper. This whole day has flipped me on my head.

The man smirks. "Didn't seem fair for you to have to take the bus after enduring dinner with my family." I chuckle and shake my head. He tilts his head toward my front door. "I'll walk you up." Those strong fingers graze the small of my back again.

Lord, what is this man doing to me?

We climb up the few rickety stairs to my porch and stand toe-to-toe at my door.

His eyes snap down to my mouth. His gaze locks there. He winces.

"What the hell is wrong with your face, King?" I tip my chin up at his distraught expression.

His wince deepens. "I have a feeling I'm about to get head-butted into a coma."

Surprised laughter bursts past my mouth.

Shit—Cannon Kingston is actually brave enough to try and kiss me?

My eyes go to his lips. They look soft and delicious.

I'm tough. I'm loyal. I'm self-sufficient. But I'm also a woman. And I'll be honest here—in this moment, there's nothing I want more than to kiss this man despite everything that's at stake.

"Might be worth it." My fingers curl in his collar and I tug him toward me.

He grins, all sexy and lopsided as he leans closer. "Yeah, it might be."

"Or maybe not," I taunt, shrugging a shoulder. "I guess there's only one way to find out."

His big palm cups the back of my head, messing up my hair. He lowers his face some more. "You're annoying." I hear the laughter in his voice. He plunges his fingers into my hair and yanks my head back.

And then our mouths collide.

Instantly, I'm swept away by the intensity of Cannon's hold on me. The momentum from the contact has me crashing into the door.

It's a bloodthirsty kiss. There's no build up, no soft intro, no tender prelude. It's just lust. Hard, hot and so very possessive.

My pulse pounds in places it's never pounded before. My head, my stomach, my breasts, the space between my thighs. I relinquish my good sense. My arms lock around his neck, my only hope of keeping upright on these wobbly knees.

Meanwhile, he touches me all over all over all over. He cups a hand on my hip then his groping fingers slide down to my ass. He gives a good squeeze before his touch moves up my back, my neck and into my hair again.

And why does this feel so good? Why does it feel so right? Why does it feel like I could kiss this man for the rest of the night, until the sun is creeping up the horizon? Hell, I want to do a whole lot more than kissing.

Even as I'm drowning in the kiss, the voice of reason

manages to surface for air. I can't sleep with Cannon. If I do, there's no way I won't catch feelings for the charming bastard.

Sex would be a very bad idea. I'm already in a vulnerable position. He holds the power in this agreement of ours. It would be foolish of me to delude myself into believing for one second that we're on equal footing.

I untangle my lips from his and take a step back. My bones tremble beneath my heated skin. I pat him high on the chest. "Good night, King." My voice is breathier than it should be. Dammit.

He takes a step back. Licks his lips. Blinks through his lust. "Good night, Stormy ."

I watch from my doorway as my fake fiancé backs down the stairs to his car sporting one hell of a boner. I'm way too turned on to gloat.

22

CANNON

I'm supposed to be having a bachelor party. I'm supposed to be in a sweaty strip club drinking dubious shots and having random women shake their over-bronzed cleavage in my face. That's what regular guys do the night before they marry the love of their life.

Regular guys are idiots.

My engagement is as phony as they come, yet the only woman I want to see naked right now is the one who'll be dressed in fields of white, walking down the aisle toward me tomorrow afternoon.

I can't stop thinking about Alexia but really, what's new? My every waking hour is populated with thoughts of her.

For the past few days, it's that kiss that's been replaying in my head. The way she felt, the way she sounded, the way she tasted. I'm not sure I can wait until the altar to kiss her again, to do more than that.

. . .

"Bro, you're up." My attention snaps over my shoulder to where Walker is waiting impatiently, cue stick in hand. Eyes on me, he tips back his beer.

We're here in his quaint hunting cabin on the edge of the family farm. It's a quiet evening, just him, our dad and me. I think their role is supposed to be getting me shit-faced and watching me make terrible decisions I'll regret in the morning but so far, they've been doing a terrible job.

"Yeah." I shake my head and approach the pool table in the middle of my brother's man cave. I lean down and take a shot. It's pure shit.

With that silent judgmental stare of his, he rounds the table and effortlessly knocks three balls into the hole.

He chuckles under his breath. "Look, dude. Nobody's forcing you to be here so don't feel obligated to stay."

I stare incredulously. "Wait...you kicking me out of my lame-ass bachelor party?"

"You're obviously not into it and I've got pig stalls to clean, so..."

I raise both brows in disbelief.

He shrugs, regretting nothing.

. . .

I THROW a glance at my father. He's slouched in a recliner, mouth agape, fast asleep. No help there. "Some drinking buddies, you two are."

"DAD and I both know you don't want to be here drinking beer with us...She's been on your mind this whole time. No shame in it. She's yours. Go to her."

Fuck—she *is* mine. Or at least, I have the right to pretend that she is and that she wants to belong to me.

I give up. I can't fake this anymore. I need to see her.

I fling my stick onto the table and throw up both hands in surrender. "I'm out."

I text Alexia as I'm walking to my car on the edge of the dirt lane.

CANNON: **where r u**

IT TAKES her no time to respond.

ALEXIA: **Frosty Pitcher. Impromptu bachelorette party**
She attaches a selfie. Tongue out, hair wild, baby doll eyes squinting at the camera. And she's not wearing nearly enough clothes.

I message her back immediately.

CANNON: **I'm on my way**

. . .

ALEXIA: **What? Ur on ur way? Why?**

I GET INTO MY CAR.

CANNON: **just get ready, Stormy**

I TOSS the phone onto the passenger's seat and grin. She keeps blowing up my phone—of course she does—but I ignore her damn messages, my cock aching for the minute I'll have her in my arms.

SHE'S the first thing I see as I step into the Frosty Pitcher.

She's on a table, in a mini skirt and a tiny white tank top with the word Bride scribbled across the front in black Sharpie.

Even with half the girls in town dancing around her, Alexia is the center of the universe.

SHE SPINS AROUND and from across the room, our eyes meet. *Fuck, she's beautiful.*

A GRIN SLIDES across my face as I push through the pulsing crowd, moving toward her.

. . .

But a blonde, pint-sized woman steps into my path. Iris. Two other women flank her sides.

Penny gives me a nervous smile. "Hey Cannon."

"Hey Penny." I turn to the rest of the group. "How can I help you ladies?"

A chirpy-looking girl stretches a hand out to me. "I'm Jessa. Lexi's sister. I don't know if you remember me from the coffee shop the other—"

Iris slaps Jessa's hand out of the air. "Long story short. We're Lexi's friends and we love her and we just want to make sure you know that we're backing her up."

Jessa interjects. "The entire town is backing her up." When I glare, she smiles sweetly.

"And we know where you live," Penny adds and I'm only half-sure she's joking.

Iris shoots daggers at me. "So if you hurt her, we won't hesitate to hurt you back."

From across the room Lexi's eyes are on us and she's laughing and dancing and laughing and dancing and from the way she's laughing I can tell that I probably look like a deer in the headlights surrounded by this tribe of protective women.

"Look, Alexia is fully clear on exactly what she's getting into. We have a crystal clear contract." Am I nuts? Why am I giving these women details protected by my NDA? I continue to throw all business sense out the window when it comes to Stormy.

. . .

"What we're saying is, don't hurt her..." Penny begs softly. "Just...don't hurt her."

I see the genuine concern in her face. God, people really *do* love that girl. They're loyal to her and she deserves every bit of that devotion. And every second I spend with her, she inspires my devotion, too.

Alexia bursts through the crowd, barging in between her friends and me. "Okay, this was amusing for the first few minutes, but enough...I can hold my own and we all know it."

She hooks an arm through mine and guides me away from her protesting friends, straight into the thick of the dancefloor.

She faces me. "King why are you here?" Challenge glints in her eyes beneath the flashing strobe lights.

"To take you home."

She scoffs. "To take me home?" She plants both fists on her hips. "Who said I'm ready to go home? You don't seem to realize that I'm a grown woman, an independent wom—"

I hook an arm around her waist, pull her flush against me and shut her up with a kiss. Right there in the middle of the dancefloor.

. . .

HER BODY MELTS AGAINST MINE, her objections dissolve with each stroke of our tongues together. I kiss her until neither of us can breathe.

She licks her swollen lips and swallows. "On second thought, I think I'm ready to go now."

Smirking, I lace my fingers through hers as she urgently tugs me out the door.

23

LEXI

My heart is a thumping, pounding mess as Cannon's car glides up the driveway to his mansion. The landscaping is impeccable. Spotlights illuminate the facade of the majestic building.

But I'm not here to admire the architecture. There's a sculpture of a man in the driver's seat and I'm here to get his cock.

I lean across the console and taste the salty flesh of his neck. I don't know how much longer I can wait.

He's had his hand on my thigh throughout the drive, his broad, warm fingertips flirting with the edge of my skirt, detonating an electric storm at the apex of my thighs. I feel like I'm losing my mind with need.

We roll into a garage that's bigger than my entire house. There are already two luxury cars parked inside.

Cannon jumps out from behind the wheel and in a flash he's at my door. He's not big on chivalry but I'm about to fuck a man who clearly has no right being near my body. The least I can do is make him work for it a little...He's gonna open my door.

I wait until he does and then I step out.

His fingers slide into my hair and he kisses me. Hard and wild. Jamming me against the side of the car, running his hands up and down my body as I fist the front of his shirt to drag him closer. My head is light when we pull apart for air.

"You're sexy as fuck, woman."

I look into his caramel eyes, wondering what it is about this man that makes me so stupid with lust. "I hate to admit it but you're pretty damn sexy yourself."

We stumble into the house, hands all over each other. He grabs me by my belt loop and pulls me down a long marble hallway.

One second, he's hauling me up into his arms and he's marching through the house like a caveman on a mission.

The next second, he's kicking open a heavy oak door.

Then I'm on my back, plush clean bedding haloing around me as I watch Cannon rip his sweater over his head.

I must be staring, gape-jawed as his muscle-cut torso comes into view. He smirks. "You gonna take those panties off, Stormy, or do I have to do all the work around here?"

I ROLL MY EYES. "For somebody with a boner that borderline looks like a medical emergency, you really do waste a lot of time talking shit."

EYES GLINTING, he growls. "Take. Those. Panties. Off."

STATIC ELECTRICITY POURS into my belly at the threatening tone.

Every nerve ending misfires.

Cutting my eyes at him, I do exactly as he says.

Now, he's kneeling on the carpet, spreading my legs apart. Big, hot palms voyage across my skin and his soft lips follow the path. Then, he's stroking my clit, kissing my folds, driving me wild. Cannon is putting in work but I'm the one panting hard, sweating.

This feels amazing.

I focus on the pleasure so I can avoid the fact that I'm scared, terrified. I have no right to be in this man's bed. Tomorrow, we'll exchange counterfeit vows and he'll become my fake husband. Fucking him tonight really isn't the brightest idea I've ever had.

He looks up from where he's kneeling and when our eyes meet, he gives me the most self-satisfied smirk I've ever seen. "On your knees, Stormy. Let me eat that pretty pussy from behind."

"Now, that's the kind of order I can obey." In an instant, I'm on my belly, ass in the air.

With renewed motivation, he dives back in, face buried in my ass. Licking and stroking and groaning into my folds until my spine is arching and I'm fisting the sheets at the height of my orgasm.

Violent aftershocks of pleasure pulse through my limbs and my chest heaves with labored breaths.

A gentleman would give me a second to recover but Cannon Kingston is no gentleman. He's a bastard.

HE FLIPS me over like a pancake and grabs a condom from his bedside drawer as he climbs over me. He slides on the condom and takes a second to grin in my face. "You're so pretty when you're horny and compliant."

I HOOK an arm around his neck and yank him in for a kiss as my pussy swallows him to the hilt. I moan. "Shut up and fuck me, asshole."

AND GOD, it's a tight fit. He's so big. Thick and long and so, so hard. He pumps into me. Smooth, long thrusts. Taking his time. Luxuriating. Enjoying my every whimper and moan as he tugs on my hair.

OVERWHELMED, I close my eyes. For something so wrong, it feels so right, so right, so right.

I know I'm going to fall for him, I know I'm going to regret it. But when it comes to this guy, I can't help myself. Where he's concerned, my good sense fails me every time.

Now, he's moving faster, hitting deeper, going harder. I'm groaning. Louder and louder, begging him not to stop.

It's official. I'm screwed. I'm addicted to everything this man does.

His hand smooths up the front of my throat and tips my chin up. He growls near my ear. "Open your eyes, Stormy. I want you looking at me when I make you come."

HIS THUMB FINDS my clit in a smooth back and forth motion. He fucks me harder now. A hot gush of arousal pours out of my pussy. "Oh shit," I groan.

. . .

He smirks. "What is it, darling?" He asks sweetly as his thumb works faster.

"Just make me come, you sadist." The only reason I'm not strangling him right now is because I want this orgasm more than anything.

He grabs my hips for leverage. He bares down. That move unleashes the orgasm. Wave after hot, rippling wave of pleasure washing over me.

He leans down to kiss me, to swallow my moans while pouring his sexy sounds into me.

He's coming too. His muscles tense under my fingertips, his breathing hitches. I watch in awe as pleasure ripples through the big, powerful body hunched above me. I never realized he could be even more handsome but in this vulnerable moment, he is.

We lie immobile, side by side. A little voice reminds me that I need boundaries if this fake relationship is going to stay fake.

I blink up at the vaulted ceiling, waiting for a rush of common sense to crash into me, to shove me out of this bed, out of this house.

It never comes.

Even more troubling? When Cannon rolls over and

lazily wraps an arm around my waist while kissing my spine, I don't get up and run, screaming. Instead, I sink deeper into his hold and drift off into an easy sleep.

At three in the morning, I wake up in a strange room, on a massive bed that's softer than a cloud. I'm nose to nose with a sexy, gorgeous, naked super villain who makes my girlie bits flutter. And I realize, to my horror, that my heart is fluttering, too.

Fuck. This is wrong.

This wasn't part of our agreement. If I allow myself to indulge in his rockhard body and his butter-soft kisses, I'll only end up hurt.

Mournfully, I untangle my limbs from his and roll to the edge of the mattress.

Just as I'm about to swing my feet to the floor and make my great escape, his arm tightens around my belly. He flings his leg around my waist. His voice is groggy and thick with sleep. "Get your beautiful ass back here, Stormy. I'm a spooner."

And just like that, my hot-off-the-presses decision to run away from this man goes *poof!* and a second later his light snores and my loud doubts fill my head.

24

LEXI

"If I get married one day, you *have* to do my flowers, too." Jessa spins around with my bouquet, humming to the quiet music wafting from the speakers. It's like she's reenacting a scene from *The Sound of Music*. "I can't get over how perfect these look."

Iris grins up at my sister from where she's arranging a small basket of rose petals for Callie, my little flower girl. Meanwhile, Penny is across the room, giving my wedding gown one final steam.

Since I'm getting married on the rooftop in a couple hours, we're all sardined into the back of the bridal boutique. Having my girls here, fawning all over the place and tending to my every need, is the only typical part of my wedding day.

I never imagined I'd be marrying a billionaire. I never imagined the wedding would be all for show. I never imagined I'd be saying my vows all while fully aware of the ticking clock looming above the relationship.

Yet, here I am getting ready to walk down the aisle to a

man who doesn't love me, a man who fucked me senseless just last night.

"Are you tossing your bouquet afterward?" Miss Lucille asks while poking me in the scalp with another bobby pin. The woman is like a bobby pin ninja. Bless her heart for taking on the task of wrangling my her into order in this humidity. I've been sitting here an hour already, and my ass is officially numb.

"I don't know. Maybe?" When planning a quickie wedding with only a week's notice, certain small details tend to fall through the cracks, I guess.

Penny gives me a cautious look. "I don't know if a bouquet toss is the best idea. We're gonna be on a rooftop, after all."

Jessa sniffs the flowers and sighs. "I'd go headfirst over the safety railing to catch these beauties. Especially if it raises my chance of finding my own Prince Charming."

"I'd hardly call Cannon Kingston Prince Charming," Iris mutters. She perches on the edge of the counter and gives me a concerned look.

Jessa giggles. "Okay, he's a bit of an asshole. But assholes need love, too."

"Assholes need love the most," Miss Lucille says sagely. "But never at the price of your own self-respect." The cringe on her face tells me that was a hard-earned lesson for her. She's not fully on-board with this whole marriage thing. I can tell she's been biting her tongue.

Jessa gently sets the bouquet into a vase of water. "Call me naive but I still think that Lexi and her rich prince could fall in love and live happily ever after." She pops a kiss against my cheek and twirls off on a cloud of cotton candy and whatnot.

A week ago, I would have laughed at my sister's wishful

thinking. But today...my heart is more open to the possibility. Because despite my rough edges, I *do* believe in happily ever afters like all girls do. Maybe I could have my moment, too. With Cannon Kingston.

If I've learned anything this week, it's that Cannon and I have undeniable chemistry. As soon as he's within touching distance, my body knows it. And the things we did to each other last night? Well, let's just say I didn't tell the girls about that. I know I shouldn't be withholding the juicy bits from my friends but all these feelings are new. I need time to sit with them.

I won't admit how many times I've thought about Cannon's lips, his hands, his cock. I won't talk about how much he tasted like desperation and hunger, about how he moved with urgency and passion. Or, how much I want to feel him again.

My stomach buzzes at the realization that I will. In just a short time, I'll be his lawfully-wedded wife and he'll be putting his mouth on me again.

Iris comes closer and keeps her voice low. "Are you sure you're okay with all this, Lexi? You can still walk away."

My friend has finally explained why she's been so hostile toward Cannon. Apparently, she and his younger brother, Jude, were sort of rivals in college. The few times that Cannon hung around in their circle, he didn't leave a favorable impression. Not that hard to believe since the man usually makes a point of being a bastard. Anyway, the fact that he doesn't even seem to remember her years later has cemented my friend's resentment toward him.

"I'm sure. I'll be fine." I say it with a smile. A smile I hope is convincing. Beneath the surface, my nerves are brittle and raw. I'm charging blindly into unknown territory with this marriage.

"You're not doing this just for me, are you? I couldn't live with that." Concern mars her beautiful face.

"I mean, partially. But not just you. Me. You. Your mom. This whole town." *Cannon.* "We're all going to benefit from this arrangement. I know this is the right decision."

"Would you hate me if I didn't open the sandwich shop back up?"

"What?! Why?" My surprise sends my head rearing back. Miss Lucille yanks on a chunk of my hair to scold me. *Ouch!*

"I've done a lot of thinking over the past couple weeks, and it just doesn't feel right. My cash flow is really low anyway, and I have some other business ideas I want to explore. The sandwich shop was my dream when I was a married woman, but now...I picture my future differently."

I want to hug my girl, but her mom will smack me with a hair brush if I move again. Instead, I reach out and grab Iris's hand. "Don't feel bad. I get it. You need a new...you."

The bell dings from the front of the shop, signalling that someone has come through the door. Penny dashes off to check, and in a moment, she's escorting an older gentleman into the room. He's smartly dressed and has a complete head of gray hair. Uneasiness crawls up my spine at the sight of him.

"Ms. Robson?" the man asks, looking straight at me.

"Present." Who is this guy? God, I hope he's not the fake marriage police, here to throw my ass in jail for marriage fraud or something like that.

He has a tight smile when he approaches me. He offers me his hand to shake. "I'm Cannon's attorney, Frank Lawman. Can I get a word with you?"

I'm not sure if knowing the man's identity makes me feel any better. Slowly, I rise from my seat, my friends all focused on me. "Of course." I walk down the short hallway to my messy office and he follows me.

Once I've closed the door, he speaks. "I'm here to collect your signed paperwork."

My brain short wires. "Paperwork?"

The old man lowers his voice. "The prenuptial agreement and NDA, ma'am."

My stomach knots and any delusions of a happy ending for Cannon and me go pop-pop-pop. "Oh. *Right*. Those."

I bend into my desk drawer and collect the documents I signed a few days ago. Some of the pages are a little wrinkled from my pouring over them again and again. "You sure used some big words in there," I laugh nervously to disguise the fact that I'm in over my head.

The lawyer doesn't laugh along.

With shaky hands, I flip through the pages one last time hoping I haven't overlooked some fine print where I inadvertently pledge my left lung to my fake husband should the need arise. I bite my lip to keep it from quivering as I quickly review the terms.

No sexual or romantic relationships with third parties during the course of my marriage. No financial entitlements aside from the compensation explicitly agreed to before the wedding ceremony. And in big, bold font, as though it's the most important section of the paperwork...When this is all over, both parties are bound to keep their mouths shut and peacefully walk away.

The language of the prenup is so ugly. Like a dirty accusation. Like I'm nothing but a low golddigger trying to scheme my way into some rich boy's trust fund.

It's downright insulting. I didn't initiate any of this. I was just living my life, trying to run my business and spend time with my friends. But this is the corner I've found myself backed into.

All these damn legal documents just serve to remind me of the power imbalance in our situation. I really am at my groom-to-be's mercy. It's downright insulting. And more than anything, it's another flashing warning not to let my guard down with this guy.

It's a not-so-subtle reminder that I have no future with Cannon Kingston. This isn't the happy ending I now find myself craving. It's a business deal and I have to accept that despite what my heart wants.

This is so dangerous.

The scales of power in this situation are tipped sharply in Cannon's favor. He has the money. He has the options. He has the high-priced lawyer who looks like he could burn down my life with a few quick strokes of his expensive pen.

Satisfied that spousal organ donation isn't one of the terms of the agreement, I hand over both stacks of documents to my fake fiancé's lawyer.

He hands me a check.

True to his word, Cannon has dropped a *huge* chunk of change on this deal. Yet somehow, I've never felt so cheap.

"I can't say I've ever been in this position before," the man mumbles awkwardly, seeming at a loss for the polite thing to say as he slides the paperwork into his briefcase. "Best wishes on your wedding day...?"

I nod, giving him an A for effort. He walks out, leaving me with an achy feeling in my chest.

So much for fairytales.

25

CANNON

I never put much thought into my wedding day. I guess most guys don't. But now that the moment is here, my nerves are beating me like a motherfucker. Of all the feelings I'd anticipated, being scared shitless was not one of them. My chest is pounding so hard. I can feel a thousand anxious thoughts throbbing inside my head.

What the fuck is wrong with me?

I stand at the makeshift altar on the rooftop above the bridal shop. My eyes scan over the crowd. There are more people than I expected to see today, despite our efforts to keep this small. In the groom's section, there are my parents, Walker, and best of all, my grandfather. The people who matter most to me. Well, most of them. I know I said I didn't care who shows up but it feels a little odd that my other two brothers aren't here. I'm feeling the absence of Jude and Eli.

Meanwhile, Lexi's section is overflowing—of course it is, given how popular she is around town—many of them I recognize as the people I evicted.

Not awkward at all.

She wasn't exaggerating when she talked about the

other business owners. She really cares for each and every one of these individuals, and it's clear they support her, too. All of Crescent Harbor loves the woman. And as I'm standing here on this rooftop overlooking the town, the idea that I could fall a little bit in love with her doesn't seem so farfetched anymore. Maybe, some way this fake marriage could lead to real feelings.

Why the hell not? Everything about Alexia Robson feels made for me. Never have I met a woman who could take my bullshit and meet me blow for blow. And the way her body feels under my hands, the way her lips meld with mine makes me second guess myself.

I try hard to not feel like a fraud up here. With Walker and my father's dark gazes on me, it's hard to ignore the fact that I'm lying to everyone. I try to focus on Ma's eager smile instead.

The gentle sounds of a harp fill the air, and my pulse races. Jessa accompanies Callie down the small aisle. My niece beams at Lexi's sister as she sprinkles the carpet with flower petals. I smile at the sight. Callie might be a tiny mischievous monkey most days, but today, she's on her best behavior.

The unmistakable sound of the traditional wedding march commences, signaling that my bride is next to follow. Moments move by in sort of a slow, watery blur. Lexi appears at the other end of the aisle. She looks like a dream in white silk and lace. The crowd gasps at the sight of her but she can't take her eyes off of me. I can't take my eyes off of her, either.

At first, her expression is guarded, like she's having second thoughts, like she might back out at the last minute. But then I give her a smile and I'm sure that all the raw emotions coursing through me bleed out onto my face.

Fuck, I'm scared too, I'm anxious, I'm nervous. Still, I know there's no one else I'd rather see at the foot of that aisle wearing my mother's wedding dress.

Her gaze is tentative. Then she breathes deep and she lets go. A smile spreads like beautiful wings across her face. It lights me up from the inside out and all the things I was worried about a second ago disappear. She glides down the aisle with such grace but I still see wild flickers of mischief in her big, blue eyes.

I've never wanted anyone so badly. This woman is dangerous for me.

When she reaches me, I twist my fingers with hers. I'm dying to touch every inch of her, but for now, I'll settle for her hands. Even those have the power to burn me. We exchange vows and rings in front of my family and her friends, and for the first time today, I don't have an ounce of guilt. Right now, Lexi is mine, and that's all that matters.

When the pastor finally pronounces us husband and wife, I yank her into my arms and hold her flush against my pounding heart. Her shiny, babydoll stare tells me she feels my lust for her lengthening along her stomach. I smirk at our little secret.

Then, I fucking claim her.

Right there in front of everyone, I take her mouth with mine and I kiss her like I mean every vow, every promise I just made.

She pulls out of the kiss and grins up at me with perfectly smudged lipstick. "If we don't stop making out up here at the altar, someone's going to call the fire department to pry us apart."

Sassy thing. Chuckling, I smack her ass.

An hour later, as we're swaying together under the twinkling string lights at our reception, I hold her body snug against mine as we move to the sound of Michael Bublé. I don't even care that the couples dancing around us are staring. This thing with Lexi may have started out as a strict business agreement, but I've never felt something so real in my life.

"It's not polite to stare," she teases even though she can't seem to look away, either.

"You look really good, Mrs. Kingston," I growl into her ear. "Fucking beautiful."

Her body shivers against mine, and I revel in the vibration. Her fingers tangle in the too-long hair at the base of my neck.

"You don't look too bad yourself, Mr. Kingston." She isn't able to hide the tremor in her voice, and I swear, all it does is make me harder.

I'm trying to be smart about this. But the clear-headed businessman persona is no match for this lust that's clouding my head. My hands are fisting the material of her dress on her lower back, struggling with the growing urge to roam her perfect body.

It's a fight I'm losing. Quickly and painfully.

I know I can't keep my hands off of her one minute longer.

"Come with me," I demand, my eyes fixed on hers, making my intent clear. My plans are far from pure, but Lexi's hungry gaze tells me she doesn't want pure.

Her answer is just a quick nod, and that's enough for me.

I slip my fingers through hers and discreetly slip her down the fire escape.

26

LEXI

I fumble with my keys at the backdoor of the bridal boutique. My heart thrashes against my ribcage, a rabid animal hurling itself at a chainlink fence.

Am I really going to have a quickie with my fake husband at our wedding reception? With our guests upstairs waiting for us to cut the cake?

Even in my blindingly horny state, it seems like a really, really bad idea.

But Cannon's hot, hard frame pulses with lust and impatience behind me. His hand covers mine, deftly turning the key in the lock. He slides his big body around me and nudges the door open with his broad shoulder.

When I hesitate to enter, his voice rumbles and his lips curl with a dangerous smirk. "Get your sexy ass in here before I do something indecent to you against the side of that compost bin in the alley." He holds the door open with his foot.

I roll my eyes even as my pulse rehearses an erratic tap dance at the base of my throat. "Well, you're just a mack daddy, aren't you? Is this the state of chivalry in the twenty-first century?"

Grunting out a laugh, he fists the satin skirt of my gown and yanks me through the doorway. "My cock is gonna have the time of his life inside that sassy mouth of yours."

I run my hands down the muscled planes of his wide chest. "Keep talking like that and your cock is gonna need reconstructive surgery by the time I'm done with it."

My groom chuckles again. "I'm not sure if that's sexy-talk or if it's an actual threat of violence but either way, I'm diggin' it, honey." He winks.

I yelp when he shoves me against the nearest wall. His fingers plunge into my hair, his open lips collide with mine. He kisses me deep, hard. My breasts feel soft, tingly, hot. A greedy tremor stutters through my pussy.

He tastes like a man. A little bit of mint, a little bit of whiskey and a whole lot of something primal that makes me hungry to taste the rest of him.

My arms loop around the back of his neck, refusing to let him move. He palms my ass before his big paws slide beneath my skirt. The heel of his hand grinds into my clit and my body clenches all over.

Still, my self-preservation whispers in my ear, *He's a rich, selfish bastard who's using you as his chess piece in his game.*

Fuck!

I pull back and stare at his gorgeous, stoic face. *Why can't I just walk away?* "This is so stupid," I whisper more to myself than to him.

He watches me, his features suddenly perfectly sober. "I don't understand it either, Stormy." His mouth comes close to my ear, brushing my cheek. "It's an animal attraction. It doesn't have to make sense."

I pull in a breath and I'm done trying to rationalize this. I'm done trying to convince myself that this is a bad idea. I want it too much. It's been too long since I've had a man's hands on my body. And the fact of the matter is, men like Cannon Kingston —Dominant. Sexy. Irresistible—they don't come around very often. There's no point in trying to fight this desire.

My fingers curl into the waistband of his pants and I drag him down the dark hallway. We end up in the stockroom.

Amusement twinkles in his eyes as I take complete control. I'm shoving him against a wall of shelves and scaling his body like a rock climber in heat.

He tugs on my hair and his delicious mouth is on mine again. Our tongues play together. Tasting. Exploring. Devouring. Then, he's kissing my neck, soft lips and rough stubble sweeping across the sensitive flesh.

And goosebumps.

Goosebumps everywhere.

I experience a level of arousal I thought only existed in romance novels. And maybe at Jason Momoa fan meet-and-greets. I murmur pure gibberish out loud.

I feel Cannon smile against my throat. His hand slips out of my hair, crawling down my chest to cup my breast, to palm it roughly. I moan.

I arch my spine, serving up my tiny boobs like a bite-sized offering. He pries down the neckline of my bodice and his lips cover one nipple, sucking it into the warmth of his mouth.

"Feels so good," I whisper, my hands navigating the vast plains of his shoulders.

His other hand moves down my back, fingertips playing connect the dots along my spine. He chuffs. "Stormy, I'm about to upgrade your definition of 'feels so good'. Permanently."

He lets me unfasten the buttons of his shirt. He lets me draw my palms over his tight deltoids. He lets me taste the bronzed skin of his collarbone.

But when I reach for his waistband and start lowering myself to my knees, he grabs me by the waist and backs me up against my work table. "Fuck chivalry. I'm eating first, baby."

And then he's on his knees.

Spreading my legs wide.

Licking and sucking his way up the inside of my thigh.

Removing my garter with his teeth.

He draws his tongue along the lacy edge of my white underwear and stares up at me with a half-smile that could single handedly melt what's left of the Arctic. "Your panties are in the way," he announces.

The soft flutter of his warm breath against my thigh makes me tighten my grip on the edge of the counter. My voice is thick and raspy and desperate. "So, take them off."

A second later, my panties are on the floor. Cannon props my ass on the edge of the counter and hooks my leg over his shoulder like a man about to feast. He tilts my pelvis to spread my pussy wider. He tongues my clit, slow and hard. Swirling, sliding. Lingering on the bud for long moments before plunging deep into my channel.

I lie back and clench my knees against his head as if holding on for dear life. When he drives a finger inside me and sucks my clit into his mouth, I expel a long, loud moan that bounces off the walls.

Just as my legs start to tremble and my skin starts to prickle and my vision starts to melt at the corners, Cannon rises to his feet. He scrapes my overstimulated body off the table and spins me around so that I'm facedown on the now-warm fibreboard.

"I want you just like this, Alexia." The no-nonsense edge in his voice has my body in full compliance. "Bend over for me just like this."

I hear the crinkle of a condom wrapper ripping open. Before I can throw a glance over my shoulder, he's breaching me with his long, fat cock. "Shit—why the fuck are you so big?" I groan.

"Too much for you, Stormy?" he taunts through gritted teeth as he surges forward into the tight grip of my pussy. "You can't handle it?"

I jerk my hips back again and again, frantically swallowing that dick like it's my life's purpose.

"I can take it," I groan. "I can take it."

I may require a lifetime of osteopathy after tonight but for now, I press my cheek to the counter and take him to the hilt. Each thrust is a powerful expression of his masculinity. The man fucks like a warrior, like a conqueror, like a man on a mission to mark unclaimed territory. And turned on as I am, submission is an easy choice.

The dull throb of the music from our wedding reception upstairs is our only reminder that a world exists outside of these walls. In this moment, all I'm aware of is him.

The orgasm starts as a tingle on the soles of my feet. By the time I take a breath, it's burning its way up my thighs. It explodes with seismic force at my core.

My belly is full of fire. My mind is consumed by flames. My body seizes in surrender and I chant Cannon's name as we both plunge over the edge.

His arms come around me. I melt in his possessive hold as we recover from the orgasm. My body is blissfully sedated but now, my brain is asking questions.

Do I know what the hell I'm doing? How am I supposed to protect my heart? How am I going to survive falling for my fake husband?

The clear-eyed look on Cannon's face tells me I'm stuck in limbo all by myself. He's already buttoned his fly and tucked his rumpled shirt back into his waistband.

From over by the door, he stretches a hand out to me. "Come on, Mrs. Kingston. We don't want to keep our guests waiting for us to cut the cake."

27

LEXI

I'm curled up on the plush, oversized sofa in Cannon's massive living room, still recovering from the wedding reception. In addition to my head-splitting hangover, every single part of my body hurts. After an entire day of pretending to have my shit together in those four-inch heels yesterday plus endless hours of tearing up the dance floor with my friends and the newly-wed, all-night-long sex-a-thon that followed, I can barely move a limb.

How come no one ever told me that getting fake-married is a heck of a workout?

So today, I'm keeping a low profile, sipping on coffee while I read the tattered self-help book I found on Cannon's coffee table. The book is sort of gloomy though I have to admit that it's super interesting. Still, every few minutes, I find my brain wandering off with thoughts of my new hubby. I don't know what's coming over me.

He locked himself in his ridiculously-huge home office much of the afternoon, doing Cannon-like things. Though I'm tempted to go off in search of him, I've decided to stay put. Last night I got lost on my way from his bedroom to the kitchen. I had to text him to come rescue me and it took an agonizing three minutes and forty-six seconds for help to arrive.

I grin shamelessly thinking about the things I did to him in that long stretch of hallway as a 'thank you' for saving me.

He strides into the living room, and it suddenly feels like we've been apart for days, instead of just a few hours. During our time apart, I swear this man has only grown more delicious. How is it possible that I want him naked again?

And he's wearing those sexy reading glasses.

Oh my gosh—*delicious*!

I've had more sex in the past twenty-four hours than I've had in a year. Yet, every time my fake groom stalks into the room, I crave him all over again. The way that man moves, his body should be illegal.

There's too much distance between our skin right now. My body actually mourns. This is going to be a problem. A big, big problem. I'm scared that, when this is all over, my body won't know how to handle life without Cannon Kingston's attention.

I set my coffee cup on the table beside the couch. "Hi," I say with a shy grin and I barely even recognize myself with the way I'm behaving. There's this tension in the air that practically sizzles.

I'm not going to lie to myself. It's hot but overwhelming. I'm downright terrified of it. Sex was not part of our agreement, and I'm not sure how to handle all this.

"Hey," he answers finally. He eyes my coffee cup, a tiny frown creasing the space between his brows. Silently, I wonder if I did something wrong.

I feel a bucket of ice drop into my stomach. "D-did you sign the paperwork to take over the company?" In other words, are you already here to kick me out? Is that what he's been working on all afternoon in his office? I'm scared to find out the answer.

I'm trying desperately to keep my grip on reality. This marriage is only temporary. That's why I haven't packed up my entire life and hired a moving truck. I haven't claimed closet space in Cannon's bedroom.

For now, I'm living out of a suitcase parked in a corner of his walk-in closet. Logically, I know I can't let myself get comfortable in this life. Keeping my heart in check is proving to be a bit of a challenge, though.

"The lawyers are still going over the paperwork, but everything should be done in a few weeks." His words are cool and aloof but a sense of relief washes over me because it means I get to hold onto this fairytale. At least for a while longer.

He runs his thumb along his bottom lip as he studies me. He hesitates. "Have you eaten?"

"I haven't," I respond after a pause. I sort of got caught up in the book and lost track of time, honestly.

I see his gaze narrowing on the book in my hands. He smiles. "*Lessons the Successful Man Must Never Forget.* That's my favorite read."

"I know."

He narrows his eyes playfully and any traces of grumpy Cannon vanish. "You know?"

"You told me about this book during our date before we met your family," I remind him.

"I'm just surprised you remembered..." He watches me thoughtfully.

"Don't look so impressed," I warn him. "To be honest, I'm finding this book to be a bit morbid. If this is your life's manifesto, it's no wonder you're so cynical."

"Hey, now," Cannon reprimands, closing the distance to steal the book from me. He scoops my legs off of the couch. He drapes them across his thighs when he sits next to me.

My skin burns against his. This man has no idea what he does to me.

He opens the tattered book and flips through the yellowing pages. I lose track of time again as Cannon reads several pages out loud. I do my best to focus on the contents of the book but instead I get lost in the vibrations of his gravel-velour voice.

When he finishes, he shuts the book and stares at me with so much hope. He looks boyish, eager for my approval. I laugh a little. "As I said, morbid as hell!" Then I scoot a little closer. "But there *are* some real gems of wisdom in there."

Cannon leans in suddenly and kisses me hard with those talented lips. When he pulls back, I need to know whatever is going through his mind. I whisper, heart thudding. "You're staring again, King."

He grins *that way* and a tingle slings up my thighs. Sexy little fucker he is. "I like when you wear your hair like that." His fingers dive into my dark, knotted roots.

I belt out an unrestricted laugh. "Um, this hair is not a fashion statement. It's a sad display of neglect." I haven't even brushed it today and it's still heavy with the styling product Miss Lucille piled into it yesterday.

"Well, it's sexy as fuck."

Heat flares in my cheeks when this man admits that he's attracted to me. "You might need to have your vision checked," I say in a self-conscious voice that doesn't even sound like me. I tap the frame of his glasses with a fingertip.

He cocks his head in annoyance. "Stop deflecting my compliments, Alexia. And stop making excuses for who you are. Just be yourself." He hesitates for half a second. "Because I like your..." His hand gestures vaguely in my direction. "...*self*."

The climate in the room shifts. On the heels of his tender confession, he wears this raw, exposed look on his face. Those addictive lips of his cover mine before I've even decided how to feel. The kiss is soft and mind-melting.

He pulls back with a barely there smile. "You wanna grab dinner and catch a movie or something?" I've never known Cannon to sound so unsure. But then again, we're both well aware that dinner and movie dates were definitely not part of our arrangement.

"Okay." I chew on my bottom lip to fight back a grin, but it still finds its way through.

He eases off the couch. "Okay then. I'll go call the movie theatre to reserve some tickets. Does 6:30 sound good for dinner?"

I'm still gnawing on my lip. "Sounds great."

Butterflies swirl in my gut as he walks away.

It's just dinner and a movie. I shouldn't be all knotted up like this.

Boy, I sure am in trouble.

28

LEXI

I wiggle, getting cozy in my theater seat as movie trailers roll. Cannon is out in the lobby somewhere, finishing a business call with his lawyer and I'm the only person in the room.

All throughout dinner, I badgered him to tell me what movie we're watching but he just stuffed his face with burgers and fries while stubbornly refusing to answer.

The man is infuriating.

Just as I'm starting to think my date has bailed on me, he stalks into the theater, hands full. He carries in a huge bucket of popcorn, two drinks and enough candy to send a preschool class over the edge. My stomach is still loaded from our fast food dinner so I really doubt I'll be participating in the pig-out.

"Thank you," I whisper as he hands me a large, heavy cup. "What movie are we watching?"

"You'll see." The white of his teeth glows as he grins back at me in the dark room.

"You're such a butthead." I elbow him in the ribs. "It's

probably a shitty movie since *literally* no one else is here." Seriously. That cannot be a good sign.

"Well, it's not my preferred choice of movie, but the reason the theater is empty is because I rented it out."

I blink. And then I blink some more.

"You rented out the *entire* theater," I deadpan. I think there was a question in there, but my brain can't handle things like verbal punctuation right now.

"Yeah." He shrugs like it's no big deal. Like this is a regular, everyday occurrence. The man just rented out *an entire movie theater*!

Before I can tell him how ridiculously over-the-top he is, the movie starts playing. I freeze. I'd recognize the opening scene of this movie blindfolded.

Pride and Prejudice.

My favorite movie in the whole wide world.

"Oh my god!" I shriek, way too loudly. My voice bounces off the walls. I throw my arms around Cannon, accidentally sending the popcorn bucket and all of its contents flying. Popcorn rains down on the seats and floor around us, like buttery confetti.

I never pegged Cannon Kingston as a romantic, but now, I know without a doubt that this man has a secret soft side.

Cannon ignores the spilled popcorn and settles into his seat. He throws an arm around my shoulders.

I continue rambling in shock, my eyes blurry with tears.

He sends a smirk in my direction and presses a finger to his lips. "Shh…"

The man is such an asshole. An asshole I have a huge crush on. So, I grab his face in my hands and kiss his stupid mouth.

29

CANNON

Slipping on my earbuds, I jog down Hart Road in the direction of downtown Crescent Harbor. There's a Taylor Swift song in my head and a crazy smile spread flush across my face as my running shoes steadily hit the pavement.

I tip an invisible hat at the old man working on the flowerbeds in his front yard beneath the early morning sun. When I come across the faded markings of a hopscotch pattern chalked into the middle of the quiet sidewalk, I can barely restrain myself from scampering through it like a kindergartener.

Fuck, I'm...*happy.*

The word tastes funny in my mouth.

It's been two weeks of wedded bliss and Alexia is turning everything upside down for me. Or maybe she's turning things right side up. She brings out parts of me I haven't seen in years. Parts of me I buried to make it in the competitive world of business, to survive the sting of betrayal that comes when you let your guard down and trust the wrong people. And I know she's cantankerous and combative and borderline crazy but I can see beneath all that. I can see that she's *good*.

She cares about people. She values friendship. She's loyal. She puts her heart into protecting the ones she loves.

And I want to be one of those lucky bastards that woman shares her heart with. I want to claim space in her life.

I'm willing to do whatever it takes—demolish a fortress, dig a tunnel, build a bridge—whatever it takes to get into her heart. She's worth the effort.

Maintaining my steady pace, I cross the bridge squinting against the blinding sun in my eyes. But as I turn onto Promenade Street, my blood runs cold in my veins and my heart grows erratic.

There's a police cruiser and two moving vans in front of Lexi's shop.

Fuck! No, no, no!

I pick up my pace and before long I've broken into a breathless sprint. Everything on my peripheries fades. All I can see is the two muscle-bound assholes carrying my wife's sewing table up the moving truck ramp.

"Hey!" I clip out, shaking an arm in the air to grab their attention. "Hey, fuckers! Stop!"

Eyes snap in my direction momentarily but they continue loading the table into the truck anyway.

"Put that down!" I bark at them. "Put that fucking table down!"

The men glance back at me before sharing a *who-the-heck-is-this-lunatic?* expression.

"Are you fucking deaf?" I yell. "Put the table down!"

As I'm closing in on the moving truck, a round-bellied man comes ambling out the door, holding a clipboard in one hand and a box overflowing with wedding veils under the other arm. He tucks the clipboard under his arm and extends a hand to me. "Mr. Kingston? Hi, I'm—"

I yank the box out of his hold. "What the fuck is going on here?" I glance toward the windows. Sheets of old newspaper obscure my view of the inside. Through the door, I can see a group of men taking down the chandelier.

The man blinks up at me. "I'm—I'm Ron, the owner of the company coordinating the remaining evictions. Like you expected us to." He waves the list of non-paying tenants in my face.

His words jab like a broom handle to the stomach. *Dammit! Dammit, dammit, dammit!*

Storming past the bored-looking sheriff's deputy eating donut holes and playing Candy Crush on his phone, I burst into the shop. The place is in disarray. Bridal gowns shoved carelessly into garbage bags. Naked mannequins facedown on the floor. Light fixtures hanging by the wires.

Dammit!

The deputy lethargically steps into the boutique. "Sir, is there a problem here?"

I hear Ron's confused voice somewhere behind me. "This is what you requested. Six evictions. Sally sent over instructions. Before she left on her vacation."

Fuuuccckkkk! I want to scream.

I *did* give Sally instructions to coordinate the evictions. *Before* I knew that Kingston Realties was in trouble. *Before* I made Alexia my wife. *Before* I started giving a damn about her feelings. Then I sent Sally off on vacation so I wouldn't have to deal with her crochety ass for a while. And I got so damn caught up in things with Alexia that I forgot to axe the legal proceedings. Fuck. All this is *my* fault.

I drop the box to the floor and wipe sweat from my forehead. *Fuuucccckkkk!*

One of the moving guys comes inside and grabs a decorative mirror from the corner. I spin at him so fast he jumps a foot back. "If you dare touch that..."

At my threat, he backtracks out the front door with both hands in the air. "Jeez, man. Just doing my job."

I turn to Ron. "I need you to shut this down. Right now."

The man's eyebrows knit on a frown. "Mr. Kingston, I don't understand what's going on here."

"Get your men and get out of here!"

Taking a step back, he shakes his head. "I can't do that. Do you understand how much I had to pay these movers? To get them here at this time? We cancelled three other jobs to reserve the day for you."

My jaw clenches with irritation. "You will be fully remunerated, Ron." I stick my hand into my pocket and pull out my cellphone. "I'll have my assistant send you a check from my company's bank account by the end of the week—"

"No. Cash!" My head snaps up at the old man. His eyes are wide and resolved. "No, I need cash, Mr. Kingston. No cheques. No wire transfers. None of that. My daughter needs her medication today." His eyes narrow. His voice quivers but he doesn't back down.

I try to negotiate. "I'll transfer the money into your account in a matter of hours."

"No. Cash."

It's a standoff.

He doesn't soften under my unflinching glare. "I have bills to pay..." he tells me.

I dig into my pocket and all I have is a bank card. I usually have a wad of cash on hand but I left it at home since I was going for a jog. I glance at the watch I pull from my pocket. I don't have much longer until Lexi shows up to start her day. Panic crackles through me. I don't want this to be the scene she meets when she gets here.

I'm trying to get this girl to like me, for heaven's sake.

I stick an appeasing hand out to the mover. "Wait here." I pace sideways toward the door. "Wait here and don't you move," I tell him. "I'll be right back with the money. And don't let those movers touch anything. Not one thing."

I don't wait for his answer. I don't have the time.

All I know is I'm running—not jogging—full-on running. Sprinting down the winding sidewalk, jetting in the direction of the bank, darting around the slow-moving locals congregated in the middle of the sidewalk to spread the latest gossip, zooming across the street, barely missing a collision with that rusty, junk-hauling pickup truck from the other day.

My feet can hardly keep up with my racing mind. All I know is I have to fix this before Alexia finds out.

There's a line-up at the bank and only one functioning ATM. From the back of the line, I bounce about on my soles, impatience crawling up the legs of my sweatpants like fire ants.

I'm jumpy, pacing anxiously, peeking over the shoulder of the shaggy-haired guy in front of me with the too-big business suit and the too-eager look on his face. He glances at me with an agitated expression.

"You mind if I cut in front of you?" My voice is gruff and much less than friendly. I brush sweat from my forehead with the back of my hand.

He recoils and gives me a terrified look. "I-I...but I've got a job interview..."

I shoulder my way in front of him and crowd the machine. "And I've got a life-threatening a emergency." It's not a stretch. If Stormy sees what I've done to her bridal shop, there's no telling *how* she'll kill me.

The twenty-something man at the front of the line steps aside, making space for me. "It's all yours, sir."

I must look like a maniac right now. My hair dripping sweat. My face red from exertion. My T-shirt soaked through. And I'm sure my body is leaking desperation.

There's a young mother who takes a step back and holds her gurgling baby closer to her chest. I look at the woman over my back as I punch in my pass code. "You don't mind if I cut ahead, do you?"

She gives me a synthetic smile. It might as well be polyester. "No, no. Go for it." She looks a bit afraid.

I withdraw as much money as the old machine will let me.

"Thank you," I say, shoving hundred dollar bills at each person as I go. Lexi would give me shit if she saw me trying to pay my way out of being a jerk right now. But I don't really have a choice in this situation. "Buy yourselves something nice," I tell the mother. "You deserve it." Their eyes bulge and their jaws drop collectively as they snatch the offerings from my hand. "Here ya go. Have a nice day."

I rocket out the door, shoving the money and my wallet in the pocket of my pants as I go.

And I run. I run as if my fucking life depends on it. I run through red lights. I run despite the burn in my lungs. I run.

Ron is standing outside the door as I approach, his eyes narrow, his lips thin. But I made it. I made it in time. A mix of hope and relief swoops through me.

I slap the wad of bills into his outstretched hand and he gives me a disapproving headshake. But I don't care about his opinion, I just need these movers to put everything back into place before Lexi shows up.

I hunch forward, bracing my knees and struggling to catch my breath. "Get that furniture back inside," I bark at the movers, my oxygen-deprived lungs screaming. "Hurry the fuck up. Get them back in there before the owner shows up."

Hearing her voice from over my shoulder is like being dashed with a bucket of ice water and then getting a livewire thrown at me. "Too late, asshole."

30

LEXI

My chest is so hot with rage, I fully expect my heart to catch fire and burn right through my skin.

That fucker!

Slowly, Cannon turns around. His gaze collides with mine and all I feel is rage. I am so angry with him. So angry with the situation. But more than anything, I am *so* angry with myself. Why did I let myself trust him?

I woke up this morning, feeling something like love for this man. I woke up hoping for forever with him. But he betrayed me.

His lips move but no words come out. His shoulders slump with defeat. Deep in those caramel eyes, I catch a glimpse of something I've never seen on him before. Something hollow and shadowy.

Maybe it's remorse. Maybe it's shame or guilt. Maybe it's just my mind playing tricks on me, telling me it's impossible that I let someone this vile get so close. I'm not quite sure.

He approaches me, arms outstretched like a shield. In an appeasing tone, he starts. "Look, Lexi—"

Before he can get another word out, I rush at him. My finger jabs him in the chest like an ice pick. "Dick!"

"Look, I—"

My fingernail strikes again. "Dick!"

His irises flash with frustration. "Are you going to let me explain?"

"No, actually."

Cannon's fingers latch around my wrist and I have a mind to clock him in the nose but as mad as I am, his touch has a way of interrupting the anger receptors in my brain. I let him pull me down the hall to the stockroom.

He cups the back of his head with his palm. "I know I probably look like the biggest asshole right now."

"You do."

His chest fills up when he takes a hard breath. "You don't have any reason to trust me."

"Thanks for reminding me of that. Because I forgot for *one* second, I put my guard down for *one* second..."

I know not to trust men like him. Brash, rich, beautiful. It's a lesson I learned a long damn time ago. Girls like me don't get happy endings with guys like him.

I had walls up, I had gates and fences with barbed wire curled around the top. But I let Cannon in anyway. I gave him the key and the passcode and I left the damn door open for him to storm inside. And he stole my dreams.

"You lied to me. You used me to get your father to hand over Kingston Realties to you. Now, your going to kick me and my friends out anyway." I take a slow step back and fold my arms across my stomach, an unconscious effort to press down the turbulent emotions spinning there.

He grabs me by the shoulders and forces me to look at him. "This was an honest mistake, Alexia. Please believe me. I asked Sally to make arrangements for the evictions and then I sent her on vacation to get her out of my face." I sense the frustration in his words. "I got so caught up in the wedding plans, hell, I got so caught up catching feelings for you that I completely forgot to call off the evictions."

"Catching feelings?!" I scoff bitterly.

"Yes, fuck. Yes, Alexia. I have...*feelings* for you."

My weak little heart gives a hopeful flutter but no way am I falling for that line. Cannon Kingston is as ruthless as they come, and deceitful to the core. There's no way I'm letting him fool me again.

I shoulder my way past him. "You can take your 'feelings' and shove them, King."

"I made a mistake and I'm trying to fix it. I sent the men away. I called off the evictions." His words are frantic. His body pulses with frustrated energy. "I'll get a construction crew in here to get everything in order. I can fix it." He pleads gruffly. "Let me fix it, Alexia."

Over his shoulder, I see the movers hurrying to put my furniture back inside the boutique.

It makes my blood boil. They shouldn't have touched my stuff in the first place.

I put two years of sweat and tears into that place. And Cannon Kingston tore it down in a matter of minutes.

My eyes land hard on his face. I can feel the prickle of tears. I hate the part of me that actually wants to believe him. "Yeah, you're going to fix it, King. In the meantime, I'm going to go take a look at that prenup of ours. Because in case you forgot, I have rights too in our deal."

On that subtle threat, I stomp into my office and slam the door.

31

LEXI

"Alexia dahling, I'm thinking a floor-length regency-style mirror would be stunning along the back wall. Maybe something in sterling silver or rose gold to compliment the accents on the crown molding?"

Dahlia Windsor glances at me over her shoulder. The woman's designer stilettos pummel the freshly-buffed hardwood with each quick, purposeful step. Her feathery mid-Atlantic accent mixes with the sounds of drilling and hammering echoing through the empty bridal shop.

She adjusts the fur-trimmed collar of her pink pantsuit. "And I found a beautiful white leather chaise lounge we could place along the front window. It would go perfectly with the powder blue Bhadohi area rug." The interior designer rests a hand on my shoulder and lowers her voice. "It was pricey but Mr. Kingston said to make sure you get everything you like. He said the price tag is secondary to your satisfaction." She winks and fluffs up her salon-bleached hair.

A heated blush explodes across my cheek. "Well, that's...lovely."

Cannon has been seriously obnoxious in his efforts to get back into my good graces over the past few days. He started with the typical apology gifts—extravagant bouquets, expensive jewelry, designer clothes, a chocolate basket that almost did me in.

I think he expected me to land in a swoony pile at his feet once he started flinging money around to get his way. But when his efforts didn't have the desired effect, he upped his game.

He hired the best construction company in the tri-county area to repair the damage the movers made when they tore my shop apart. Then he flew in a sought-after interior designer all the way from New York City to give my boutique the right aesthetic. Dahlia has a bottomless expense account and she's not conservative about putting it to use.

The woman slaps a pile of wallpaper swatches into my hand and wanders off to answer her ringing phone.

The construction crew buzzes efficiently around the space, getting the boutique back in working order. They started by patching up the holes in the wall and laying down a fresh coat of paint. Now, they're reinstalling the fixtures and the equipment.

I've lost two days of business thanks to this whole debacle and I've been in here with the construction crew, doing my best to make sure we can get the place reopened in two or three days tops. I don't know if that's realistic, though. The boutique is a mess. With dust and paint buckets everywhere, and newspaper covering the windows. Plus, Dahlia has a long list of upgrades she intends to implement. We have a lot of work ahead of us.

I approach a scruffy-chinned man wearing a Hartley Construction T-shirt. "Excuse me, do you mind moving that shelf a little to the left?"

He lowers his power drill and glances at me over his back. "Sure thing," Leo says.

I bite the inside of my mouth. "I don't mean to be nit-picky. It's just—"

"Mr. Kingston said to give you whatever it is you want." He bends at the waist in a regal bow. "He said to give you the royal treatment."

I barely resist rolling my eyes. "That's what *Mr. Kingston* said, huh?"

Leo grins widely. "That's what he said."

I won't lie, having King so adamant to win my forgiveness has been kind of satisfying. I have to keep reminding myself that that's not the point. I don't want to bring Cannon to his knees just for the heck of it.

But I *do* need him to understand that he can't just go, throwing his weight—and his wallet—around to get the things he wants. I need him to actually start taking other people's feelings into account and recognizing that his brazen actions can be hurtful in a way that money can't fix.

Okay, the eviction debacle may have been a mistake. But it could have all been avoided if he hadn't been so damn invested in his power games, using legal threats and writing fat checks to manipulate me into marrying him.

I need him to take his assholery down a notch.

No matter how tempting and handsome he is, I can't let myself give in to a bully.

That's why I've been staying at my own house ever since the whole eviction mess. Yes, I realize that moving out of his mansion is a violation of our prenup but *he* broke our deal first when those movers showed up at my boutique. As much as I miss the charming asshole, I can't just go back to him and act like what he did is okay.

The construction worker stands there looking at me. "Mr. Kingston is *very* sorry, y'know?" He wears a half-grin. "Very sorry."

"Did he tell you to say that, too?" I question, fanning out my wallpaper samples on the counter.

Leo's boss, Charlie, marches around the corner with a box of tiles in his arms and gives me a big nod. "Yup. We have no idea what the poor guy did but he told us to apologize *profusely* on his behalf."

I tilt my head at them, feigning annoyance.

Charlie shrugs a shoulder. "Hey...men mess up sometimes."

"A lot," Dahlia interjects.

"Even men with a lot of money," Leo says.

"*Especially* men with a lot of money." Dahlia sagely lifts a manicured brow.

"And he's trying to make it up to you," the boss continues.

"Us guys, we don't go throwing out apologies all willy nilly. So if he's going to these lengths—" Leo points his chin around the room. "—he must mean it."

Sometimes apologies aren't enough. Sometimes it's best to protect your heart and stand your ground. I don't say that to the workers. No need to drag them into my marital beef. Instead, I give them a little smile. "I'll keep all that in mind."

My defences are weakening but I can't lose my head over this.

I grab my purse from under the cash register and sling the strap across my chest. "I'm gonna get going for the night," I tell the workers. I need to get some rest because tomorrow's going to be another long day. "You have the keys. Call me on my cell if anything comes up."

Dahlia smiles and wiggles her elegant fingers at me as she answers another phone call.

"Will do, boss. Good night." Charlie salutes me.

Leo calls after me with another smirk. "Think about the apology."

I roll my eyes again and it's no use fighting against the smile trying to break free across my face.

Cannon Kingston is such an asshole. A fucking antihero. A shameless bastard. He has his *construction workers* doing his bidding for him. Talk about using your powers for evil.

As I push the newspaper-covered glass open with my butt and step outside into the crisp, dark night, I renew my determination to resist him. I won't let him buy his way back into my good graces.

32

CANNON

She hasn't come home in days and it's driving me crazy.

I park across the street from Alexia's shop. I arrive just in time to see her step out the front door and take off down the sidewalk on foot.

At that, I hop out of my car and take off in her direction without giving it much thought. She startles when she hears my footsteps pounding toward her.

"Just me," I call out with my hands wide.

I know better than to sneak up on an unsuspecting woman after dark. And a woman like Lexi? Yeah, she's bound to have pepper spray in her bag.

She shoots me a dirty look but doesn't stop walking. Okay. I may deserve that, but I don't have the patience for this sassy shit today. My whole world is off-balance without her in it and I can't even hold up my tough facade right now.

Suddenly, I'm mad at myself. I have three luxury cars sitting idle in my garage. Yet, my wife is roaming around on foot in the middle of the night. I need to fix that.

I grab Lexi's hand, tugging her back in the direction of my car. "Come on. I'll give you a lift home."

She rips her hand back and I'm not surprised. But at least, she finally stops walking, pausing with her fist on her hip to scowl at me. "I'm not going anywhere with you. Take your fancy car and go back to your fancy house and leave me alone."

"Not happening, Stormy. You're my wife. It's bad enough that I've had to sleep without you in my bed these last few nights. There's no way I'm letting you walk the streets alone at this hour. Let me give you a ride."

"I'll have to give you a 'hell no' on that one." Then she pivots and continues to speed walk into the darkness.

I growl audibly and grind my molars for half a second before chasing after her again. She's marching at lightning speed and before I know it, we've walked three blocks. "Now you have me walking you home? Is this some kind of power trip for you?"

She doesn't bother to answer. Why haven't I turned around and gone back into my warm ride? I could be at my house and tipping back a scotch in minutes. I don't want to be out here in the damp cold with an angry woman who's determined to be unreasonable.

Yet... I can't walk away. When Alexia's near, I can't ever walk away. Even when she grates on my last damn nerve, I find her magnetically refreshing.

She shivers visibly, and I roll my eyes. The irony is thick, almost as obvious as Lexi's misery out here in the cold. Her top is thin, and I approve of that, but it's obvious she didn't plan for this little stroll home after work today.

I want to let her suffer because—come on—it's Illinois. If you know anything about the weather here, you prepare for blistering heat, snow, and spring rain to all go down in the same twenty-four hour span. Plus, she's being stubborn just for the fuck of it so I don't know why I feel the need to save her.

But for some unfamiliar reason, it causes me physical pain to see Alexia uncomfortable. I grudgingly peel off my jacket and wrap it around her narrow shoulders as we continue to walk into the dark unknown.

"Thanks," she mumbles. She's clearly not thrilled to accept my help, but she must be too cold to fight me. I'll tuck that into the win column.

"You're welcome, Stormy."

She eyes me briefly, likely trying to determine whether I'm being genuine. I am.

"It's not safe for a woman to walk around alone at night." I try to speak softly but I can't remove the edge from my voice, even though I'm trying to be a decent human being.

"I'll take my chances on the 'rough streets' of Crescent Harbor," she says sarcastically. "But it's *you* I'm not safe alone with."

Ouch! That stings...

She turns up a narrow sidewalk toward her tiny house, and I follow. My eyes enjoy the view. I'm trying to be a gentleman for once but I just can't fight my lust when it comes to Stormy. I laid in bed last night, struggling not to picture her next to me, on top of me, beneath me, saying my name and writhing with pleasure. I hold onto a shred of hope of somehow making that vision my reality tonight.

I stand behind her as she unlocks her door, ready to follow her inside so we can continue this discussion. Hopefully, it'll lead to something more.

The door pops open and she turns back around, facing me. I wasn't expecting that move, so now we're just inches apart. We're so close, I can smell her grapefruit shampoo.

Her scent alone just made my hopeful cock stand at attention. I want this woman so much it's driving me crazy.

"I deserve another chance."

"You don't *deserve* shit."

She meets my gaze, and then her eyes drop to my lips. Fuck all her stubborn grandstanding. She wants me as much as I want her.

I lean in, ready to take her cherry red mouth. "Come home, Alexia..." I can admit I sound like an entitled prick.

Two tiny hands halt me in my tracks. She tilts her head to gesture toward her house. "I am home."

She backs away, one step at a time.

"Have a lovely fucking night, Mr. Billions. I hope your moneybags like spooning."

I stand there like a goon, watching her step inside and slam the door in my face.

Stormy has more spunk than ever. I hate to admit to myself how much I admire that.

I might just have to tame the woman after all.

33

LEXI

Faith Monroe-Masters steps out of the changing room in a silky, Greecian-style gown. She angles herself in front of the mirror and squeals. "I think this is the one."

Her sisters sit hip-to-hip on the brand new chaise lounge in the showroom.

"It is *gorgeous*." Grace puts down her teacup and stands to examine the gown closer.

Faith turns to me and grins. "My husband and I are renewing our vows for the third time."

I circle around her, making adjustments to the fabric. I glance up with bulging eyes. "The *third* time?"

She giggles. "We didn't quite get it right the first time," she explains. "Let's just say our first wedding was..."

"A drunken Vegas debacle." Lily, the third Monroe sister, mumbles into her teacup. "You're totally overcompensating."

Faith grins with an eyeroll. "You're one to talk, Miss Let's-Rush-Down-To-The-Courthouse-Before-My-Water- Breaks."

When Grace snorts laughter, Lily strolls over and jabs a

finger into her shoulder. "Don't even get started or I'm telling Lexi the story about you and your husband and the tantric yoga retreat."

"Ooh! Sounds *spicy*!" I coo.

Grace turns chili pepper red as she circles around the mini platform where Faith is standing. "Let's just focus on the gown shopping, shall we?"

I laugh.

I love these girls. They're a trio of gorgeous bombshells who share a close bond. They drove up from Reyfield this morning just to check out the shop. For some odd reason, it feels like I know them even though I'm sure I've never met them before.

In any case, I'm happy to announce that Renewed Gowns is officially back in business. The place is dreamy. A modern blend of rustic and regency elements.

Even Iris, who is decidedly *not* Team Cannon, had to admit that my fake husband went above and beyond.

Cannon waved his credit card like a magic wand and in one week, he turned my shop into everything I've been working toward for the past two years. I'm trying to keep my resolve, y'all, because Cannon doesn't deserve a pat on the back for fixing things when he's the one who tore them down, but I *miss* him. And each time I step back to look at my renovated boutique, a little more of the ice around my heart dissolves.

I'm the worst at holding a grudge.

And business has been super busy since I re-opened. It's like the brides-to-be of Crescent Harbor and the surrounding areas somehow sniffed me out. I have several appointments booked for this afternoon alone. Good thing Jessa is coming by after lunch to give me a hand.

Across the street, I can see the Hartley Construction

guys setting up to commence renovation work on the old craft store. The owner is thrilled to be back in business after the whole eviction scare and she's working harder than ever to increase her sales and catch up on her bills. This morning, I saw her handing out flyers for a knitting workshop she has planned for next week.

The seasonal tourists are starting to trickle into town, frequenting businesses that, just weeks ago, were coming up against the threat of eviction.

There's a note of hope in the air all across Crescent Harbor.

And as much as I despise him, I can't deny the role my bastard husband played in that.

Lily tilts her chin at my wedding ring as I'm bagging up Faith's dress. "What about you, Lexi? What was your wedding like?"

I stop to twirl the glittery diamond around on my finger. My prenup prohibits me from removing it during my marriage. But even in the absence of the clause, I don't think I'd be able to take it off regardless of how 'in limbo' things are with me and Cannon right now.

Stupid, stupid heart.

I wish I could just shut down my feelings and coast through the marriage until the time comes to dissolve this situationship but the truth is, I miss my bastard husband. I miss his cocky grin. I miss his smart-ass comments. I miss the way he would wrap my leg over his right before he'd drift off to sleep.

I even miss his snoring.

I smile at the women. "We got married right here, up on the rooftop, actually. It was a small ceremony. I wore my mother-in-law's dress."

The sisters' eyes go cartoonishly wide and they coo in

unison about how sweet and dreamy the entire thing sounds.

The hole in my heart aches and stretches wider as memories of my wedding day play out in my head. *God, I need him back.*

Faith leans on the counter and props her chin in her palm. "I'm so glad we came here, Lexi. I feel like a huge load just rolled off my shoulders."

"I'm glad you came, too." I come around the counter to drape the garment bag over her arm. "How did you find me anyway?"

"Grace found your shopping app this morning and insisted that we drive up here," Lily supplies.

I blink at them. "My shopping app? I don't have a shopping app."

"Yes, you do," Grace says, squinting at me. She holds up her phone.

I take the device into my hand and blink down at the screen. That's my logo and branding. Those are pictures of my boutique.

Instantly, I know exactly who's behind this.

34

CANNON

The day I've been working toward is finally here.

Frank has performed his due diligence on the legal documents and if he tells me everything looks good, I trust him. Within the hour, the papers should be signed and finalized. I'm about to become the legal owner of Kingston Realty Holdings.

It's a full family affair. I'm seated at our headquarters, crowded around the conference table with my parents and two of my brothers. My father's lawyer is present, too, and he's droning on and on.

I've seen Jude drift off at least twice. I don't blame him. The legal stuff is mind-numbing. I'm just thankful he took a quick trip down here to make this transaction happen.

My mother must be tired too because she suggests we take a quick coffee break. I step out into the hall, but don't head to the coffee pot with them. My nerves are already jumping; the last thing I need is more caffeine right now.

Dad strolls over to me where I'm pacing the worn, navy carpet. His heavy hand clamps down on my shoulder, bringing me to a halt. "Son, I just wanted to talk to you for a minute."

The look on his face makes me nervous. Is he going to back out? Is he going to spill the beans to Ma?

"I want you to know I feel comfortable signing over the business. I see now that I was wrong about you and your new wife. Yes, the wedding was quick but you and Lexi look solid. A lot like your mother and me."

"Thanks, Dad," I answer.

Guilt claws its way up my chest. When my family asked why my new bride didn't accompany me to the signing, I told them she had to work today. Luckily, they bought my excuse.

My family has no idea that I couldn't even keep my fake marriage afloat until the damn signing. I've estranged my wife over a stupid mistake.

Alexia moved back to her place. Out of respect for the terms of our prenuptial agreement, she's been discreet about the break down of our sham relationship. But she wants nothing to do with me. I texted her four times this morning, telling her the signing is today. She never answered. As pissed as she is at me, I'm willing to bet she deleted every one of those messages without reading them. She can't just up and disappear on me like that. It's a violation of our contract.

But I don't give two shits about the contract.

What matters is that she's cut me off, she won't speak to me and everything is meaningless if she's not by my side sharing it with me.

Fuck—I miss her.

I miss the way she keeps me on my toes. I miss the way my face fucking hurts from smiling so often when I'm with her. I miss the way she makes me happy. And here I am, having to fake a smile and pretend life's just peachy so my father doesn't back out of this deal.

Dad leans in, with a half hug. "I'm proud of you, son."

The words land in my gut with a bitter splash. Christ, I hope he'll still feel that way when all of this is said and done. I want to do right by him and Gramps. I want to fix the mess I've made with my wife. *Damn, no pressure, Cannon.*

After Ma and my brothers refuel, we shuffle back into the conference room. I'm antsy. I want to get this over with. I might blow a gasket if anyone suggests another break.

Dad's lawyer continues his speech while shoving document after document in front of each of us. "These documents state that Mr. Jude Kingston and Mr. Walker Kingston are selling their shares to Mr. Cannon Kingston." My brothers scribble their signatures. "I want to make sure it's clear though that Mr. Eli Kingston's shares will remain in trust. When he's released from incarceration, he can make the decision whether to keep his shares or sell them to you, Cannon."

I grumble hotly, "Great! I'm in business with a convicted white collar criminal!"

"I know in my heart he didn't do it," my mother insists, her voice a little watery. And now I'm making Ma cry.

I'm *winning* today.

My father groans, resting his hand on hers. "No need for anyone to get worked up. Eli's not on trial here with his family. He's serving his time. Let's just focus on the matter in front of us."

I sigh, but I'm sure it comes out more like a growl.

Dad's lawyer distracts me by handing me four thousand other documents to sign and initial. My family files out one by one while I scribble until my hand aches.

The second I finish the last page, the lawyer snatches the

documents then he hurries out of the office, leaving me alone in the room.

It's official. I am the owner of Kingston Realty Holdings.

No outside investor is going to swoop in and take away Gramps's company. No one is going to demolish all of the small businesses in town and erect ugly factories.

I lean back, waiting for the wave of satisfaction to wash over me. It never comes. Because Lexi should be here now. She should be witnessing it. I saved my grandfather's company with her help and it feels wrong that she's not here to celebrate with me.

Somehow, in just the short time we've been living as husband and wife, this crazy woman has become my confidant. She's the first person I want to run to now that I've achieved my objective. I just want to see her proud of me.

I hadn't realized until my movie theater surprise how much I enjoyed seeing Lexi happy. There's a lot about her that I'm quickly discovering, and a lot about her that I'm enjoying.

I reach for my phone, but I stop myself when I realize that if I tell her I own the company, she'll want to put an end to our sham relationship and go back to her normal life. I don't want that. I don't want to end our relationship.

I want to keep my wife for real.

The hollow feeling inside of me grows wider and deeper as I drive home. I'm acutely aware of how very alone I am.

I park in my garage and enter the house through the kitchen entrance. The high ceilings loom above me and the walls threaten to close in and swallow me up.

But when I step into the kitchen, I swear I feel the nerve endings in my scalp tingle. I catch hints of grapefruit shampoo.

Lexi is standing in the doorway, a frown etched deep on her beautiful face.

35
LEXI

God—I'm supposed to be stronger than this.

I've always considered myself a tough girl. But this husband of mine, he has a way of breaking me, stripping me down to the vulnerable woman beneath all my damn bravado.

I couldn't stay away from him any longer.

Halfway home after work, I turned around and came here. I paced the living room floor.

While I waited for him, I planned out what I'd say. I was going to yell, I was going to scream, I was going to let him know how very, very pissed I am over what he did.

When I heard the garage door open, I came into the kitchen to give him a piece of my mind, to let this asshole know exactly what I think of him.

I did not come in here to be pushed up against the cold, stainless steel refrigerator, to have my skirt hiked up over my ass and my legs tangled around his waist, to have my wet, wet panties shoved to the side, to have this jerk hammering an exquisitely brutal rhythm into my throbbing core.

But the second I walked in, he pinned me with those

caramel eyes, the scorching lust melting every defence I ever built against him. Then we were charging across the room, colliding with the urgency of a magnet seeking out a bar of iron.

His lips were on my throat, his hand was between my thighs and I forgot the textbook of reasons why I hate this man.

Because when he touches me like that, what is English?

What is grammar and syntax and punctuation?

When he touches me like that, the only words in my vocabulary are "please" and "yes" and "more."

"God, I've fucking missed you." He breathes against my neck before kissing a path down between my breasts.

I missed you, too.

The words are right there, locked in my throat. My pride and self-preservation won't allow me to let them out. Because this man hurt me. Even though he might not have meant to.

He plucked my heart from the safe cocoon it's been buried in and he took it so high with hope, so high with need.

And then he let it fall.

The last thing I want is to give him the chance to hurt me again. But I'm too far gone now. I can't just walk away.

I brace his cheeks with my palms and I kiss him so hard.

And we fuck. On the table. Bent over the sink. Against the refrigerator. Frantic, pulsing bodies making careless promises in the dark.

My armor cracks open under the pull of the orgasm. The sounds of my ecstasy echo off the pots and pans hanging from the wall. Cannon is right there with me, coming hard in the throbbing grip of my pussy.

Together, we slide down to the kitchen floor, my back

nestled against his strong chest. His lips press against my scalp when he brings me into his arms.

"I'm sorry..."

He whispers the words so softly. They get caught in my messy hair. Seated in his lap, I crane my neck to look into his face because I'm not sure I heard him right.

He lifts my chin to press his mouth to mine. It's a sweet, innocent kiss, full of relief and adoration. He looks me in the eyes and says it again. "I'm sorry, Alexia. I'm sorry that I hurt you."

From his expression, I can tell that the words taste foreign on his tongue. This is difficult for him. But he's genuine.

I pull his arms tighter around me, my silent way of accepting his apology. He presses a soft kiss to my temple and then another to my cheek, my jaw, the spot beneath my ear. He holds me like I mean something to him.

And now here I am, shaking in his arms on the cold tile floor, orgasm still screaming in my veins. And I know, I just know, I just know...I'm falling for the bastard.

36

CANNON

Lexi puts me to work the second I step into the bridal shop at lunchtime. I pretend to be a grumpy asshole about it, but deep down, I'm enjoying this. Honestly, I'm just glad to be back on her good side.

The relief I feel that she came back to me, I can't describe it. If the way she kissed me and touched me and moaned my name last night is any indication, I'd guess that she's forgiven me, but I'm not taking any chances. I'm not too proud to grovel until I'm sure she knows she can't live without me.

After a heated battle at the kitchen table, I managed to convince her to drive the BMW this morning. That's an encouraging sign. And she looked damn good behind the wheel of that sleek black luxury car.

I hid my grin behind my coffee mug as she reluctantly took the keys from my hand, grumbling under her breath about being a strong, independent woman who can find her way to work without my assistance.

Blah-blah-blah.

I finally talked her down by assuring her that the car is a loan, not a hand-out.

Anyway, I haven't been able to get her off my mind since she left for work this morning. I was sitting in my executive office at the new and improved Kingston Realties when I gave in to my need to come see her over lunch. I didn't fight the urge. Instead, I left my newly-hired office staff to run the business for the afternoon while I swung by the florist for a bouquet of pink daisies. Just a little something to decorate my wife's shop and brighten her day.

Good thing I showed up when I did because with a shop full of customers, I could see that she desperately needed a hand.

Stormy would never ask for help outright though. She's the most fiercely independent woman I know. I might have to drop some hints about her hiring some part-time employees if business continues to pick up.

I'm not embarrassed to admit that I don't know a whole lot about wedding dresses, so I can't say how helpful I am. I mostly just serve as her errand boy, running around her renovated shop fetching order forms and things from high shelves, and helping blushing brides-to-be carry their purchases to their cars.

Despite the menial tasks, I'm enjoying the opportunity to spend time with Lexi, especially after she cut me off for a whole miserable week. And seeing her like this—thriving in her element—it turns me on.

Though I'm learning that nearly everything Lexi does turns me on. Even when she argues with me, I have to struggle not to strip her clothes off.

I wink at her from across the shop as I carry a large box to a customer's car. I take pride in the way my wife's cheeks redden. I may not know what she's thinking most of the time, but it's clear that her body reacts to me. And maybe—just maybe—she's really not mad at me anymore.

But I'm keeping a secret from her. It hangs above me like a stupid cloud of doom, like this constant reminder that I'm a lying asshole. I need to tell Lexi that I am the rightful owner of Kingston Realty Holdings. But I can't. Because once she knows that, she'll walk away from me and I don't want to give her up.

Yup, I'm a selfish bastard.

When I come back inside, Alexia's rummaging around her counter. "Have you seen a yellow paper?" She's a little frantic, which I've learned is sort of her habitual mode when she's at work. "It's about this big." She holds up her hands. "It's a carbon copy of an invoice I need." She continues flipping things apart.

I put a steady hand on hers. "Where's the last place you remember seeing it?"

She chews on her bottom lip, and I'm dying to do the same. Then she snaps her long fingers and points at me. "In my office. Can you man the counter while I go look for it? Should just be a minute...Or ten." She grins.

"I'm yours." I say too quickly. Then I realize that I mean it in more ways than one.

She pauses, her babydoll eyes telling me that she caught my slip of the tongue. Lucky for me, she doesn't reject me outright because I wouldn't be able to handle that now.

I'm in too deep.

She runs off to the back to find her invoice, and I stand at the counter, probably looking out of place in here. There are a handful of customers in the shop, who are browsing through different gowns and headwear.

I'm impressed with the business Lexi's put together and I'm relieved that the renovations have been to her liking.

She may be a bit disorganized at times, but she really seems to have thought of everything.

I like that in a woman. I like that in Lexi.

The bell above the front entrance signals a new patron, and I look up to find the local mailman approaching. "Hey man," I greet him.

He tips his chin. "Hey, Mr. Kingston." He sets a huge, battered cardboard box on the counter before wiping off a bead of sweat from his bald head. This box has clearly seen better days. It's dented on the sides and smashed on the top. It's a miracle it hasn't disintegrated.

"Is this a delivery for Alexia?" I ask.

"No," he grunts. "It's a return-to-sender. The package is undeliverable due to..." He looks down, reading something from his electronic tablet. "Incorrect address."

A quick peek at the label shows Lexi as the original sender. I'm guessing she made a mistake writing down someone's address. "Alright. I'll let her know," I say, as the postal worker tiredly walks out of the store.

I carefully grip the sides of the large box, lifting it off the front counter, so I can drop it off in the back for her. I only make it three steps before the tape lets out. The bottom flaps fly open and the box's contents fall to the floor in a heap. Brightly-colored phallic objects hit my shoes and bounce and roll, littering the rug around me.

"Goddamn," I huff, tossing the destroyed box to the floor.

Dildos.

Dildos everywhere.

"What in the hell?" I muse out loud.

Several gasps capture my attention. There's a conservative woman less than three feet away that is looking at me like I just flashed my junk at an elderly church group. I see a younger mother who's holding the hand of a small girl. Her jaw drops and she immediately claps a hand over her child's eyes. A middle-aged man who's standing by the jewelry case gives me a dirty glare.

The customers hurry out, seemingly horrified by the scene. What a bunch of prudes. I shouldn't laugh but I can't hold it back.

I grab one toy and stroll down the hall to Alexia's office in the back. She's seated at her desk, trying to sort through a mess of receipts. I watch silently for a minute, leaning on the door jam.

When she looks up at me, her jaw drops. In one hand, I'm holding an extra large purple dildo, flicking it back and forth.

Wearing a devilish smirk, I fight back a laugh. "Oh, so this is what my new wife is into, huh?"

37

LEXI

"Oh my god. Oh my god. Oh my god."

I rush to the front of my boutique, dropping to my knees to pick up the scattered dildos. I start tossing them into the broken cardboard box before I even realize that it has no bottom to it. Cannon approaches, setting down a fresh box that he must have found from my recycling bin.

"Where is everyone?" I gasp in horror. "I thought the shop was still full." Surely Cannon didn't scare everyone away in the two minutes I left him in charge.

He shrugs. "They left."

"They left? All of them?"

Cannon nods. "Sorry. A hundred bouncing dildos doesn't bode well in a conservative town like Crescent Harbor. This isn't exactly a progressive community."

"Oh god," I groan for the millionth time. "These stupid dildos are ruining my life!"

He laughs. "Care to explain? Where exactly were you shipping these toys to? Is there a remote female village charity somewhere that doesn't have access to men? I knew you were generous, but I had no idea…"

"You think you're funny, don't you?" I narrow my gaze on his amused face.

He leans down and starts helping me toss sex toys into the box. "Can't help it, babe."

I ignore the way my tummy flip flops at the endearment.

"This was all Iris's doing ," I start, while we both drop silicone body parts into a box. It's like déjà-vu. "It was the weekend that her husband served her divorce papers. There may have been too much wine. And too much male-bashing. And Penny had this really great coupon. At some point, Iris drunk ordered enough dildos to keep her sexually-satisfied for multiple lifetimes. But when she came to her senses and she had a meltdown. I gave her the cash I had on hand and told her she'd pay me back once she got her refund. And now, here we are…"

He smiles at me before leaning forward and pressing his full lips to my forehead. "Those women are nuts. But you're a fucking great friend."

It's stupid how hard my stomach flutters with his mouth on me. The tender embrace has me feeling all kinds of raw and vulnerable.

After we clean up, Cannon tells me the mailman mentioned an incorrect address. I double check the label, comparing it to the printout Iris gave me. The address is one hundred percent correct. I don't understand.

"I told you these things were cursed," I mumble, bringing up Google to search the company. Maybe their postal address is different than their physical address.

When I finally find the evil dildo company, Google displays bright red letters, "Closed" right under the company's name.

"No, no, no," I say, clicking through several recent comments to confirm what the search engine tells me. "It's closed. The company closed down!"

Cannon leans over my shoulder. "A dildo manufacturer going out of business? This does not look well for the male population. If no one needs dicks anymore, what are—"

I smack his chest. "Stop it. This is *bad*. If the vendor went out of business, that means I don't get my money back. Do you know how much a zillion dildos cost? Let's just say, Kingston Realties won't get their rent next month if I can't get my refund."

He wraps his strong arms around me. "Okay. Calm down."

I growl at him. I hate when he tells me to calm down.

"You're sleeping with your landlord. I'm sure you can negotiate a rent deadline extension."

My eyes spin and I smack his chest.

He gives a flash of those perfect teeth. "In all seriousness, didn't you read chapter two of Gramps' book? Let's stop considering this a problem. Instead, see it as an opportunity."

I shake my head. Now's not the time for Cannon's Self-Help Book of the Month Club. I need to come up with a plan to get my money back.

"An opportunity?" I ask skeptically.

My hubby's hand engulfs mine as he leads me to the front door of my shop. He smirks. "Lock up, and let me show you how to hustle like a billionaire, Stormy."

38

CANNON

I carry the cardboard box that serves as a temporary home to Lexi's many, many dildos. She walks beside me, asking me a half-dozen times where we're going. I can tell she's freaked out about walking around town with sex toys in broad daylight.

I lead my wife across the street to the local lingerie shop that's on the end of the block. Lexi stays quiet but skeptical while I charm the business owner. The woman is an eccentric little thing with over-dyed hair and an eyebrow piercing. "How's business going, ma'am?" I ask, wearing a good-natured smile.

I listen attentively as the woman talks, going on and on about the woes of owning an underwear shop in a town like Crescent Harbor. Meanwhile Lexi smirks beside me. I think she's onto my plan now.

"I have a deal for you that may open up a whole new stream of revenue for you." The owner leans on the cracked counter, intrigued. I take a few items out of the box. I don't miss the way her eyes light up with my product demonstration. "I have at least eight of these." I wave a crystal butt plug around. "And nine more of these bad boys." I show her a hot pink g-spot massager. "Oh, and you'll have customers lining the block to get one of these." I slide a glittery spanking paddle her way.

When I hold up a tiny hand-held vibrator and flip it on, the loud buzz draws a few more spectators. Customers begin crowding around the front of the store for the impromptu sex toy swap meet. I dust off my sales skills and the women in the lingerie shop hang onto my every word. "Stay with me here. Imagine... no, I want you to *visualize* using one of these with your partner."

"Where does that go?" a wrinkly woman in a buttoned-up cardigan whispers, eyes glinting with interest. She clutches her pearl necklace.

I wink despite my desire to barf. "If you chose the right partner, he should know exactly where to put it."

The woman moans.

I feel Lexi shudder next to me. She might be a tad bit embarrassed, but I imagine she's turned on, too.

"How much for the vibrator?" One lady at the back calls out.

I look at my bride, raising my brow. "Thirty. That one is thirty dollars," she announces with authority.

That's my girl.

Hands shoot up. Dollar bills are thrust toward us. One young guy who hung near the back of the store earlier comes forward and discreetly slips me some cash for one of the glow-in-the-dark cock rings. I hand him the sex toy without any questions asked.

This is a judgment-free zone.

By the time the crowd thins out, I calculate that we've sold twelve vibrators and eight dildos. Definitely good results for fifteen minutes of work.

I apologize to the owner, not meaning to take any of her business, but she waves her hand dismissively. "No, I should be thanking you. I've been considering installing a sex toy vending machine in here—y'know, those are *huge* in Japan—but I wasn't sure that Crescent Harbor was the right market. Well, you just did my market research for me, dear. These babies will fly off the shelves." She grins.

Lexi speaks up, with a smile. "Make us a deal, and you can snatch up the bulk of our inventory today."

The woman takes most of our stock aside from the cracked butt-plugs and some other things that must have gotten damaged during shipping. But Lexi is undoubtedly in a better position than when we walked in.

When we leave the lingerie shop, the grin on my wife's face tells me she's satisfied with the outcome of our little business trip.

Either that, or she saw me slip one of the dildos from the box into my pocket.

I have a strong suspicion that my wife will be interested in trying this one out.

We stroll out, hand in hand, now that I no longer have to lug that box around. Her eyes are full of awe and mischief when she glances up from my side. I know those eyes. Those are her horny eyes, and I one hundred percent approve. And more than that, I'm relieve to find that all traces of resentment from earlier are gone. *Maybe I still have a shot with her...*

We're in no hurry, taking the long way around Main Street on our way back to the bridal boutique. We pass under the scaffolding the Hartley Construction workers are setting up in front of the coffee shop. We'll be seeing a lot more of them in the coming months since I awarded them the renovation contract for all of Kingston Realties's crumbling properties.

Charlie and Leo grin when they see Lexi's fingers intertwined with mine. I give them a grateful chin tip that my wife doesn't notice.

Her phone belts out a now-familiar chime. An alert of a new customer booking an appointment for a bridal gown consultation. A smile pulls across her face and she squeezes my hand. "Thank you for the app."

Looking at that smile, I feel a little bit like a superhero. I shrug a shoulder and try to play it off. "I'm a glorified software developer. That's how I made my fortune. The least I could do was build an app to help my wife."

One of those nights when she was refusing to take my calls, I couldn't get her off my brain. Out of boredom and frustration, I started poking around on my computer and a few hours later, I managed to develop a basic piece of software to help promote the bridal boutique.

Alexia's eyes narrow on me. "*You* built the app?"

"Yes. That surprises you?"

She shakes her head thoughtfully. "I just assumed that you'd tossed around some money and pawned off the task on someone else."

"Wow, you really don't have a high estimate of me." Yet another repercussion of me being an asshole to her one time too many. I'm going to have to fix that.

We both know I don't deserve a parade. The damage caused by the almost-eviction was *my* fault. Cleaning up my mess was the right thing to do. Simple as that.

She sets a hand on my bicep and we stop walking in the middle of the sidewalk. "Don't get me wrong—I *am* grateful for the renovations you did at the boutique. I would have had to save up forever to accomplish that on my own...But you hurt me, King. You can't do that again. You can't just throw a pipe-bomb into someone's life and then expect a pat on the back for rebuilding the world you blew up." She flinches subtly. "Do you know how it felt when I showed up at work and I saw those men tearing my shop apart? I was sick, Cannon. Sick to my stomach. Helpless. Powerless." She holds her thumb and forefinger an inch apart. "You made me feel *this* big."

The look on her face. I hate that I'm the one who caused her that pain.

I grapple for what to say. All I come up with is another apology. I cup her jaw. "Let me show you that I'm sorry, Alexia. Let me make it up to you."

She searches my eyes. I hope to god I look as genuine as I feel. She folds her arms across her middle, a defensive posture. Finally, she whispers. "Fine...I'll give you another chance. Just don't hurt me again."

A flood of relief sweeps in and loosens the tightness in my chest. "I won't hurt you. I promise." I peel a thick clump of hair from her face and rest my lips against her forehead, sealing our pact with a tender kiss.

She doesn't pull away. Instead, she leans into my embrace, softening in my hold. I want to lift her chin and press my mouth to hers. I want to pour my apology into a passionate kiss, but we're drawing a bit of an audience. I think she senses it, too. She's smiling as she eases away and links our fingers together.

We continue our stroll down Promenade Street and I try to convince myself that the hand-holding is just a show for our spectators. But I know fully well, that's a damn lie. I have the most beautiful woman walking beside me and I feel like the luckiest bastard. I can't *not* be touching her right now.

Stormy and I pass an obscure shop, and I can't even tell what the business does. "They'd make a lot more money if they updated their branding," I state off-handedly. "I'm sure the locals know what they do, but if they want to grab the attention of visitors, their marketing needs to be clearer."

She cocks her head at the weird sign. "Huh. I guess you're right." She pulls a paper napkin out of her jeans then steals a pen from my shirt pocket. She jots something down as we continue to walk along the sidewalk.

"What are you doing?"

"Taking notes. I want to tell Hector your advice. He mentioned to me a couple weeks ago that he was struggling."

Shit. She's always thinking about how she can help someone else. I admire that about her. It makes me want to do more for the people in my own life, to make sure they know I give a damn about them.

We stroll a bit further.

"If the ice cream shop adds a juice bar, they'd maintain margins through the winter months." I point at another storefront as we continue to walk. "Those guys would triple their profits at the hardware store if they started carrying farm equipment. Walker always has to order his equipment from out of state since he can't source them locally."

We pass a dozen businesses, walking down each side of the street. Lexi continues to make notes and I ramble on with business advice that comes to mind for each organization.

For me, this is fun. Just a mental exercise for the day. But I can't understand why it feels so good to impress Alexia. I'm crazy about the way she's looking at me right now.

We pass the sandwich shop, which I see is still closed.

"When will Iris be ready to reopen? I have some ideas on helping her improve her perishable inventory, to optimize her COGS." I'll admit to having an ulterior motive for wanting to help my wife's bestie. Iris doesn't like me and I suspect that winning over Alexia would be a heck of a lot easier if she did.

Lexi gazes at the empty shop. "Iris isn't interested in reopening her place. She told me she wants to move on to something new."

"Sometimes it's good to move onto something new," I answer.

She meets my stare then. "Yeah, you might be right."

"I think you mean, *I'm always right*." I bump my elbow into her ribs. She shoves her scrap of paper back into her pocket, and I move like I'm going to take the pen from her. Instead, I intertwine my fingers with hers again.

"Thanks for sharing your godly wisdom," she quips. "I'm excited to go back and give everyone your ideas. You should consider a side gig in consulting, you know."

Right now, I'm more than content with what I have right here. Walking through town with Alexia at my side? Feeling her warmth press into my palm? Having this feisty woman look at me like I'm a frigging superhero?

Sign me the fuck up.

The only thing lingering on my list for the day is taking this woman home and putting this dildo to good use.

39

CANNON

Renewed Gowns is closed on Saturday morning for some final renovations. We leave it in the competent hands of the Hartley Constructions team and I keep my beautiful wife at home.

We lie around in bed, in no real rush to face the outside world. I, for one, am perfectly content to spend the day inside the blanket fort we've built in our bed.

Her stomach roars and she attempts to untangle herself from the sheets. I pull her back and volunteer to make us breakfast in bed just to keep her locked up in my room a little longer. My kitchen skills are shit so we end up eating burnt toast with butter and bitter coffee. I accompany the 'meal' with a tub of strawberry yogurt that's dangerously close to its expiration date.

Alexia shamelessly mocks my lack of cooking skills. I feign hurt feelings and get an apology in the form of the best blow job of my life. Stormy's a swallower and that's a win-win proposition. I let her ride my face to a screaming orgasm in return.

I find a box of playing cards in my bedside drawer. She

teaches me some game I've never heard of and I swear she's just making up the rules as we go. But I don't care because —*man*—I'm happy. Happier than I've ever been.

I've travelled the world, mingled with dignitaries, I even went onboard a spacecraft once. Yet somehow, all those events pale in comparison to a quiet morning at home, playing and bantering with this wild, perfect creature.

This is crazy. After the way things ended with Margot, I should have trust issues, I should fear commitment, I should be repelled by the idea of a relationship. Yet here I am, diving headfirst with Alexia.

A voice in my head tells me I need to back the heck up but caring about this woman feels easy. Natural. Inevitable.

She grins at me and braves a sip of the now-cold coffee. That smile melts into a cringe as the brew goes down. Her eyes water. "Wow, that was pretty disgusting." She rests the mug on the bedside table and a river of brown liquid slides down the side of the cup to pool at the base.

I don't give a fuck. She's sloppy and she's messy and she's mine.

Sometime in the mid-afternoon, I drag myself into the bathroom for hygiene stuff. I lean close to the mirror with my toothbrush in hand and I can hardly recognize the grinning fool staring back at me.

This is *not* the man I was when I drove into Crescent Harbor with nothing but revenge on my mind. Alexia Robson has changed me. She has softened me. And I can't bring myself to apologize.

Moments later, she stumbles in wearing only her tiny panties, looking like she got fucked hard all night. She did. And I still want more of her.

I can't help it, I grab her by the waist and lift her onto the counter. "You're fucking beautiful. You know that?"

She touches my face. "*You're* beautiful, Kingston." Her eyes twinkle with reverence.

I yank her head back to kiss her mouth then I pull off her panties. Her morning breath could wipe out mass civilizations but still, I just want to kiss up on her. I can't stop.

Her moans surge and fade in the quiet room as I taste her gorgeous, little breasts and finger her to the peak one more time. My arms circle her back to hold her as she recovers.

Minutes later, she slides off the counter, grinning, and tries to bump me out of the way with her narrow hip. She fails. I roll my eyes and move aside to let her grab her toothbrush.

As she's brushing her teeth, a text message comes in on my phone on the counter. Absently, I swipe to unlock the screen. I glance down and...

Holy clitoris!

"Da fuck is wrong with that woman?!" I mutter to myself, staring at the picture in disbelief.

Lexi sets down her toothbrush and pops up over my shoulder. "What's that?" She stares at the phone with a cocked brow, tone heavy with curiosity.

"Nudes from my ex," I groan. "Again." A quick glance in the mirror confirms that my expression is just as traumatized as I feel.

"Can I see?" Not a hint of jealousy in her cool, unaffected tone.

"Knock yourself out."

My wife eagerly snatches the phone from my hand and leans against the marble counter next to me. Not an inch of fabric covering her perfect skin, not a self-conscious bone in that tempting body. I run a brush through my hair and tie it into a quick knot at the base of my neck.

"Oh, I almost bought a clit ring just like that!"

I snort— actually snort with laughter—as I pick up my razor from the counter. This woman is something else.

She expands the picture with her fingers. "And gorgeous tits, by the way." I hear nothing but amusement in her voice. She swigs some mouthwash.

"They'd better be gorgeous. I spent a fortune on them."

She looks up at me with wide eyes and roughly coughs out a laugh. I have to thump her a few times on the upper back because, choking to death on some Listerine? I don't want my wife to go out like that.

Once she recovers, I press kisses all over her smirking face. "You're amazing."

The look in her eyes is pure and genuine. "I'm really sorry that bitch hurt you..." Alexia is loyal to the bone and that only makes me want her more.

And the funny thing? I'm not sorry. I'm not sorry that Margot turned out to be a shitty human being and that she thought fucking my clueless best friend was the way to get ahead. Because if she hadn't made that colossal mistake, I wouldn't be standing in my bathroom in quiet Crescent Harbor with my hands all over the most beautiful woman I've ever seen.

Nah, Margot did me a favor.

Lexi goes over and sits on the edge of the bathtub. "I'm in the mood for a bath. Join me?"

I'm 6'2 and thirty years old. I have no right trying to squeeze myself into a bathtub, dammit. But I can't deny my wife anything.

Minutes later, we're together in the tub with warm bubbles up to our chins. Touching and murmuring sweet nothings in between long, lazy kisses. Like we have nothing to do and nowhere to go.

I pull back and look into those crystalline eyes. I want to know every little thing about her. "What's your backstory, Stormy? Tell me about your family."

As soon as I say it, she pivots around and sinks into my hold. She pulls my biceps around her, back slick against my chest. She shrinks like a child seeking out refuge, protection.

I'll do whatever it takes to get her to relax, to see that she's safe in my arms. I grab her grapefruit shampoo from the corner of the tub. I squirt some into my hand and she giggles. "What are you doing?"

"Washing your hair." I kiss the side of her neck.

"Uh, I usually leave that to the professionals." Her tone is skeptical.

"Don't worry about it."

She writhes as I draw my sudsy fingers through her thick, tangled hair. "I hope you know what you're getting yourself into."

I circle my fingertips into her scalp, massaging deeply. She moans. "I've got it under control."

Still trying to keep the conversation off of her past, she continues to stall. "Are we gonna address your hair fetish at some point or are we just gonna keep sweeping it under the rug?"

"What are you talking about?" I feign ignorance then lean in and jokingly make a big show of sniffing her hair. She squirms as I continue to touch her. "Sit still."

I don't have a hair fetish. I have an Alexia fetish. I don't think there's a twelve-step program for that.

"Your family, Stormy."

I'm being persistent as hell but I've been curious. I've tried to bring it up on a thousand different occasions. She's changed the subject every time. I'm not letting her get away with it today.

She shrinks some more. "I grew up in Cowersville."

"Cowersville? Never heard of it."

She laughs morosely. "Lucky you. It's a little town somewhere between Reyfield and Copper Heights, tucked into a corner where no one is supposed to find it." She absently scoops a handful of bubbles and lets the suds slip between her fingers.

Sensing how uncomfortable this conversation is making her, I continue rubbing her scalp.

"When I was small, Dad owned this furniture and appliance store he ran downtown. It wasn't huge but I guess he did okay for himself. Provided for a family of four. Every Friday after work, his first purchase would be a case of beer and a pile of lottery tickets and after the news, me and Jessa would sandwich him on the old living room couch while he watched the winning numbers pop up on the TV screen. Every week, he'd lose. Jessa would start to cry and he'd promise to win the next week..." A rueful tone laces her voice.

She chews on the nail of her thumb as she continues to bare her soul.

"And then, one Friday night, he did. Every single one of his numbers came. We won two and a half million dollars."

"Wow..." I mutter.

She drops her head and shakes it. "The first thing Mom wanted was a house. A big one. In the most expensive area of Chicago. Nice cars. A cabin. Then, Jessa and I were in private school. Forget keeping up with the Jones's. We were burning through money fast to keep up with the Coventry's and the Kenworth's. But in the eyes of those old money aristocrats, me and my sister never quite measured up at school. The way they looked at us...made me wish I were invisible." Lexi continues to bare her soul. "But Mom kept trying and trying and spending more money to try and keep up." She wipes her cheeks and I imagine the tears streaking down her face. "Eventually we were broke. We were worse off than before we won the lotto..."

"Fuck, Alexia..." I spin her around to look at her face.

"I guess I never forgave my parents for that." She drops her stare. "I mean, winning the lotto was our shot, y'know. We could have built something good, solid. If Dad had invested in the business, opened another location, ordered more product. Instead, he wasted every dime. We had to move into a trailer park. We didn't even have anything in the fridge to eat some nights. It was my friends in the neighborhood who stepped in to fill our bellies. My parents never bothered to make a backup plan. Dad didn't even *try* to recover from that failure. His drinking spiralled out of control. He just gave up on life."

Resentment bleeds from her features and I don't blame her one bit. Her parents squandered what could have been a promising future.

Now, it all makes sense to me. I understand why she fought so hard to save Renewed Gowns, why she was willing to do anything to save her fellow business owners around town, why she was willing to marry the complete stranger who posed a threat to her little world.

I feel like such an asshole.

She goes back to biting her nail. "We had this neighbor a few trailers down from us. Mrs. Tremblay. She was a sassy old thing who was a hoarder like nobody's business. But she was kind. She took me under her wing. She taught me to sew. And right before she got moved into a nursing home, she handed me a big, fat envelop stuffed with crumpled five-dollar bills. I used it to get out of Cowersville and open my shop."

This bath is supposed to be relaxing but I watch as the tension in her shoulders increases with each word. My fingers move down to her shoulders, slicking across her smooth skin.

"That's why I hustle so hard when it comes to my business. I'm dead-set on not making the mistakes my parents did. I want to make sure that when I have my own family, they'll be secure."

I almost blurt out that I've got it covered, that she won't have to worry about providing for her family because it's a family we'll create together and I've got a fuck-ton of money and I'll be there right by her side.

But saying that would be insane. Stormy is just my temporary wife and we both know it.

"I *had* to do better for Jessa and me. We couldn't stay in that toxic environment. That's why we left. That's why we never looked back. It's not that I don't love my parents." Guilt bleeds from her words and I sense her overwhelming need to explain herself, to prove to me that she's a good person. Not that I'm doubting her. "But they fucked up. I just resent them so much for the mistakes they made."

I wrap her up and rest my chin on her shoulder. My blood boils just beneath the surface. I'm pissed that the adults in her life didn't look out for her.

"They're just in denial about *everything*. They have issues but neither of my parents will address it. This is why I stay away from them. They're a mess and they won't let me help in any meaningful way that counts. All they do is ask me for money." Shampoo suds dripping down her face, she scrunches up her nose and speaks quietly. "You think I'm a loser, don't you? I'm all fucked up."

"What?" I say in response to the guilty expression on her

face. Shock takes hold of my system. How could this incredible woman doubt her worth?

She whispers. "I don't deserve a guy like you."

I make a silent pledge to her, right there and right then. I will *never* be the one to make her feel like that again.

I trace an invisible line down the bridge of her nose and over the swell of her lips. "Don't you ever fucking say that, Alexia. You're a Kingston now. You're my wife. You deserve the whole damn world." *And I'll make sure you get it.*

Then, I kiss her. Hard.

40

LEXI

A loud screech jolts me out of a dream on Sunday morning. I lay there, a little bleary-eyed, until I recognize the sound. A child. A child yelling and squealing at the top of their lungs.

Cannon didn't mention that we were having company, so I quickly throw on some clothes and tiptoe downstairs. If I'm going to be murdered today by a tiny person, it seems important that it doesn't happen when I'm half-naked.

When I approach the living room, I hear more voices. Then I catch sight of Cannon on his knees in front of the couch, throwing blown-up balloons in the air. His niece is there catching them. And squealing. Cannon's parents are here, too, watching the commotion.

I move to stand next to them by the fireplace, reaching down to hug Mrs. Kingston. I smile, enjoying the scene of my fake husband playing with a kid. Last time I checked, Callie wasn't Uncle Cannon's biggest fan but maybe she's warming up to him now.

The sight of them together has thoughts running through my traitorous brain that have no business being there. Like...would Cannon Kingston be a good father? Does he actually like kids?

I round the couch to get in on the balloon-throwing fun. That's when I get a better view of the little girl. I can't help but gasp out loud.

The poor child has absolutely no eyebrows.

Like, none at all.

Just gorgeous bright eyes, wispy eyelashes, and then...forehead.

Diana laughs at my reaction. She comes over and lays a hand on my arm. "She got her hands on Lucas's electric shaver this morning and gave herself a bit of a makeover. I nearly had a heart attack when she ran out of the bathroom."

"Wow," I say on an exhale.

Kids are terrifying creatures. And suddenly, I want a whole batch of them with Cannon.

"I'm just relieved I found her before she shaved off a patch of that glorious Kingston hair!" The woman tenderly strokes her grandchild's blond ringlets.

Mr. Kingston laughs and drapes an arm around his wife's shoulder. "I think she's pulling off the new look pretty well. Right, Princess Callie?"

The little girl beams at her grandfather and nods. "'Yes, Papa!"

Cannon plops down on the couch and hauls her into his lap. "This kid is Eli, two-point-oh. Remember that time Walker fell asleep in the toolshed and Eli got his hands on a pair of old garden pruners? Let's just say it took a few weeks for my oldest brother to grow into his free haircut..."

The family laughs at the shared memory and their closeness warms me to the tips of my toes. I want to be in on their inside jokes, I want to make memories with them, too.

...Also, I make a mental note to hide all cutting devices around the Kingston family. They're a wild bunch, and this darling girl is the biggest handful of all.

Cannon hooks an arm around my leg, causing me to collapse onto the couch next to him. My heart thuds when our eyes meet. "We're going to babysit today," he announces, looking straight at me to gauge my reaction.

"Oh! Okay, that sounds...lovely," I respond, hoping I've covered up my initial fumbling shock.

"I think my parents are overdue for a day off and could use some alone time together." He jerks his eyebrows suggestively. "It's important, y'know?"

Cannon's parents eye me. Or rather, I catch them looking at my hair. My cheeks heat up. I totally forgot to look in the mirror on my way down. I can only imagine how bad my bedhead is right now.

When Mr. and Mrs. Kingston share a knowing grin, they confirm it.

I really need to get my priorities straight. Apparently, it's important to me to be dressed if I'm going to be murdered by home invaders, but I didn't consider actually making myself presentable.

Next time, I need to put more thought into that. I can't expect a funeral home to detangle my hair, can I?

"Young, in love, and up all night, huh? I sure remember those days," Diana comments. Her husband elbows her playfully in the ribs.

Cannon drapes an arm around my shoulder and squeezes me to his side. "Hey now. Don't make my new bride blush."

I can actually feel the redness climb to my ears. Lord. Is anything sacred in this family?

A doubtful look comes over Mrs. Kingston's face. "I don't

feel right about dumping a child on you both so soon after your wedding," she hedges. "You should be enjoying as much alone time as you can get right now."

I stand and grab my mother-in-law's hands. "Truly, it's no problem at all, Diana. It'll be fun, right?" I smile, looking at Callie.

"Yeeesss!" She's currently using the couch as her personal trampoline.

"Oh, okay," Cannon's mom concedes. "If you're sure it's all right with you. But you two will be going on a honeymoon soon, right?"

A honeymoon?

I have to admit that I've been imagining a honeymoon. A little getaway to somewhere tropical where we could sit in a cabana by the ocean and Cannon would eat mangoes and pineapples out of my cleavage. If this were a normal marriage, we would have exchanged vows and then immediately whisked away on a romantic vacation for two. But everything about this relationship has been far from conventional. Is it wrong that part of me is holding onto wishes for that kind of normalcy with him?

Cannon avoids my eyes and shoots out the vaguest answer ever. "In time."

My hopeful heart sinks. Just another reminder that our time together has a looming expiration date.

His parents don't pick up on the tension.

"Okay love birds, let me know what you decide. I'm happy to help with the arrangements." His mother smiles.

Hugs are exchanged, and we stand together at the door waving them off as the car drives away.

I feel a tug on my leg. When I look down, Callie grins up at me.

Now, how to keep an eyebrowless four-year-old entertained?

41

CANNON

My mother left us with enough lasagna to feed an army, so after watching cartoons and chasing balloons all morning, the three of us enjoy lunch together.

Lexi flutters around my kitchen, warming everything up. She brings our plates into the dining room, serving Callie and me. Just when I think she's going to join us, she rushes back to grab a glass of juice for each of us.

"Can you handle a big girl glass?" Lexi asks the little girl, setting a tumbler in front of her. "Your Uncle Cannon doesn't have any kid cups for us." She gives me a mock glare. Callie joins in because she's a hater like that.

I can't help but chuckle.

My wife looks at me with twinkling eyes. "Can I get you guys anything else?" she asks, tenderness in her movements as she strokes my niece's curly blonde head.

"Good grief, woman. You can just sit and eat with us," I demand with a half-smile.

Lexi grins back at me as she drops into her seat, and it stirs something deep inside me. I've never seen a woman with a more genuine smile. When she looks at me like that, I nearly forget everything shitty in my life. She's this bright, shiny object that I just want to cling to for dear life. There's no way I'm letting her go.

This wasn't part of the plan. But who fucking cares? She's my wife. The woman who screamed my name last night. The woman I left blissfully-satisfied in my bed this morning.

I'm going to keep her. Even though she doesn't know it yet.

Now that I've had a taste of the real thing, there's no way I'm going back to settling for the kind of woman who pretended to love me in exchange for the benefits that come with being the trophy on a billionaire's arm.

I need to tell her that Kingston Realties is mine. But before I do that, I need to make sure she knows she's mine, too.

Lexi notices Callie just sitting there staring at her plate, not eating. "What's wrong, sweetheart?"

"Grandma cuts it up for me."

"*Oh*, of course she does." My wife hops up, not hesitating to help her out as she kneels on the floor. "What about the bread? Does she cut that too?" Lexi asks with exaggerated, wide eyes.

The little girl giggles at her. "No. That's silly. You just bite it." Then she demonstrates by taking a huge, unlady-like bite out of her garlic bread.

"You're right. Silly me." Lexi chides herself, shaking her head. It's obvious she's doing all this just to make the child feel more comfortable. It means a lot, considering my niece's quiet reserve around me.

In recent years, I haven't always been present for my loved ones. But after hearing about Stormy's fucked up childhood, it's suddenly really important to me to improve my relationship with my family. It's not something I've talked about with her, but in all the little things she does, it feels like she already knows.

And I want her to feel included. She couldn't form a bond with her own family? Fuck 'em. She can have a place in mine.

I continue to sneak glances at my wife throughout the meal. I'm not sure I could explain it even if I tried, but hanging out with her in this way just feels...right. I like the way she interacts with my family. I like the way she makes me feel.

It's all...It's *different* for me.

I've never invested emotionally into a relationship. Not even with Margot. That kind of investment always seemed too high-risk. But Alexia is stirring something inside me. Like I'm trying a rare delicacy for the first time, surprised to discover exactly how delicious it really is.

I'm nearly finished with my lunch when my cell phone rings in my pocket. Sliding it out, I see that it's Frank.

"I've got to take this. Are you guys good here?" I'm already rising from the table when Alexia nods and tells me to go ahead.

"Frank, what do you have?" I answer, striding down the hallway to take the call in my office.

Things have stalled on my revenge plans over the past few weeks while we focused on organizing the wedding and the business arrangements. And that fight with Lexi had me out of commission for days. I need to get things back on track, I guess. But to be honest, my appetite for blood isn't as voracious as it was when I just showed up in town.

Frank spends the next ten minutes explaining to me

that, again, he's been hitting some dead ends in his execution of my request.

"I don't understand. I thought I handed you airtight instructions here. I wanted this done weeks ago."

"I know, but I'm still bound to work within the limits of the law, Cannon. And I would advise you to do the same. What you've proposed in the latest workup was not ethical. Or legal."

My palm slams down onto my desk and I growl into the phone.

Dammit!

I take three steps forward, and then get shoved two back. It's frustrating.

The sounds of Alexia and Callie laughing in the kitchen make their way into my office. I feel a pang knowing that I'm missing out on whatever fun they're having together. I'd rather be with them instead of stuck in here dealing with this bullshit.

"Do whatever you've got to do, Frank."

It's getting to the point where I'm about ready to drop the whole revenge thing and move on with my damn life.

Callie's innocent laughter floats up to my office. Warmth surges through the beating lump of muscle in my chest. Thinking back to Alexia's traumatic upbringing, it feels wrong that I'm not doing everything in my power to give my niece the sort of childhood she deserves.

"Also, I need you to redirect some of your resources," I tell Frank.

"Oh?" I can almost hear the man's bushy brow jut up.

"I need you to find a way to get my brother out of jail."

42

LEXI

Cannon's niece and I finish up lunch on our own, and she keeps me quite entertained. If I've learned anything about four-year-olds today, it's that they are brutally—and innocently—honest. Sometimes it makes me want to hug her. Other times, I think she's been invaded by tiny jerkface aliens.

"You're really pretty."

"It smells funny in here."

"Your fingers are too long."

"There's food in your teeth."

And on that note, we move our party into the master bathroom upstairs to wash up. And, she's one-hundred percent right, I do have parsley in my teeth. I thank her for sparing me further embarrassment there. Better to hear it from her than from Cannon, right?

She eyes me carefully when I apply a fresh layer of a nude lipstick. Even though I'm not working today, I have this urge to look my best around Cannon. I want him to be attracted to me, but I'm not going to analyze that too deeply. Ignoring these feelings seems like the smarter decision.

"Can I do makeup?" she asks sweetly. I'm starting to get used to looking at her without eyebrows. Maybe I could actually draw some on her. I've seen the way her uncle fights back a laugh each time he's caught off guard by the sight of her. A little eyebrow therapy could certainly help with that. I think.

"Okay, hop up here," I say, as I lift her to the counter top. "Sit still, and I'll do your makeup. Just a little though, so we don't get in trouble."

"Then I do yours?" She bats her blonde lashes at me. Man, Cannon's right. She's *good*. I can't tell her no. The poor girl doesn't even have a mother to do these sorts of things with. Thank goodness she's living with her grandparents though. I know Mrs. Kingston is great with her.

"Absolutely," I promise.

I draw on an excellent pair of new brows, dab a bit of color on her cheeks, and add some pale pink lipstick to her lips. She lights up when I hand her a hand mirror, remarking on her own beauty. She really is adorable.

Then she turns the tables on me, making me sit on the floor while she works her magic on my face. When she rubs lipstick on my eyelids, I decide I'm too terrified to see the finished product. Callie chews on her bottom lip, pure concentration eating up her expression. She designs my new look, taking twice the time I did on hers.

When she eventually begins singing the alphabet, I hum along with her. She's smart and so confident, though she somehow squeezes two S's into her lineup.

My face is downright atrocious, and I just pray that Cannon doesn't walk into the room anytime soon. There's lipstick on my eyelids, cheek, *and* lips, of course. There are several uneven lines drawn on my forehead with my eyeliner pencil. Thank god she didn't grab the waterproof liner.

I catch her yawning, so I put her down for a nap in one of the upstairs guest rooms. As I tuck her in, she begs for me to sing.

I have to struggle not to make an ugly face. "I'm a horrible singer. Really horrible," I explain. "I don't think you want to hear me sing."

She yawns again, snuggling down under the covers. "Please. My Papa is a horrible singer, too. It's okay."

I chuckle. She's got a point. Like always.

I sing through that *Twinkle, Twinkle* song twice. It's the only kid song I can remember right now, and even still, I had to get assistance with a few lyrics on the first run through.

After I'm convinced she's asleep—and that no razors or scissors are left nearby—I scrub my face clean and then move back downstairs. I keep myself busy, tidying the kitchen, straightening up the living room, and picking up the toys strewn across the floor.

Just as I fall into a chair to rest my feet, I hear a tiny pitter patter on the hardwood floor. Callie crawls into my lap, still groggy. "Up already?" I bury my nose in her blonde curls and inhale her sweet bubblegum shampoo.

I have no clue how long she normally naps, but it's been about an hour, so we'll call that success.

A moment later, heavier footsteps approach from the hallway. I smile at Cannon as he enters the living room. I haven't seen him all afternoon and my heart flutters to acknowledge that.

His eyes soften at the sight of me with the child all curled up in my arms. "Who wants to go swimming?" he asks.

"I do! I do!" A tiny hand shoots upward. She's wide awake now.

After changing into our suits, the three of us goof around in the in-ground pool in the backyard.

Cannon holds onto his niece's belly, guiding her around the water while she kicks and splashes and giggles. Her makeup is long gone. After a few more sessions in the pool, I bet we'll have her swimming on her own. I should pick up some floaties for her next time I'm in town.

Whoa! Where did that thought come from?

It's like I'm quickly losing sight of the fact that this marriage of mine has no future. Cannon and I haven't discussed our status directly but there's no need. His expectations are clearly outlined in the prenup his lawyer prepared before we said our vows. As soon as he gains control of Kingston Realties, he'll have no further use for me. The contract made that clear.

The momentum of that reminder nearly knocks me off my feet. Suddenly, I feel a little bit afraid because Cannon owning Kingston Realties would mean he doesn't need me anymore. It would mean he could terminate our agreement at any moment and throw me away. And these emotions percolating in my heart wouldn't even matter.

If things feel different between us now, it's because *I'm* the one losing sight of our situation's reality.

"Ouch! Water in my eyes! My eyes!" Callie shouts.

I rush out of the pool to grab one of the beach towels I brought out. Cannon sits his niece in one of the pool chairs. He crouches down beside her and holds her tiny, wrinkly hand as I wrap her up, taking extra care to wipe all traces of water from her little eyes. I feel a pang at the man's tender concern as we care for the little girl.

Yeah, this guy is definitely baby daddy material.

I wish I knew how to turn these thoughts off but with each moment we spend together, I fall a little deeper.

When Callie has recovered, I stand, needing to put some space between Cannon and me. But he comes up behind me. His dripping arms wrap around my shivering body and he kisses the top of my head. I should fight it, I should pull away. But I melt into the feeling of being tightly secured in his embrace, safe in his—

The asshole straps me to his chest and launches himself into the pool. I barely have time to scream before the water swallows us both. We break the surface with a *splash*!

I flail in his hold. His niece's shrieks of amusement fill the air.

I swim back to the surface, ready for revenge. "You're going to pay for this, Cannon Kingston!" I threaten, splashing in his direction.

Before I can put my plan of attack into motion, I catch sight of his father approaching the pool.

The man has a wide grin spread across his dashing face. "Looks like Princess Callie is the babysitter, huh?" he comments with a laugh as he scoops up his granddaughter.

She slings an arm around his neck and points at the pool. "Uncle Cannon is so silly, Papa!"

Laughing, he stamps a kiss on her cheek. "Ready to go, Princess?"

"I want to stay," she begs. "We're having fun!"

"Sorry, bug. Nana's got our dinner started, and these two look like they need a break." Mr. Kingston sets her back on her feet as Cannon and I climb out of the pool.

We take Callie inside and I get her into some dry clothes. She complies but makes sure to pout as much as humanly possible the entire time.

At the front door, I kneel in front of her, wrapping my arms around her tiny form. "You can come back real soon."

Pleading eyes move between Cannon and me. "Promise, Aunt Lexi and Uncle Cannon? *Promise*?"

"Pinky promise," her uncle confirms, making my heart swell. In fact, I think it's on the edge of bursting right here on the front mat.

This is the most fun I've had in one day for as long as I can remember. And I'm the girl who loves tearing up the Frosty Pitcher on a Friday night.

These people...they're just so easy to be around. They love each other and it *shows*.

I want to be a part of that.

43

CANNON

"You'll get much faster service if you go to the bar," Penny says, practically batting her eyes at Walker from across the table. I guess she would know since she works here most of the week.

Right now, she's just a lowly patron like the rest of us, and getting good service is nearly impossible. We've been waiting *forever* to get another round of drinks.

"Sounds like a good idea." A slow smile unfolds across my brother's scruffy face as his eyes linger on his 'friend'.

They sit there unmoving, wearing identical goofy expressions. It's like they think the whole damn world has stopped just for them to keep staring at each other.

Walker doesn't usually come to the bar. Silently, I wonder how Penny managed to bribe him into getting out of the house.

Jessa has been dominating the conversation with her bubbly personality. Tucked into my side, Lexi has been too busy laughing at her sister's ramblings to notice Iris shooting me suspicious glares half the night. As for Penny and Walker, they've been sharing annoying, forlorn glances since we got here and at this point, I can say with certainty that everybody at the table would pitch in to get them a room at a nearby motel just to relieve them of their repressed sexual tension.

I elbow my dumbass brother in the ribs. "We gonna get that beer or what?" He and I are tragically outnumbered by the ladies in our group, so I don't mind getting a break from the estrogen for a minute.

Walker peels his gaze away from Penny just long enough to glare at me and shuffle out of the booth. I plant a quick kiss on Alexia's cheek and grin at the hint of a blush that crops up her neck. Walker and I leave the ladies at the table and head for the counter.

The two of us weave through the sports crowd of the Frosty Pitcher to grab refills for our table. There aren't many places to hang out on a Sunday afternoon here in Crescent Harbor, so it's packed from wall to wall. Flat screens line the bar, and Jude's Iowa Paragons team blasts on the surround sound speakers in an early preseason game. My little brother is a bit of a legend around here, even though he was drafted out of state.

It's a good five minutes before Walker and I are able to grab some empty bar stools, and I split my time between watching Lexi laughing with her girlfriends and watching my brother Jude dominate on the television.

I put in our order with the bartender, and I'm vaguely aware of Walker grumbling some shit in my ear while I stare across the room. I love the way Alexia laughs. It's loud and unbridled and so damn sexy. Even though I can't hear her from this far away, it's easy to imagine the sensual tones of her voice.

Somehow the sight of her enjoying herself is even hotter than the sound. She throws her head back, and her wild hair bounces, reaching down her spine. My eyes follow the column of her throat, and my fingers itch to reach out and touch the soft skin there.

Walker is still running his mouth, and I'm trying my damndest to listen while I continue to watch Stormy.

"I'm surprised to see you two still together since the business deal is final. What's up with that?"

"Hmm?" I'm hedging. I still haven't told her the truth. The objective of our marriage—getting control of my family company—has been achieved and I've been withholding that information from my wife. I'm practically holding her hostage.

"Lexi. You like her, don't you?"

Man, my brother sure is dragging me into the deep end here. I'm not really ready to address what is going on inside my head, largely because I still don't even fucking know. How can I explain something I don't even understand?

But I do know Walker. And I know he'll call me out on my shit if I try to lie or change the subject.

Ruefully, I nod and glance at him. I feel like I'm signing my own death certificate here. "More than that...Brother, I think I might be in love."

44

LEXI

I'm surrounded by my favorite people tonight. The guys are just across the room, and Jessa, Iris, and Penny are crowded into a corner booth with me.

Iris is telling us all about her latest business idea. She recently had some big plans that sounded promising, but those weren't netting any quick revenue. I offered to bring her on at the boutique—at least temporarily—since business has really picked up after Cannon started that shopping app and online ads for me. But she refused my help because she wants to do this on her own. I know she's struggling. I just hope her new idea comes through for her, fast.

While my bestie talks, my gaze keeps averting to watch Penny. She thinks she's being stealthy, stealing quick, longing glances at Walker. I wouldn't be surprised if she went and clocked in, just for the excuse to go serve Walker his beer.

I hate that the two of them waste time dating other people. It's so dumb. They'd be cute together. I hope they quit running in circles around each other and just get it on.

Jessa shoves her empty glass aside and waggles her

brows at me. "Okay. I just have to say it—you and Cannon were looking pretty cozy a few minutes ago."

Good god, she's a persistent little thing. Jessa has been bugging me for days to find out what's going on between me and my groom. My friends know we've been sleeping together, but other than that, I've been holding the details close to the vest.

Penny speaks up, traitorously backing up my annoying little sister. "I was thinking the same thing. You have to spill, lady. What is going on with you two? Do you have feelings for him? Like *more* than fake wife feelings?" Her grin is downright evil.

Based on their expressions, it seems like my girls already know the answers to those questions. *The jerks*. I sure wish they'd fill me in because I'm still trying to figure this all out.

It's like Cannon can feel my stare, because a second later, his caramel eyes meet mine. My insides coil and flip. I'm still trying to understand his effect on me. Why is it so darn strong?

After a blushing glance toward the object of our conversation, I sigh heavily, giving in to their peer pressure. "I'm trying really hard to convince myself that I don't." Deep down I know that what I feel for Cannon is stronger than anything I've ever experienced. I know that it's love.

I'm freaking myself out trying to come to grips with those scary feelings. I try to slam the door on them quickly and with force. But those fuckers fight back.

"Oh, I knew it!" Jessa claps. "I told you. You two are going to get your happily ever after. You just wait."

Penny leans across the table to grip my arm. "You deserve this, Lexi. You deserve a man who looks at you the way Cannon has been looking at you all night."

Iris doesn't seem quite as thrilled as the others. "You

need to protect yourself and your heart, Lexi. I have a funny feeling about that man." I know that her shitty experiences with Kirk have left her jaded. I don't blame her, but I refuse to think that all men are as awful as her ex.

They can't be.

I've seen with my own eyes that assumptions can be wrong. Cannon has proved me wrong again and again. He's not the selfish bastard I thought he was the day he sat barking orders at my sister across the coffee shop. We've both come a long way since then.

Now, he fucks me every night. He eats breakfast with me every morning. He comes by the shop with a different kind of flowers every day at lunch. He snuggles up with me to read personal development books after dinner. And then, he fucks me all over again.

"I'll be fine." I tell Iris, even though I'm really not so sure if that's true.

"Just promise me you'll be careful," she pleads.

I nod, unable to voice the words of an outright lie. I'm scared it might be too late to be careful.

I like him. A lot. And every time I think about the upcoming dissolution of our marriage, a heavy rock settles at the bottom of my stomach.

Yes, this marriage was only supposed to be temporary. Logically, I know that Cannon and I could never work out in the long run We're opposites in every way that counts...but I'm not ready for this to end.

I steal another glance at Cannon right as the bartender sets our drinks on the counter. But this time, my husband's eyes don't meet mine. His attention is firmly locked on the television in front of him. I watch as his hand freezes with his beer bottle suspended midway to his mouth. His expression drops right before my eyes.

In a heartbeat, the room erupts in shouting and swearing. I blink in confusion as the entire bar roars with loud, angry yelling. People are jumping out of their seats and screaming at the football game.

I shift my attention toward the television closest to our table and I gasp. Now, the whole world is moving in slow motion.

I'm on my feet, too. *Oh my god. No, no, no, no.*

Jude Kingston lays helpless on the football field, gripping his leg. An agonizing expression twists his face as coaches and medical staff surround him.

Moving on pure instinct, I'm shoving through the crowd, trying to find my way across the bar to get to Cannon. I don't stop until my arms are wrapped around his shoulders. His wide eyes don't leave the screen, but I know he feels my presence, because he reaches up and tightly grips my hand.

Together, we watch in horror as Cannon's youngest brother is carted off the field.

45

CANNON

"Dammit!" I shout, punching my steering wheel as I make a left turn. "Why won't anybody return my calls? Can you look in my phone for another number?"

Lexi plucks my phone from where I threw it into the cupholder after my last failed attempt to contact my brother's agent. "Of course." She quietly searches for the name I give her.

She hasn't said much since we left the bar, but she lets me know she's here for me with small, comforting touches. It's soothing.

Margot would have been more concerned with filming her commentary on Jude's injury to post on her Instagram stories than with checking in to make sure I'm okay, and I would have blown a damn gasket by now.

I appreciate Alexia's quiet, calming presence, but still, I'm desperate to find out what's going on with Jude. I'm at my wit's end searching for someone who will pick up their damn phone. Watching him being carted off the football field was one of the hardest things I've had to do. Jude can be an absolute shithead, but he's *my* shithead, and I'd do anything for him.

Right now, I need to know how he is. I need to know *where* he is.

The Paragon team manager doesn't pick up either. Christ, I'm about to ask Lexi to pull up the team roster list, so I can find someone who might know about Jude's condition right now. Someone who might actually be close to their cell phone at half time. I'm fucking grasping at straws here.

Why is no one answering their damn phone?!

My own phone buzzes in Lexi's hands, and I ask her to put it on speaker.

"Jude?" I'm still holding out hope that my brother is *fine*. He just pulled a muscle or had an agonizing leg cramp. He's just hanging out in the locker room, laughing with a trainer while I lose my bloody mind over here. I'm hoping hard for that.

"No, this is his agent, Paul Price. I saw that you called. Cannon Kingston, right?" My hopes wither and dry up on the backroads of Crescent Harbor, Illinois.

"Yes, that's me. I've been trying to get ahold of Jude or find someone that knows what's going on with him. Is he okay?" My gut churns with dread. It can't be a good sign if his agent is calling. It can't be good if Jude is unable to call me himself.

His agent talks too fast, giving me a speedy update, like he's being charged for talk time. Before I can ask any questions, he quickly ends the call, saying he has a dozen other calls to make. The man asks me to pass along the update to the rest of my family.

My mind instantly goes to mom. *Shit...*

When he hangs up, Alexia is looking at me with wide

eyes from the passenger seat, but still, she doesn't intrude. She doesn't badger. She just rubs the back of my neck while I drive.

"Can I dial your parents for you?" she offers quietly.

I nod, my throat tight. "Yeah, my parents."

She takes my phone and does just that, and all too soon, my mother is answering the call.

"Oh, Cannon. Tell us you have some news," Ma begs with an anxious desperation that's all too familiar. "We can't get through to anyone." I know she and Dad had to have been sitting at home, watching Jude's game.

My father speaks. "Son, tell us your brother's going to be okay."

I relay the update from Jude's agent. "He dislocated his kneecap."

"Oh god," Ma wails, her voice cracking with panic.

"Were they able to pop it back in?" Dad asks.

"I think so. But that's not the worst of it," I pinch the bridge of my nose. "A dislocated kneecap isn't a big deal on its own, but the early scans are showing a significant tear in his ACL. He's already going into surgery."

I hear my dad swear, and my mother cries harder. Lexi squeezes my thigh.

"He's all alone. He's all alone, Lucas. We have to get up there," I hear my mom speaking in the background. Her voice is distant like she's moved away from the phone.

In an instant, my mother is packing their bags and making arrangements with Walker to pick up Callie. The little girl will stay with him for a couple days, while our parents handle things with Jude. My father is telling me that he and mom plan to drive up to Iowa tonight.

"Call me when you guys get there?"

"Of course, son," Dad says, his voice gruffer than usual, and then we end the call.

Later that evening, I'm still sitting in my dark home office. I'm staring at the wall, considering whether to dial Jude's agent again. I know he probably doesn't have another update for me, but I can't help it. Right now, that man is my only bridge to my brother.

Alexia steps into the room, quietly padding over to my desk. She's been my rock tonight, here with me every single step of the way.

She's wearing this silky, little sleep set and I'm immediately distracted in all the best ways. I watch her carefully, assessing every move she makes. Every expression. Every breath she takes. My wife comes behind me, her hands finding my tense shoulders.

I am in love with this woman.

Why did it take so long for me to realize it? One look at her, and it's like I'm waking up from the longest, deepest sleep.

Now, I just wish I knew when it happened. Was it when I was watching her fix that coffee machine at Jittery Joe's? Was it when we were together on the dance floor at the Frosty Pitcher? Or, did I fall in love with her while reciting our vows?

I groan, because her massage feels perfect. Still, that's not exactly what I need right now. I reach up, grabbing her wrist and pulling until she falls sideways into my lap. She lets out a surprised exhale, staring back into my penetrating gaze.

In a way, I feel like I'm looking at her for the very first time. She's not just the feisty, wild-haired bridal attendant who never passes up the chance to fight with me.

No, Lexi is my wife. And I love her.

And I want to show her in ways I can't explain with words.

I rise to my feet, lifting her perfect body along with me. She kisses my face as I walk down the hall, carrying her to our bed. I lay her down on the mattress, eagerly stripping her naked before running my hungry palms all over her skin.

When I crawl over her sprawled form, she whispers my name. That sound is my undoing.

I love her.

But if I say it out loud, she'll protest. She'll remind me that this wasn't part of the deal.

So, I move slow, appreciating every moment. Appreciating every touch. Every shiver. Every moan.

This time, I don't fuck her. This time, I spend the whole night making love to my wife.

46

LEXI

"Okay. Serious question here," I deadpan. "How in the world do you fold a fitted sheet?"

Cannon's mom laughs at me, patting me on the back. "Oh you have come to the right place, dear."

Now, we're in the oversized laundry room at the Kingston's inn, and I'm spending the afternoon with Diana. Cannon, his father, and Walker are off doing boy stuff around the farm while Eli's daughter tags along. Cannon told me last night that his mom has been having a rough time. They only spent a couple days in Iowa, but she's not taking Jude's injury very well.

His surgery was successful, but the outlook is bleak. Jude may never play football again, and the family is all taking it hard. I suggested to Cannon that we come out to the farm today, so I could try to take his mother's mind off things. I'm trying my best, but the poor woman keeps changing the topic back to her son.

"I know he's so fortunate that he'll be able to walk again, but it just tears me up that his life will never be the same. Did you know he started playing when he was four?"

I shake my head. "Wow. So young. Did the others play sports?"

"Oh, here and there. Cannon was more interested in solo sports."

I laugh. "Yep, that sounds like Cannon. He has to be his own boss." The woman laughs along.

I shift my weight around on my feet. What was I thinking wearing heels out there? I should stop trying to impress my fake in-laws and start using common sense. We're working on our second load of laundry. I never realized how much linen you go through when running an inn. This is ridiculous.

Diana notices me shifting about in my shoes. "Those look terribly uncomfortable, dear."

"Pain is part of the game, isn't it?" I wince.

"Kick those suckers off," she prods me, sliding out of her own flats. "If you don't tell, I won't either." The woman grins.

I laugh. "My lips are sealed." I toe out of my shoes, leaving them under our waist-tall work table. Barefoot, we work side-by-side.

Chipped nail polish, don't care.

"How do you get the whites so white?" I've never seen such milk-white sheets.

Diana shows me the special detergent she uses. I'm going to learn so much today. It makes my heart swell. I'm probably annoying Cannon's mother with all the questions, but I never really had this kind of relationship with my own mom. There's not a lot I can say she taught me.

"We need some music," Diana decides, after we work in silence for a few minutes.

"Agreed." I pull up an app on my phone, finding a good, upbeat oldies playlist. The woman comments on each song, tying each back to a happy memory while we dance around the laundry room in between loads.

Things are cheerful for a while, but then a heavy sigh leaves Diana's lips. "I'm so heartbroken for my boy but I'm thankful for your support during these hard times. Cannon always needed a good, strong woman to stabilize him." She smiles. "Don't tell the boys, but Lord, I always wished for a daughter."

And I always wished for a mother.

I laugh lightly. "Your secret is safe with me."

"Cannon is going to owe you a long footrub tonight," she laughs as I wiggle my toes against the tile floor.

I grin. How can I not when she mentions my man? It's already been too many hours since I last saw him. "Y'know what? I think I really like that idea."

Diana sighs contentedly. "He's been so busy since he took over Kingston Realties from his father. I'm glad you two make time for each other."

I'm busy wrestling another fitted sheet into submission and almost miss what Diana is saying. "Wait. Took over what?"

She blinks. "Kingston Realties, of course."

My movements halt and I eyeball my mother-in-law. "He *took over*? When?"

Her brows scrunch with confusion. "It's been a while now, dear. I-I thought he would have told you."

Well, he most certainly did not tell me. I think I would have remembered a conversation like that.

Honey, I'm home. By the way, I own the family company now. I don't need you to be my fake wife anymore.

Okay, great. Where do I sign? Oh, and I burned the meatloaf again, sorry.

Yeah. I think I would have remembered that.

When I don't say anything, she waves her hand dismissively. "Oh, Lucas was the same way. He never liked to bring work home with him. I'm sure Cannon would prefer to skip all that and enjoy the honeymoon phase with his new bride." Her eyes tell me she's not convinced with her reasoning.

I don't understand.

His father signed over Kingston Realty Holdings, and Cannon never told me? We spend all our free time together now. How did that not come up? I feel betrayed, especially since it felt like walls were starting to crumble between us.

But maybe...

Maybe Cannon didn't want to tell me because he knew what that would mean. It would mean the end of our arrangement. It would mean being honest with ourselves about what's *really* going on between us. Maybe Cannon lied just to make our relationship last longer. Without actually hearing those things from him, this is purely wishful thinking on my part.

Right now, I'm so very confused.

Diana takes my hand and gives it a squeeze. "I was never really close with Eli's wife. I knew deep down she wasn't a good woman or mother. But you..." Mrs. Kingston points a smile in my direction. "You're different. You're a good person, Lexi. I can sense these things."

I smile, but it's forced.

Guilt is starting to weigh me down. This woman has fully bought into my relationship with her son. I shouldn't be lying to a sweet lady like Diana. She's exactly the type of mom I wish I had, and here I am, deceiving her.

I'm not a good person, as she suggests. This is not what a good person does.

My stomach is churning, and suddenly I feel short of breath.

I'm not sure if I'm going to puke or cry or pass out. I politely excuse myself, running off in search of the nearest bathroom. I open a narrow door and dart inside, only to find myself in a small broom closet.

Ugh. Just my luck.

I lean on the wooden shelves, bent over, trying to suck in much-needed oxygen. I am such a horrible, shitty person. Tears well up and there's nothing I can do to stop them from falling.

Diana is going to be so devastated when this all blows up. My soul aches because I genuinely care about her. Once Cannon and I are through, I will also lose, not only the man I'm head over heels for, but also this wonderful family. The family I always wanted and never had.

I have no idea how much time has passed, but my ears perk up when I hear Cannon's voice calling my name. Doors are opening and closing nearby, and then, the door to the broom closet opens.

He crouches down to eye level. "Lexi, what in the world? What's wrong? Ma's been looking for you. She's worried." God, of course she is. That poor, sweet woman.

I shake my head.

"Answer me, babe. Are you okay? Why are you so pale?" His brows are pinched, his beautiful face marred with concern. He presses the back of his hand to my forehead. "Why are you hiding in here?"

"I just..." I don't want to add to the burdens he's dealing with. But every day that goes by, I'm getting more and more attached to this fake, temporary life. I'm not being careful at all. I pull him fully into the closet and close the door behind him. "I feel bad about what we're doing."

Cannon flicks on a light switch. "What do you mean?" he asks, his brows low.

My words are quiet and shaky. "I just feel bad about the people who are going to get hurt in all this. Y'know, like your mom. She's so sweet, and she's been working so hard to include me in the family. I feel like I'm betraying her." My voice cracks.

"You're not. This is all on me."

"They trust us, Cannon. Your entire family trusts us. Your mom, your dad, your niece. And we're doing...*this*. It's a mockery of their trust. I mean we are *actually* married. I don't think our lie could get much bigger than that, and here we are keeping up this charade."

He drapes his arms around my waist. "It'll be okay."

Good god, is he delusional? How is this not a big deal? How is he *not* as freaked out as I am? Does he not care about anyone's feelings?

No, I refuse to believe that. I know he cares about his family. It shows in so much that he does, even if he tries to appear stoic and detached. I've been around Cannon enough to know that he's more than just skin deep. Way, way more.

"But this relationship isn't real," I whisper, eyes falling to his chest.

He drops his forehead to mine. "Maybe it is real," he tells me, his voice low and hoarse. "Or maybe it could be. For me, it could be."

I think I stop breathing altogether. My head snaps up to look him in the face.

Did he just say...?

Cannon reads the question in my wide eyes. Slowly, he nods, no hesitation in his words. "I love you, Alexia."

He doesn't give me a second to respond. He moves

quickly as if he's afraid of what I might say. He covers my mouth with a long, deep kiss.

He holds me in his warm, strong arms, easing the fears and anxiety he doesn't even know I have.

I kiss him back, I kiss him back, I kiss him back, my own heart nearly bursting with love.

I think my fake marriage just became real.

47

LEXI

Things are insane at the shop this week. I can hardly catch my breath in between customers. Thankfully, Jessa, Penny and Iris have been taking turns helping me out when their schedules permit. Penny is in the trenches with me today.

I'm literally about to drop when Cannon's mother hustles into the shop right before lunch time. An excited grin breaks out across my face when the bell dings above her head.

"Hello there. Are you here to shop for a wedding gown?" I tease.

"I can do you one better than that. I'm here to help," Diana tells me as she slips out of her cardigan. "If you need a hand, of course."

The offer catches me by surprise but I'm not about to turn it down, especially during this rush. "Absolutely. I'd love that." I step away from the woman I'm assisting to give my mother-in-law a quick hug and hang her sweater over the back of my chair.

Diana tells me to put her to work and I pair her up with a rosy twenty-something who has no idea what she'd like. "Oh, how do I decide?" the girl groans. "You have so many beautiful gowns in here. And so much other stuff, too. Headpieces, hair clips. Maybe you can help with that, too?"

Cannon's mother drapes a comforting arm around the flustered woman. "Don't worry, dear. I've got you covered." She throws me a wink over the customer's shoulder and I grin.

Penny and Diana flit around the shop, grabbing different options for their brides. I'm busy boxing up some jewelry and accessories for the customer at the cash register but I'm smiling because I've always dreamed that business could be this busy. It's fulfilling. And so much of this success is due to the handsome jerk who coerced me into marrying him.

Never in a million years did I think I'd end up in love with this man, *happy* with this man. Things have unfolded in a way I could not have foreseen. We're good together. We make each other better.

He's changed in so many wonderful ways. He's more focused on his family and the important relationships in his life. Seeing him care for his parents, play with his niece and joke around with his brothers has split my heart wide open for the man. He's even taken me along to visit his grandfather a few times over the past few weeks. He's brought me right into his world.

Cannon's love has changed me, too. I've let my guard down. It's a relief not having to constantly lug that hard persona around all the time. With him, I can be vulnerable and open. And he's teaching me so much about running my business and I'm seeing the results in my bank balance each week. Plus, he doesn't complain too much when I drag him to the Frosty Pitcher on the weekend to hang out with my girlfriends.

I just can't list all the ways this man has made me happy. And I spend all my time dreaming up ways to return the favor.

As if summoned by my hopeful thoughts, a white Tesla pulls up behind the BMW right in front of the bridal shop.

My body responds viscerally to the man. Instantly, I want to go to him.

Before I can get my over-excited hormones under control, a beat-up truck overflowing with junk swerves recklessly toward the curb right behind my husband's sleek sportscar. The driver tries to squeeze the vehicle into a parking space that's obviously too small. My gaze settles on the weathered face of the man gripping the wheel. I'd know that red baseball cap and those jean overalls anywhere.

My skin tightens defensively. *Oh no.*

I watch in horror as the nose of the old rust-bucket plows into the tail end of Cannon's pristine, white sportscar.

Oh no, times two.

Cannon jumps out of his car with a bouquet of yellow tulips in hand. He flings those suckers to the ground and stalks toward the skinny, graying driver who's slowly clambering onto the sidewalk.

This is about to get nasty.

If I could fit, I'd crawl right into this cardboard box and ship myself to Canada. But if I have any hope of preventing the bloodbath that's about to go down, I have to intervene. Now.

"E-excuse me," I tell my customers as I quickly circle the cash register and head for the door.

I burst onto the sidewalk just in time to hear Cannon yell. "You rear-ended my damn car, man!"

The old man parks both fists on his hips with an easygoing smile on his face. "It'll be fine, pretty boy. It's a simple fix. We can tow it to my workshop and, in an hour or two, it'll be good as new." He leans closer to inspect the damage.

"You won't lay a finger on my car." Cannon stands protectively in front of the vehicle. He takes a glimpse at the old truck. "Y'know, there's a by-law limiting the amount of junk you can haul around in this town. If you can't follow the fucking rules, maybe you should drive back into the hole in the ground you crawled out of, you piece of shit!"

My husband's harsh words are a slug to the gut.

Hot, electric thorns of rage needle the back of my neck. "Why don't you tell the old man how you *really* feel, King?" I spit out sarcastically, my voice rough with anger.

Both men swing their heads to me.

Cannon grinds his teeth. "Go back inside, Alexia. Now. I've got this taken care of."

Of all the times for him to be a chauvinistic pig, now is *not* it.

He stomps a step closer to the old man who bravely squares his body like he's ready to scrap.

Are you fucking kidding me right now?

I shoulder my way between the two neanderthals and plant a firm palm into the middle of my husband's strong chest. "Back the fuck up, Kingston..." I narrow my fiery gaze on his face. "This is my *dad*."

His eyes volley between my father and me. I can feel my shop full of customers doing the same.

Bubbling feelings of inferiority surge up from my cellular memory. I get flashbacks of being shunned by those rich kids from private school, of seeing that foreclosure notice on our gaudy, over-the-top mansion in the hills, of having to pack up, tuck tail and move back to the trailer park.

It's been a long damn time since I've felt this humiliated. I'm Cinderella and my carriage just turned into a pumpkin right here on the sidewalk.

I spin to my father. His clothes are filthy, his hair is greasy and his truck is a rust bucket loaded with crap. It takes me back. Too far back to times I'd rather forget.

Lowering my voice, I speak to him with rounded shoulders as if that will give us a shred of privacy. "Daddy, I can't give you any money. The shop almost went bankrupt. I'm *just* starting to get back on my feet." I soften the bite in my voice. "I can't help you..."

His graying brows dip, matching the tired lines of his mouth. My dad shakes his head ruefully before eyeing the passersby who have slowed to witness the drama.

"I didn't come here to take anything from you, Lex," he says quietly and dips a hand into his pocket. "You told me you were struggling and I just sold a couple of old washing machines that I fixed up. I came by to repay some of the money I've borrowed over the past year." He tucks a wad of crumpled bills into my hand.

Head hung and shoulders caved in, he shuffles back to his truck. From behind the wheel, his gaze bounces from me to my stunned husband and back again. He shakes his head in disappointment and drives away, leaving me to drown in an ocean of shame.

My own hypocrisy strikes me in the face. I give Cannon a hard time for having a superiority complex. But I'm no better. I'm ashamed of where I come from. I got tied up in the Kingston's shiny world and forgot about my roots. And worst of all, I just betrayed my own father, acting like I'm somehow better than the people who raised me.

My dad didn't embarrass me.

I did that all by myself.

48

CANNON

She stands on the sidewalk, her babydoll eyes on the rusty truck as it bumps off down the road.

"Lexi, I—I had no idea that was your dad." I cup her shoulders and let my fingers slide down to link with hers.

She drops her head and wiggles her hands out of my grasp. "I have to...I have to go after him."

I lay a palm on the small of her back an guide her toward my car. "Get in. I'll drive."

When I glance toward the boutique window, I see my mom and Penny standing there. Ma nods, silently telling me to go take care of my wife, she's got the shop under control.

Opening the passenger side door, I usher Alexia inside. She looks broken right now, sitting stone still in the seat next to me.

When I reach over and rest my hand on her thigh, she doesn't respond. I squeeze, offering her a thread of assurance. "I'm sorry..." I whisper. "I had no way of knowing..."

She shakes her head slightly. "Yeah, well...your be-an-asshole-first-and-ask-questions later policy was bound to bite you in the ass someday."

Ouch! I deserved that.

She stays silent but as we draw closer to Lexi's hometown, I ask for the address to plug into my GPS.

She shakes her head. "GPS won't take you there." Instead she gives me play-by-play directions, leading me straight into the jaws of hell.

Each turn takes us down a street in worse shape than the previous. Houses are missing roofs. There are '4 sale' signs spray-painted on the sides of a couple homes. I see barbed wire. Boarded-up windows. Hungry dogs rummaging through trash on the side of the street.

This is not the safest neighborhood.

"Turn here." Alexia's voice is scratchy.

I pull into a crumbling trailer park and drive across a bumpy dirt path until I spot the rusty truck from earlier. She opens her door and tells me to stay put, but no fucking way. "I'm coming with you," I declare as I step out of the vehicle. This looks like the kind of place where she'd get mugged before she can even get across the yard.

She huffs. "Walk away from this sportscar and your rims will be gone before we make it up the front stairs."

I grab her wrist. "Zero fucks to give about the sportscar, Alexia."

"Please. This is embarrassing enough. I just need a minute to talk to my parents alone. Please?"

I pinch the bridge of my nose. I lean against the car. "I'm waiting right here."

Lexi's already climbing some rickety steps and banging on the door with her tiny fist. I'm on edge but she moves with confidence. Like she knows how to take care of herself here. Still, I don't like it. I'm not taking my eyes off that trailer until she comes back to me in one piece.

Her father joins her on the built-on porch. A tiny, wild-haired woman comes out after him, in a sequined mini-dress, bare feet on the wooden stairs and a cigarette pinched between her brightly-polished mauve lips. She's got big hair and frosty blue eye shadow all the way up to her penciled-in eyebrows.

One glare from the little woman and instantly, I know she's Lexi's mom. Also, I know exactly where my wife got her crazy hair and her saucy attitude from.

Arms folded tight across my chest, I watch from a distance. I can't make out what's being said but based on Alexia's body language, I assume she's apologizing to her father, making sure he's okay.

Look at the mess I've made. *Fuck, I'm such an asshole.* I wish I hadn't blown up on the man like that. At this point, the dent in my ride seems inconsequential.

I glance around and see two pale, shirtless teenagers with tattoo sleeves eyeing my car. Those scrawny cocksuckers look sketchy-as-fuck, but I'm way too pissed at this situation to be intimidated.

I casually roll my sleeves up to my elbows, revealing some tattoos of my own, and make eye contact. I have five years of jiu jitsu training under my belt and if those asshole kids come closer, I'm liable to put those martial arts classes to use. I stare them down until they move far enough away that I can breathe.

Christ. How did Alexia grow up in this shithole? I struggle even imagining her here. Suddenly, all of the rough, beautiful pieces of her personality seem to fit. Of course she'd need a spine of steel to survive in a place like this.

I watch as she and her father share a tight embrace. Fuck—I'm still beating myself up for the way I treated the man. I don't know a thing about him—except that he's a damn shitty driver—but if Alexia gets even a shred of her decency from him, then I have to think he's an all right human being.

She and her parents walk down the path in my direction. I straighten my posture.

Stormy digs the toe of her shoe into the dirt. "Mom, Dad, this is Cannon, my...my husband."

Jesus, who the hell meets their parents-in-law like this? I know the beginning of our relationship was far from conventional, but boy, my wife and I certainly deserve some sort of Nobel prize for fucked-up-ness.

"Great to meet you, Mr. Robson, Mrs. Robson."

"Hmm," the woman huffs out.

She gives me a bored expression when I offer her my hand. Instead, she looks me up and down. She focuses on my clothes, my shoes, my face, her blue eyes full of disdain, like none of what I have to offer her daughter is good enough.

Right about now, I'm tempted to agree with her assessment. After the way I acted, I feel an inch tall.

Alexia's mom wanders off, circling my car.

When she's finished with her assessment, she plants a hand on her hip, waves over her shoulder and sashays back toward her mobile home. "I guess I see why I didn't get an invite to the wedding, Mr. and Mrs. Rich Stuff. Good thing I wasn't holding my breath."

I turn my attention to my new father-in-law. "I'm very sorry about how we met and what I said." Heat climbs my tight throat. "I apologize for disrespecting you, Mr. Robson."

He heaves a breath, not bothering to accept or reject my

apology outright. "Son, you may have a 'bankful' of money but what does it matter if you make the woman who loves you feel like trash? The way you've made my baby girl feel?"

My eyes sweep momentarily to Alexia and the pain on her face makes me chafe. *Dammit.*

I shouldn't have let my temper get the better of me back there. I just never thought I'd be going head-to-head with my in-laws like an idiot. And this shame I feel is not a feeling I can buy my way out of.

My fingers cup the back of my neck. "I...I..." I stare at the man, completely at a loss for how to fix this.

"We should get going." Lexi breaks the staredown, moving back toward the passenger side of the car.

Her father walks her to her door. He presses a kiss to the top of her scalp. "Don't be a stranger," he tells her.

"I...I love you, dad." She hugs the man again.

His smile is crooked and cigarette-stained but genuine as hell. "I love you, too, baby girl." He hands me his wrinkled business card. "Sorry about your car. Here's my number if you want to take me up on that offer to fix it."

Then he limps off toward the cluttered workshop beside his mobile home.

49

CANNON

Once we're both inside, I start the car, making sure to lock the doors. We pull out of the trailer park, back onto the main road. Miles pass by. Lexi stares out the window in silence.

Something itchy crawls beneath my skin. I fucked up and I want to fix it.

"I'm sorry," I say again, watching her face to try and gauge what she's feeling.

"Yeah..." She bites on the nail of her thumb.

My anger mounts with each silent mile of highway we cruise along. The silence is excruciating. I'm uncomfortable. My own skin doesn't seem to fit right.

She continues to chew on her nail and I can tell she's sifting through painful memories. I want to help her but how am I supposed to do that when she won't let me in?

"Talk to me, Alexia." There's a domineering edge to my voice.

A full minute passes before she says, "Can you drop me off at *my* place, please?"

"Alexia, I fucked up. I get it. But I'm try—"

She cuts me off. "*Please...*" Her watery eyes tell me she doesn't have the energy to fight.

My throat is tight and hard like concrete. I can't push an answer through. Lexi doesn't speak, either.

Not until we enter Crescent Harbor and I take a left on Elgin, heading to my house, instead of the right turn that would take us toward hers.

"Cannon—I said to take me home!" She repeats in a low, firm voice. "Take. Me. Home."

I ignore her searing glare on my face and I keep on driving toward my house. *Our* house. Because she's my wife and we belong together and I'm not letting her stubborn ass walk away from me just because I made a stupid mistake.

She huffs through her nose. "Abduction? That's what you're going with? Should have known you weren't above that."

"You're my wife. We have a home together. That's where we're going." I know I sound like a crabby child but I don't give a damn.

"Cannon..." She growls my name. The uncompromising determination on her beautiful face makes me pause.

And then, without warning, I swerve.

My tires screech as I clip across the left lane and grind to a rough stop on the shoulder of the road. She braces her palms against the glove box and yelps.

"So, what? You're just *done* with me? Just like that? We're not going to have a conversation about this?" I hate the desperation in my voice.

"What's there to talk about? You're the owner of Kingston Realties now. That was your whole objective in the first place, the whole reason we got married. You got what you wanted. You don't need me anymore."

That's where she's fucking wrong. I need her more than

anything.

My fingers cup the back of her skull, tangling in her disastrous hair. My thumb slowly strokes the line of her cheekbone, brushing aside the tears that come pouring down her face.

"So you're telling me you're just walking away?" I can feel my panic rising with each word. This woman has carved out a place for herself in my life and at this point, I can't imagine going back to a world without her.

"What I'm telling you is I can't spend my life with a man who looks at me like something he rescued out of the gutter. I can't go on living in the fear that you could dispose of me at any moment. I can't be with a man who's only tolerating me out of the kindness of his heart. Because I've never felt like your equal and I don't want to feel like I'm at the mercy of the man I love."

She loves me.

I know she loves me.

But she doesn't *want* to.

She doesn't say it like it's something worth celebrating. She says it like her feelings for me are a problem urgently in need of fixing. And that fucking hurts.

"You? At *my* mercy?" I question bitterly. "I think it's the other way around, Stormy. I'm all in for you. I'm all the way committed. I'd do anything for you. And I know you love me, too. But you've been looking for a way to run from your feelings from the very beginning."

She recoils from me as if my words are radioactive. "We weren't supposed to fall in love."

"Well, newsflash—we did. So now what? Are you gonna walk away like a coward or are we gonna step up and do this thing?"

She takes a quiet moment and twists her fingers in her

lap. Heart suspended between beats, I wait for her next words. It feels like *everything* depends on her next words.

"I love you, Cannon, but I'm tired of feeling like I don't measure up. I feel inferior when I'm with you. I can't live my life like that. That's why I can't be with you."

I wince.

The sky darkens above us. Blinding headlights pour into the cabin of the car each time a vehicle passes by.

She lowers her voice and her eyes grow softer. "I'm powerless. I'm a junk yard princess and you're a king." She sucks in a breath. "Now, our arrangement is over. You can go back to your billion-dollar empire and I'll crawl back into the hole I crawled out of. Just like my parents."

This conversation is frustrating as hell. "You're twisting my fucking words, Alexia. Stop playing games."

She drops her head, defeated. "Just...just take me home."

"Fine. If this is how you want it..."

My tires scream when I make a quick U-turn on the quiet road, heading back for her house. If this is what she wants, I won't keep beating this dead horse into the ground.

When I park my car outside of Alexia's house, I feel like I'm coming out of my fucking skin. She sits next to me wordlessly, staring out into the dark night.

She doesn't look up when she speaks. "Your mom saw you arguing with my father outside of the boutique. She saw me intervene. Tell her we couldn't patch things up. You couldn't get me to listen to you and that's why we broke up. She'd find that believable. Blame it all on me."

I have to close my eyes for a second. "Shit. Here I am, hanging onto the hope that you'll change your mind and give us a chance. Meanwhile, you've got your exit strategy all mapped out."

She rears back with tears heavy on her lower lids. "This

is our way out of this fake relationship, Cannon."

"Except there's nothing fake about this relationship anymore and you know it."

She pulls on her messy hair. Frustration bleeds out in her words. "Why won't you just leave me alone? Why won't you just give up on me? What do you want from me?"

My lips hover recklessly close to hers. The words coming out of my mouth are words I've never uttered before. "Everything. I want *everything* with you, Alexia. I want a family. I want a future. I want forever."

Lexi's palm clasps over her mouth to hold back a sob. But she doesn't answer me. She doesn't tell me she wants all the things I want.

My stubborn pride kicks in. Stormy and I have a good thing going. She's the one walking away. All because I made a stupid mistake. Why am I the one groveling? Fuck this shit.

I'm done. I'm done trying to force her to love me because obviously we're not on the same page.

I lean across the middle console and shove her door open. If she wants to leave, I won't be the one holding her back.

She gives me a pained look through tired eyes. Under the spotlight of that glare, I feel like the world's biggest asshole.

But I'm done caring, done needing, done loving her.

Reverently, she sets her diamond ring on the dashboard. She walks up the path and disappears inside her house. I drive away with a giant pothole in my chest. Right where my heart used to be.

50

LEXI

Iris comes through the back door with a basket of freshly-picked sweet peppers. She pulls off her gardening gloves and dumps her mini harvest under the running water in the sink.

"You feel like leftover pasta tonight, Lex?" She throws me a concerned look from over by her fridge.

My shoulder pops up before it falls in defeat. "Sure," I croak out and pull the quilt up to my chin. I really don't care what I eat. I've lost track of how many hours I've been stretched out on this couch, stomach tense, heart sore. The same thoughts on repeat in my brain.

I shut him down, I pushed him away.

That's the last thing I want.

What I want more than anything is to be with him. I want to see him. I want to hear him. I want to smell him. Taste him. Touch him. Drown my five senses in the ocean of Cannon Kingston.

But I'd just cause myself more pain.

He and I are two mismatched shards of broken glass, trying to join together. We just don't fit.

It's time we both move on.

A long beep fills the room, alerting us that my spaghetti is sufficiently nuked. Iris brings the steaming bowl across the room and sets it on her coffee table in front of me. "How ya feeling?" she asks softly, brushing back the hair curtaining my eyes.

I purse my lips and exhale hard. "Pretty fucking crap."

It's been a week since I walked away from Cannon. A week of sleeping alone without his breath fluttering against my neck. A week of stealing glances of him from my boutique's front window as he comes and goes in the Kingston Realties building across the street. A week of missing him. And it hasn't been getting easier as the days tick by. The pain is still like razors stabbing at my soul.

Empathy fills my friend's expression. "Been there. I know it sucks, hun."

Ironic that, not too long ago, I was the one helping her mend her broken heart. Now, it's my turn.

Iris hesitates to ask. "Do you...do you love him?"

Dropping my head, I nod. I can't look her in the face when I answer. Because she warned me. She told me I'd end up crushed under a wall of hurt if I wasn't careful letting Cannon Kingston around my heart.

I didn't listen.

Look at me now.

Iris taps me on the nose, pulling me from my thoughts. "Hey," she whispers.

When I look up at her face, there's no judgment there. Only kindness, only compassion.

"Okay, the first step is admitting it. You love him. Now, what are you going to do about it?"

My eyelashes flutter, teardrops weighing them down. I

answer honestly. "I'm gonna suck it up. I'm gonna get over it. Like I've had to get over everything I've lost all my life."

Yes, I love him. I love him so much that I don't know if I'll ever make it to the other side of this pain.

But love isn't enough. Because I've always been at this man's mercy.

When he demanded that I marry him to avoid eviction.

When I walked up to moving vans outside my boutique, knowing that only he had the power to reverse their orders.

When he disrespected my father and made me feel three inches tall.

We've never been on equal footing and a relationship built on a lopsided foundation is bound to crack and crumble.

I lie on the couch barely able to move a limb. Every part of me wants to pick up the phone and call Cannon and ask if he still loves me because I'm definitely in love with him.

My good sense stops me. Barely.

Cannon and I come from very different worlds. We'd never work out and there's no point in continuing to delude ourselves and the people around us.

Iris squeezes my shoulder, a show of solidarity. "You know I've got your back, right? No matter what you decide to do?"

I bob my head against the couch cushions.

"Good." She smiles.

She leans down and pops a kiss against my forehead before heading off to put her own meal into the microwave.

51

CANNON

I promised myself I wouldn't call Alexia. That I wouldn't show up at her house, pound down her door and force her to work things out with me. That I'd just let her be.

Because she made her decision. Being afraid is more convenient to her than giving me the chance to fix the mess that I made.

But as the days wear on, I'm devolving into a state of angst that's more than a little alarming.

I can't eat. I can't sleep. I think of her every minute of every fucking day.

So, here I am at the Frosty Pitcher on Saturday night, tucked into that same booth at the back, hoping to get a glimpse of her.

This is pathetic.

Music pounds in my brain. The mass of bodies on the dancefloor blurs my vision. I'm three whiskeys deep when the front door opens. Iris and Jessa step inside, dragging a reluctant-looking Alexia along with them. I clench my whiskey glass to ground myself as I watch her shuffle across the room. When the girls approach the bar, Penny slides them a round of drinks.

Alexia's friends spend the night trying to perk her up. But Stormy sits there looking glum, a shadow of the spunky, effervescent woman I love. I think I'd feel better if I saw her dancing, if I saw her on a tabletop, grinning and moving and commanding the attention of the room. At least then I'd know that letting her go made her happy. But instead, she looks broken tonight and it's killing me to know that that's my fault.

Long moments pass until I just can't stand it anymore. My feet are far from steady as I lift out of my seat and move through the crowd in her direction. I need to talk to her. I've had too much to drink and I'm thirty seconds away from making an ass of myself. Not that I care.

...Until she turns in my direction.

As if she can sense me, she looks up and spots me coming across the bustling room.

We stare at each other.

I take in every inch of her beautiful face. Her watery babydoll eyes are hollow blue puddles. Her cherry red lips tremble with restrained words. She rises from her barstool.

She's about to come to me. Meet me halfway. At least that's what I'm hoping. But she grabs her purse and turns on her heel.

I stand there staring at the back of her head as she hustles out the door.

Fuck.

Iris is on the periphery, observing the whole interaction. Her stare meets mine. But instead of the distrustful gaze she usually reserves for me, I see compassion there. I must be in worse shape than I thought if Stormy's best friend is offering me pity instead of kicking my ass like she once threatened to.

Lugging my damaged pride, I head back to my table in the corner. I've never been this torn up over a woman. I've never found myself pining over someone who didn't want me back. I've never chased. I've never begged. I don't recognize the pathetic thing I've become.

But then again, I've never been in love. With a woman like Alexia Robson.

Grit and Grace.

A woman with a heart of gold and a spine of steel.

I take another sip of my whiskey, determined to wrangle the ailing beast in my chest and drown it in a sea of booze. A shadow stretches across my table and I look up to find Iris standing there, giving me that same pitying look.

"You mind if I sit?" She motions her cocktail glass to the empty leather bench beside me.

I give her a fleeting glance and bob my head in confirmation.

She slides into the seat. "Look—I'm gonna cut right to the point. I've had a not so favorable opinion of you all these years..."

My face snaps over to her. I narrow my eyes.

She continues. "And when you came back to town and cornered Lexi with your marriage proposal, I definitely wasn't a fan of the idea." She takes a breath. "But I've watched you two together. I've seen what you two have done for each other, what you've done for the town of Crescent Harbor...You're good together."

I shake my head at the ice cubes in my tumbler. "She doesn't want to be with me. That's her decision."

Iris sighs. "Lexi comes across as this tough badass—and she is—but she's also afraid."

"What the hell is she so afraid of?" I quip. "I've given that woman everything. I've opened myself up to her. I've included her in my family."

"And you also threatened her livelihood, coerced her into marrying you, treated her dad like crap—"

"That last one was an accident!" I vigorously defend the shards of honor I have left.

Iris speaks compassionately but steadily. "That's not the point, Cannon. You've always used your stacks of money as this pedestal you stand on top of, making yourself bigger than everybody else, getting the whole world to bend to your will. Alexia thinks she doesn't measure up. She thinks you look down on people like her, like us." She takes a breath. "If you love her—which I believe that you do—if you want her, it's time for you to get down from your high horse and show her she's your queen."

With that, Iris gracefully rises from the table and melts into the dancing crowd.

52

CANNON

This morning, I got to my office before the crack of dawn. I kept working through lunch. Didn't leave my desk until long after dark.

Had to keep myself busy somehow.

For the past thirty-six minutes, I've been sitting here in my driveway. Looking up at my mansion through the wet swish-swish of my windshield wipers. I can't bring myself to go inside.

That woman ruined this house for me.

My fucking sheets smell like grapefruit juice. Her coffee rings stain the expensive wood tables in the living room. Her laughter echoes in the long, empty hallways. Her fingerprints smudge every inch of the furniture, every inch of my heart.

She turned my house into a mess...

She also made it into a *home*.

She took it from being an expensive pile of glass and bricks and she filled it with color and joy and laughter. And that's the hardest part to admit now that she's gone.

Fuck, I miss that girl. I want to forget her. I want to hate her.

But I know it's not that simple. I know these feelings aren't disposable. I can't throw them away. Although, for some reason, she seems to think I can.

This is love, dammit. There's no 'off' button, no dimmer switch. Unless Lexi discovered one and she's hoarding that information for herself. Maybe that explains why it was so easy for her to walk away.

Iris's words of advice replay in my head. But stubbornly, I try to push them down. I won't chase Alexia down. I won't grovel. I'm holding onto my damn pride...even though I'd rather be holding my wife instead.

My phone rings in my cupholder. Lethargically, I swipe it into my hand. It's my lawyer.

"Frank, what's going on?" My head drops against the back of my seat like a cement block.

There's a hint of hesitation in his voice. "I got your message. The one requesting divorce papers? You're ready to end your marriage?"

I nod into the darkness. "How long till you can get those to me?" Time to rip off the damn bandage. Alexia has decided that she's done with this. No point in dragging it on.

The lawyer clears his throat awkwardly. "I'm emailing them to you now."

That announcement is another kick to the gut. It brings me one step closer to severing ties with the only woman I've ever loved.

His tone switches slightly, subtly becoming more upbeat as if he's trying to cheer me up. "And I finally have some good news for you."

That should get me excited but it doesn't. Because unless Frank is about to tell me he's found some obscure constitutional amendment or a new municipal by-law to force Lexi into loving me, I don't really care. Her love is the only thing I really want.

He keeps yammering. "My office is still working on putting together an appeal in Eli's case but I think we're making headway on getting him home."

I try to muster up some excitement at the prospect of my brother getting out of jail but I can barely manage two unenthusiastic words. "All right."

Frank continues. "On another note, I caught wind that there's a competitor organizing a hostile takeover of DataCo."

I furrow my brows. "Isn't that *bad* news?"

For a company like DataCo, a hostile takeover is a nightmare because it means that some third-party is trying to edge out the current board of directors and replace it completely. I don't understand why Frank would be excited about that.

"The acquirer is eyeing DataCo for mismanagement and I can't blame them. You've been in Crescent Harbor for how long now? And Carl is useless. There isn't exactly anybody steering the ship. Anyway, I was able to intercept the plan and I struck a deal with the other company."

"What kind of deal?"

"You want Carl out of DataCo? Well, this is your chance to kick him to the curb. Legally. The potential acquirer has given me written assurances that you'll retain your CEO position in exchange for your support at the shareholder vote. Carl will get the boot and you can replace him with someone who has half a brain. I'll need you back in New York to finalize the paperwork."

I respond with a drawn out silence. I know this is

supposed to be good news but I just can't bring myself to give a fuck.

"Cannon, this is what you wanted, what you've been trying to accomplish for months." The lawyer's disappointment at my lackluster response is evident.

Can I just up and leave? I'm married. I have a wife here in Crescent Harbor.

A wife who doesn't want me.

Fuck it.

I'm a miserable shit. I can't be with the woman I love. I might as well go back to New York and watch Carl suffer to keep myself entertained.

I start my engine and cut a u-turn clear across my manicured lawn.

"Get the documents ready, Frank. I'm on my way back to New York. I'll see you in the morning."

53

LEXI

It's hours after closing time. I'm perched on a stool behind the counter, distractedly tightening a loose button on a delicate satin slip dress I received in stock today.

No point in going home. As exhausted as I am, I haven't slept in days, anyway.

I set down the dress and swipe the screen of my phone to check the time. It's getting late.

As hard as I try, I can't stop myself from opening my photo gallery. I find myself scrolling through pictures of Cannon and me.

There we are. A goofy selfie from the night of our *Pride and Prejudice* movie date. A blurry image of us making funny faces with Callie when we babysat her. A picture of us slow dancing at our wedding reception. Jessa snapped that one. That's the one that gets me every time. Because the way we're looking at each other in that photo, no one would ever guess it was fake.

Maybe it never was.

God, did I make a mistake turning him down? Will I

spend the rest of my life regretting that I walked away from him?

I hate every second I spend moping. I don't have the time to sit around feeling sorry for myself. I have other things in my life to deal with.

I'm keeping my calendar packed to distract myself. I signed the boutique up for a bridal show in Chicago. A newspaper from a nearby town is coming to interview me in a few days. I'm actively trying to mend my relationship with my parents. They're visiting Jessa and me in a few days and I'm already bracing myself for the shitshow that might turn into.

I don't have the time to sit around being love sick. But I don't have the energy to be strong.

There's a knock at the door. I look up and my belly flips.

It's Diana standing there, lit up by the bulbs above the entrance.

Shit. I should have contacted her. After treating me with so much kindness, she deserved that much. I just didn't know what to say. Avoiding the conversation was a coward move, but it seemed easier than looking her in the eyes after what her son and I have done.

Gingerly, I rise from my seat. My gait is shaky as I move toward the door.

She looks hesitant too when I pull the door open.

"Hi..." She clasps her hands in front of her.

I wrap my arms around my middle to hold myself together. "Hi..."

She angles her head. "Do you have a minute to talk, dear?" She steals a glance over my shoulder.

Stepping out of the way, I sweep an arm through the air, welcoming her inside. "Sure."

She sets her purse on the counter. She looks so sad. I

hate how much I've disappointed her. "How are you doing?" I ask as I go back and slouch against the cash register.

"I'm fine," she says softly. She sets a hand on mine and looks me in the eye. "How are *you*?"

I could tell her I'm doing great but I've already told her enough lies. I decide to be honest instead. "I'm trying not to fall apart." I already feel the tears. They're getting ready to come down my cheeks.

Her gaze drops to the gown I'm mending as if she can't stand to maintain eye contact. She runs a finger along the beading.

"I sent your wedding gown off to be professionally cleaned," I tell her. "I haven't gotten it back yet but I'll let you know as soon as I do...It's the least I can do with everything that's happened."

The woman's eyes bounce to mine. "It's *your* dress, Alexia."

Ruefully, I shake my head. "I can't accept it, Diana. After the way things turned out...Maybe Jude or Walker will get married. They'll have a lovely bride and she'll be amazing and you'll get your wish to have a real daughter-in-law." *Not a fraud like me.*

It's not fair that I deprive her of the chance to gift the wedding dress to someone who deserves it more than I ever did.

Diana's shoulders heave when she exhales. She pins me with a no-nonesense look. I've never seen this side of her. "I won't beat around the bushes anymore, okay?" My spine straightens. "I wasn't born yesterday, Alexia."

"Wh-what do you mean?" My insides blister with guilt. Her crystal-blue stare feels like a spotlight on my ugly sins.

"It was awfully convenient that Cannon suddenly had a fiancée the minute his father announced he was selling the realty company. Especially since he'd dated Margot for years and never considered marriage."

My eyes widen. She knew? All along?

She drops her head and shakes it. "I know how my son is when he wants something. He pulls out all the stops. I'd never put a fake relationship past him. But I'm a sucker for a good love story. And the second Cannon walked you through my front door, I knew I was looking at a *great* love story. You couldn't see it, he couldn't see it, but I could. The way he looked at you. The way you blushed when he put an arm around your shoulder." She smiles. "And as time wore on, Cannon softened. My hard, stubborn, brutish boy softened for you, Alexia. Yes, he's a successful businessman, a powerful corporate tycoon. But your love made him into a *man*."

My tears are falling now and no amount of tissues can hold them back.

Diana grips my hand. "He's so much like his father. Lucas was the same way—hard, arrogant, ruthless—but our love was instant. We fell for each other in a heartbeat. I didn't want to deny Cannon that kind of love and I knew you'd be the woman to give it to him." She squeezes my fingers. "You are that love for him, Alexia. That in-a-heartbeat kind of love."

I'm an emotional wreck right now. After Cannon and I made a mockery of the institution of marriage and betrayed his family's trust, how can his mother still believe in us?

"I feel so shitty about what we did, Diana. Mr. Kingston only gave Cannon the business on the promise that he and I would have a future together. We broke that promise. We shattered it to bits. That feels wrong."

"Forget about the business. Forget about who'll be mad for what. If you love my son as much as he obviously loves you, it would be wrong to let this marriage go without a fight."

I drop my head and shake it. "It's a fight we can't win. We don't come from the same world."

Diana sighs. "I know you look at Kingston Realties today and all you see is its success but when Lucas met me, my father's company was in the ditch. He was a gorgeous, successful, fabulously wealthy man and I was struggling to run a crumbling business while my father drowned in depression and booze. I thought Lucas was way out of my league. We didn't come from the same world, either. But our love was so strong, there was no walking away from it." She smiles. "So you know what we did?

I stare at her hopefully, hanging on to her every word. "What did you do?"

She leans in like she's telling me a secret. "We built *our own* world. And we built it on a foundation of honesty. And we populated it with four beautiful babies. And we watered the gardens with love. And thirty-six years later, we have a *fucking* empire, Lexi...So, it doesn't matter what world you come from. It matters what world you'll build together."

At this point, I'm a sobbing mess. The woman's words strike so deep. "I was terrible to him," I mumble through the wad of Kleenex covering my mouth. "Do you think he'll forgive me?"

"Honestly, I don't know, dear," the woman says. "My Cannon is a stubborn man. But I *do* know that if I were you, I'd take the risk anyway. 'Cause that's the only way to find out."

She comes around the counter and gives me a tight hug. I whimper against her shoulder then I watch after her as she walks out the door.

With deep, long breaths, I pull myself together. I brush

my hair and wipe my tear-streaked face. "No more excuses, Lexi," I tell my reflection in the mirror. "It's time to go get your man."

Diana's words play again and again in my head as I make my way to Cannon's house.

It doesn't matter what world you come from. It matters what world you'll build together.

Cannon and I could build something beautiful together. How did I not see that before?

My calls go straight to voicemail over and over again. No answer. But when I get to his house, my passcode still works so I let myself in. I search every room. But he's not here.

I need to talk to him—tonight—so I wait. I spend the whole night waiting.

And in the morning, my raw heart seizes when I wake up all alone in his bed.

54

LEXI

Looks like I've officially begun hallucinating.

I swear, I heard him whisper my name in the middle of the night. I thought I felt his body next to me when I rolled over in his bed this morning.

And when I push open the door to Renewed Gowns at seven-thirty, I catch the scent of his musky cologne.

I freeze in the middle of the shop and close my eyes. I suck the scent deep into my lungs, taking the time to absorb it, to bathe in it. Tears leak from the corners of my eyes.

Stop deluding yourself, girl. He's gone. This really is over.

I pad over to the front desk to grab a tissue. That's when I see it. The stack of papers sitting right next to the cash register.

Dissolution papers. A simple note attached to it with a silver paper clip.

My fingers brush across the thick, ivory-toned stationery with Cannon's letterhead embossed at the top.

Got called back to New York for business. Have these papers signed and couriered to my lawyer's office.

- C

Cold. Formal. Detached.

Dissolution papers.

My husband is dissolving our marriage.

He's done fighting to save our relationship.

My heart collapses into the pool of disappointment in my gut.

I don't have the right to complain. Or to cry. I'm the one who pushed him away. He tried to work things out and I'm the one who said 'no'. I don't get to play the victim card now.

So I suck it up. I try to go about with my day. I try to serve customers and order inventory and do it all with a smile even as my heart rips at the stitches inside my chest.

By lunchtime, the lie presses heavily against my ribs. I need a few minutes alone to get myself together. I usher my final smiling customer to the door. I click the lock shut and flip the sign to the 'CLOSED' side. I pull off my annoying earrings and kick my shoes off my achy feet.

I'm trying to be strong here. I'm trying to act like none of this ever meant anything. It's time for me to just move on with my life. Because this is what we agreed to from the get-go. He fulfilled all of his promises and I fulfilled mine.

I helped him convince his father to hand over the family business. He gave my friends their shops back. He hired the best construction company around to renovate the buildings. We each got what we bargained for.

I stare down at his note again.

Got called back to New York for business. Have these papers signed and couriered to my lawyer's office.

- C

It feels unfair. Everything that we went through together, it all boils down to this? A two line note?

Ugh, fuck this!

I crumple up the sheet of paper because it's just too

painful to deal with. But as I'm about to toss it into the trash beneath my counter, I notice a big wad of the identical ivory paper stock with Cannon's letterhead lying at the bottom of my waste basket.

Heart in my throat, I reach into the garbage can. I unball the paper and smooth it across my cashier desk with my shaky, sweaty palms. My eyes scan my husband's scribbly handwriting and the angry words he bled across the page.

You know, you are so fucking stubborn, Alexia. And you have a way of pissing me off like no one I've ever met before. From the first second I saw you, I knew you'd be a headache.

...And I think I fell in love with you right then and there. At the coffee shop. While you were sweaty and disheveled and covered in coffee splatter with a screwdriver in your hand. The sexiest, friskiest, prettiest, kindest woman I've ever seen, rolling your sleeves back to help out a friend.

I'm in love with you, dammit. And the last thing I want to do is divorce you. I want to keep you and protect you and bicker with you and grow with you and love you for the rest of my life.

You've opened me in so many ways. You believe in me when I don't deserve it. You're tender with me even when I don't realize I need it. When my ego gets too big, you serve me the most delicious humble pie.

You're genuine, you're hardworking, you're sexy, you're loyal, you're down-to-earth, you have the biggest heart...Do you need me to go on? Because I will. I can list the things I love about you all day long.

Maybe I did a shit job of making you know how much you mean to me. I'd do anything for another chance.

You can go on deluding yourself, saying our relationship was never real. But I'll tell you this, Stormy; being with you changed me. You made me a better man. And there's nothing realer than that.

- C

The words seep into my soul. I can't lie to myself anymore.

Dammit. Dammit dammit dammit.

He loves me.

And I love him.

And he's in New. York. City.

And I'm going to get his ass back.

I hurriedly get my earrings on and grab my purse from under my desk. "I don't know how to get around Manhattan..." I'm mumbling to myself. "I am *so* gonna get my ass lost on the subway or get run over by a yellow cab..." Salty tears leak into my mouth as I cram my laptop and my keys and my other shit into my purse. "I don't even know his address..." I drop to my knees, scrambling for my shoes beneath the counter. "I don't even have a plan..."

But I'm willing to take the chance because I have to go get my man back.

The loud screech of tires outside draws my attention back to the shop's front glass. I look up and see my father's truck pull up at the curb, obstructing the fire hydrant and taking up half the block.

Worst timing ever.

"Oh my god, Dad." He can't just park that thing on the curb. My neighbors are gonna give me so much shit for this.

I vault to my feet so fast and rush to the door. I pound on the window and the glass slowly comes down. But when I lean into the vehicle, it's not my father who looks back at me.

Cannon's hopeful caramel eyes sweep my face. He gives me a charming half-smile that turns my knees to licorice. "Hey Stormy. Wanna go for a spin?"

55

CANNON

Lexi's beautiful eyes are wide as I jump out from behind the wheel of the old truck.

Her jaw hangs loose. "Cannon, w-what is going on? What are you doing driving my dad's truck?"

I round the hood of the vehicle and join her on the sidewalk. I give her my brashest grin although I'm a freaking hot mess on the inside.

"This is my loaner car while your dad's fixing up my sportscar. It got a little ding on the back fender a few days ago. You may have heard."

She cocks a brow. "You left my dad with your Tesla? I thought you'd gone back to New York..."

A crowd of nosy townies is already starting to gather around us.

I give zero fucks. I will make a scene out here that would put all telenovelas to shame. I don't care. I just want my wife back.

"I was on my way...And as I was passing by Cowersville, I made a little detour."

Going to Lexi's hometown hadn't been part of the plan.

I'd made up my mind that I was done fighting for her. But my heart didn't care what decision my mind had made. My heart only cared that I pull out all the stops and make things right once and for all.

So, I went back to that trailer park and took Alexia's father up on his offer to fix my car.

Stormy locks her fingers around my wrist and drags me inside her boutique. "You went to see my parents?!"

Casually, I hitch a shoulder. "We broke bread."

"Oh my god..." She looks faint. She's gonna have to get over it.

Yes, I went back to the trailer park and I sat down with my father-in-law. I looked him in the eye and admitted to being an idiot who had screwed up with his daughter. I owned up to my asshole nature, apologized to him like a man, made an earnest commitment to change.

...And then I begged him to tell me how to win back my wife's affection.

He advised me to keep it simple, to tell it to her straight.

We stand face to face in the middle of the shop. "Look, Alexia—this is my last ditch move. I've got no other tricks up my sleeve. So, I'll just tell you flat out. I'm in love with you. I get that things weren't supposed to turn out this way. I get that we were supposed to split up after we both got what we wanted out of our arrangement." I cup her cheek. "But baby, halfway through our arrangement, what I wanted changed. What I want is you. I don't care about the properties Kingston Realties owns. I don't care what Carl and Margot do with DataCo. I don't care about the dent in my car. I care about you. Only you."

I brace my hands on her hips and lift her onto the platform in the showroom. "You say I'm the one with all the power? That's where you're wrong. I put you on a fucking pedestal, Alexia. Literally. So fuck my fortune, fuck all my worldly possessions. Everything I need in this world is standing on this two-foot platform in front of me right now."

That's when the tears start streaming down her face.

"I know I'm asking a lot. I'm asking more than I deserve. But don't tell me you can't figure out how to forgive me. Don't say that to me. Please."

"Cannon, I..."

"I know you're scared. I'm scared, too. But pick me over your fear, baby. Please, pick me. Because I'm scared too, but I pick you anyway."

Alexia leans down and grabs my face in her warm hands. She kisses me with those soft, cherry-red lips and her tears leak onto my cheeks and her grapefruit-scented hair tickles my neck and everything about this feels right. "I'm sorry I pushed you away, King. I act all confident, like I know what the hell I'm doing but I don't. And I just couldn't bring myself to believe that you'd actually choose *me*."

I hiss into her hair. "You're talking crazy, Stormy. Of course I'd choose you. You're gorgeous. You're smart. You're ambitious. You speak your truth and you defend people who can't defend themselves. You're the kind of woman to build an empire with."

"Why me, King? How do you know you love me? How do you know I'm worth it? I'm damaged goods, yo..."

That makes me smile. "When I'm away from you, I'm excited to see you. And I'm also anxious that you'll pull the hard-to-get card on me again and then I'll have to chase you around the state of Illinois and seduce you all over again. Just to get you to surrender and give me a little bit of your affection." She's soft and warm in my arms. The vibrations of her laughter resonate all throughout my body. "And it's worth it, Alexia. The chase is always worth it. Because when I'm with you, I feel fulfilled, I feel smitten, I feel goddamned happy. That's how I know I love you."

When she pulls back, she's smiling. "A wise woman once said that we don't have to come from the same world. We can build a whole new world together...Do you want to do that with me, King? Can we build something new together? Something just for you and me?"

Reaching into my pocket, I pull out her wedding ring. Her eyes follow the movement. It's like dangling a bone in front of a puppy.

A corny-ass line spills from my mouth. "*A man can amass a fortune, rule a country, command an army. But he only knows true success when he has the right woman by his side to share it all with.*"

She grins. "Wait—that's a line from your grandfather's book..."

I nod. "It is." I bring her hand to my mouth and kiss her palm. "You're that woman for me, Alexia."

"Really?"

I lick my lips and nod. "Really."

A grin full of mischief takes over her face. "Cool. So, gimme my ring back." Sassy thing. I slide the ring back into its rightful place, on her hand. There's no turning back now. I'll make sure that ring stays there for the rest of her life. Her eyes twinkle. "Now, gimme your heart."

I lay a kiss on the back of her hand then settle her palm over the centre of my chest. "I did that a long time ago, Stormy. It's yours forever."

I lift her off the platform and lock her long legs around my back. She holds my face in her hands. She kisses my chin, my lips, the bridge of my nose. "I'm yours now, King. And you're mine."

"I'm yours, baby. Forever." I smirk. "I hope you know what you're getting yourself into."

She kicks her head back and laughs. I kiss my way up her throat until our lips meet and when they do, I pour every ounce of me into the kiss.

There are people at the window looking in. I don't care.

She looks at me, eyes glittering with wonder. "I love you so much, Cannon Kingston."

"I love you, Alexia Kingston." I walk her down the hallway, kick open a door and lay her on the couch in her office. I plan to taste every inch of her skin. "Now, let's get to work on our happy ever after."

56

CANNON

My beautiful wife sits cross-legged on the conference room table, feeding documents into the paper shredder. "Maybe we can go to Tortola?" She smirks at the image of the tropical beach in her hands. "I heard you own a fishing boat out there."

I throw her a smirk of my own from where I'm plucking pins out of the corkboard on the wall. "Yeah, the fishing boat was a very generous gift from an old acquaintance." My fingertips tingle at the memory of stripping the boat away from Carl. I wonder if he misses his fishing privileges...

She falls back onto the table and tosses a handful of popcorn into her mouth. She laughs evilly. "We're so bad..."

Now that Alexia and I have cut the shit and committed ourselves to each other, honeymooning is finally on the table. We just have to pick the perfect spot.

"So you really are serious about giving up on revenge on your business partner?" She turns to look at me. Her brows furrow. "'Cause to be quite fucking honest, I am *personally* offended by the idea of that asshole getting away with what he did to my man."

She rolls her eyes when I make a big show of feeding our prenup and NDA through the paper shredder. Frank will whip up some paperwork to make it official but the message is clear—Alexia's stuck with me forever. We don't need any legal mumbo jumbo standing between us.

I nudge her sweet ass to scoot across the table and make room for me. I lie beside her and throw an arm around her belly. "Baby, revenge means nothing to me if I can have you—if I can have love—instead."

She feeds me a few kernels then she kisses me on the mouth. Her voice is low and gravelly. "It is *so* sexy when you talk like that."

Lexi's horny eyes are back.

I'm never one to pass up an opportunity so I haul her on top of me. Then, we're kissing and touching, going at each other like junkies. Minutes later, she's smiling as she brings my engorged cock into her mouth.

I grind my teeth, fighting a losing battle against my self-control. "Hell, you're so fucking good at that..."

Her lips quirk around the crown. "I've had lots of practice over the past few months."

Fingers clasped around the base of my cock, she takes me deep in her throat. Again and again and again. It's embarrassing how hard I come, with my fingers tangled in her hair, my nails biting into her scalp. She swallows every drop and I haul her to her feet. "Come on, Stormy. We've got to go finish this party at home."

I plan to eat her until she's worn-out and dehydrated and struggling to remember her own name. Then, I'll fuck her mercilessly just to see her 'O' face again.

She giggles as she's straightening her clothes and I'm buckling up my belt. She wanders around the room, looking for her shoes. From the corner of my eye, I see her lean close to the remaining documents on the corkboard.

Suddenly, her fingers cover her lips and she whispers, "Are you fucking serious?"

Eyes on the papers, I come up over her shoulder as I tuck in my shirt. "What?"

She points at a corporate fact sheet on the board. "Your ex-business partner owns Vibes of Joy?"

My brow arches in question. "Vibes of Joy?"

"The company that sold Iris those crappy sex toys and vanished into thin air when it came time for the refund."

I yank the business statement off the corkboard. "No fucking way..." I mutter.

The woman from the lingerie store has bought most of the sex toy inventory off of our hands but we still have a few pieces lingering around.

Lexi stands there in shock. "That bastard." Her features tell me she's thirsty for blood.

I turn to my bride. "How do you feel about a quick trip to the Big Apple?"

She grins deviously. "Hell yes. Sounds like a honeymoon to me."

57

LEXI

Cannon breezes past the reception desk, tugging me along, fingers interlocked with mine. The gloomy-faced people crowding the depressing waiting room issue mumbled protests as we cut ahead of them.

"E-excuse me, sir!" The mousy woman at the front desk says with her fingers on her keyboard. "Excuse me! You can't go in there!"

Following after my lunatic husband, I give the woman a sheepish stare and mouth, "Sorry..."

...I'm not sorry.

Carl and Margot are shitty human beings. They've earned the steaming hot shitshow their lives are about to descend into. I'm just here for the entertainment.

We just left a meeting at Frank's office. Cannon signed the paperwork approving of the takeover that officially kicked Carl off of DataCo's board of directors. Now, it's time for the fun part...

My hubby makes his way down the brightly-lit hallway, sticking his head into each office we pass. I don't know how

Frank dug up this information about Carl's bankruptcy trustee and honestly, I'm a little scared to ask. But from what I've seen so far, this lawyer isn't afraid to do dirty work and he's worth every penny my husband pays him.

The receptionist hurry-waddles behind us, panic in her polite tone as she repeatedly asks us to leave.

"Knock, knock." Cannon casually strolls into the conference room where he spots a weary-faced, curly-headed man and a waif-thin woman with over-blonde hair sitting across from a stuffy, professional-looking dude.

The woman gasps like she's been holding her breath for the past six months.

Margot...

"Baby! I knew you'd come back for me! I knew you didn't give up on me!" She throws herself at him so fast that the blueberry muffin she's holding falls to the floor.

Cannon deftly avoids her. He loops an arm around my waist and ushers me into the room.

Professional-Looking Guy adjusts his glasses and rises to his feet. "Sir, ma'am—you can't be in here. This is a private meeting." He approaches cautiously with a hand out.

Cannon gives the man a fleeting look. "We'll only be a minute."

Carl throws a worn-down glance over his shoulder. "Man—you shouldn't have wasted your time coming here. I have nothing left for you to take from me." The guy looks sickly and dehydrated. It's obvious he doesn't know where his next meal is coming from so his plate is stacked high with complimentary pastries.

"You're still breathing so I guess that's up for me to decide." My husband smiles like the Joker.

I love it when he's all vindictive and shit.

"We didn't come to take anything," I say graciously. "In

fact, we come bearing gifts." I reverently set down my brown paper bag on the conference table.

This whole time, Margot's eyes are peeled to me. She glares and turns up her nose. "Who the hell is this bitch, Cannon? Do *not* tell me you're seeing someone else when you and I have been working on our relationship."

I'm surprised he even dignifies her with a response. "Alexia is my wife. And I'd suggest you refrain from disrespecting her again unless you want to find yourself hanging from a window by your hair extensions." He cups a hand around his mouth and lowers his voice. "My honey's got a bit of a temper. And judging by the wretched state of your life, I'm sure you know I have a temper, too."

I narrow my eyes for effect.

Margot meekly blinks away from my threatening glare and finds herself a seat.

Cannon drums his fingertips on the tabletop. "Now, moving on to the items on today's agenda." He gallantly pulls out a chair for me before dropping into the empty seat by my side. "I have become aware that Mr. Cohen is insolvent and that's a bit of a problem because it turns out that he owes my wife quite a sum of money."

The trustee looks to Carl for an explanation, eyes guarded.

My hubby continues. "The items in the bag originated from one of Mr. Cohen's businesses." With his chin, he gestures at the paper bag.

The trustee doesn't take his eyes off of Cannon as he reaches into the bag. When he pulls out the muddy, broken butt plug, the man jumps back like he just touched a rattlesnake.

"Your return policy is shit, by the way. You really need to work on that...unless you want consumer protection knocking down your door, too." Cannon breaks a piece off of a croissant and pops it into his mouth, all veiled threats and nonchalance. He feeds me a bite of his pastry.

Mmm...delicious. Tastes like victory.

Carl mumbles. "You always were such an asshole." He's red and vibrating with rage.

Cannon finishes off the croissant and hands off the Vibes of Joy invoice to the trustee. "So make sure my wife gets added to the list of creditors, m'kay?" He stands.

"That's not how this works," the trustee protests. "I can't just go adding creditors without following the proper proceed—"

Cannon gives him an exasperated look. "Can we just pretend it is? I'm going for dramatic effect here and you're cramping my style. Sheesh!"

He offers me his hand and we rise to walk out.

But Carl's resentment seemingly reaches a boiling point because out of nowhere he shrieks like a banshee and lunges for us from behind. Startled, I miss a step and stub a toe on a table leg as I duck out of the way.

In an instant, Cannon spins around protectively and his fist slams through his ex-business partner's jaw.

Now, Carl is lying on the floor. Right next to Margot's blueberry muffin.

He holds his nose and groans. My man's face turns a scary shade of red as he looms above the body curled up on the office carpet.

The trustee guy is already standing there with the conference room phone in his hand. "All right. That's it. I'm calling security." He eyes his terrified receptionist standing by the door.

With the rage he's in, I doubt that Cannon heard him. He shakes out his swollen fingers. "For the record, I wasn't willing to face jail for Margot. But for Alexia Kingston, I would *gladly* put your ass six feet under and eat my cardboard-flavored prison dinner with a smile every day for the rest of my wretched life. Remember that if you ever have the misguided idea of posing a threat to her ever again."

My heart flutters. That man's brand of romance really does it for me.

I bend and swipe the fallen invoice from the floor. "Oh here, babe." I hand it to Cannon. "Shit, we got a little blood on it."

He takes it and presses a hard kiss to the side of my face. "Don't worry. It'll still hold up in court. If it gets to that." Carl squints up at us, still holding his bleeding nose in place. "But it won't get to that. Right, Carl?"

He just groans and rolls over. Like he's completely given up on life.

My groom reaches out a hand and helps me cross over the heap of skin and bones lying on the floor. We move toward the door.

I throw a cursory glance at Cannon's pouting ex-girlfriend and motion my chin at Carl. "Come get your life, sweetheart."

I slip my hand into the crook of his arm as we stroll past the waiting room, toward the elevator. "Carl was right. You're *such* an asshole."

Cannon chuckles. "Admit that was kind of satisfying."

"It was."

We share a grin.

He brands me with a hard kiss as we get onto the elevator. He slings an arm around my neck. "Now let's go see the Statute of Liberty or some shit, shall we, Mrs. Kingston?"

I giggle. "Of course, Mr. Kingston. I'd go anywhere with you."

Made in United States
North Haven, CT
16 October 2023